Death by Muttonbird

A Lord Howe Island
Murder Mystery

Simon Dodd

Published by

DBMB PUBLISHING

Sydney Australia

www.deathbymuttonbird.com

Copyright © 2012 Simon Dodd

Thanks to Margaret Megard, Tristan Nation, Betty Dodd, Debra Steel, Julie Chatterton, Averill Chase, Bruce Griffiths, Peter Coote, Leon Fish, Maroline Megard, Jebby Phillips, the Russian & the Mexican.

ISBN 978-0-9873079-0-3 (pbk)

National Library of Australia Cataloguing-in-Publication entry

Dodd, Simon.

Death by muttonbird : a Lord Howe Island murder mystery /Simon Dodd.

ISBN 9780987307903 (pbk.)

Dewey Number: A823.4

Preface

This novel is set on an entirely fictitious Lord Howe Island that purely by coincidence and chance happens to occupy the same geographical space and have the same name as the other, real-life Lord Howe Island. That the real and non-real islands are approximately the same size and share many geographical features is pure happenstance. The characters that inhabit the fictional Lord Howe Island are in no way based on any real characters living today on the actual Lord Howe Island, nor are they intended to make fun of or offend in any way the fine people of the real Lord Howe Island, who are all intelligent, good looking, forgiving, have great senses of humour and are not in the slightest bit litigious. I hope.

28ᵗʰ September 1948 – 10:47pm

Somewhere over the Tasman Sea …

"This is RAAF No 11 Squadron Catalina A240-38. Do you read me? Over."

"We read you. And we're ready for you. What's your current position? Over."

"We are approaching the rendezvous point, and expect to be putting down in the lagoon in … hang on, mate …(muffled) What the bloody hell's going on back there? Hey! You can't come in here. Get him out! Get him out! …"

Transmission ends.

20th December 2008 – 10:47pm

As he left Lord Howe Island's Pandanus restaurant, Harvey Jacob realised he was a little more inebriated than he would usually be at that time of the evening. In fact, he wasn't usually even up at this time of night. But it wasn't often he bumped into a colleague halfway around the world.

As he walked into the humid summer night, dressed in a New York Yankees shirt, track pants tucked into his white socks, sneakers and Yankees cap sitting jauntily on his head making him look like a geriatric Dennis the Menace, the diminutive balding 63-year-old American thought to himself that he probably should have gone home an hour earlier with Matahina. But he knew that she wasn't interested in two old men talking shop, and it was becoming increasingly obvious that she wasn't interested in Harvey either.

Harvey briefly considered getting back on the 'pushbike' that the Hightide Apartments' owners had so quaintly called the bicycle they had loaned him. But in his current state of inebriation, and at his age – not to mention a total lack of street lighting – he soon decided the short walk back to the cabin would be the wisest option.

Harvey stumbled along Anderson Road, the forest of kentia palms on his right-hand side blocked out the already dark, cloudy night sky, and he began to wonder if he should have called a cab, if such a thing even existed on the island.

It was darker still when he reached Muttonbird Drive, where the deafening cries of hundreds of muttonbirds repeating their mating call, a shrill appeal that sounded like a chorus of desperate circus munchkins chanting "Pick me! Pick meeee!" sent a cold shiver down Harvey's spine. It made him think he should definitely have gone home earlier – like when the sun was still up, and the muttonbirds were still out at sea.

Sadly, this was the last thought Harvey would ever have. He couldn't see his hands in front of his face, so he had little chance of seeing whatever it was that hit him in the side of the head. All he heard was a rush of wind and a fluttering of feathers, then his own head hitting the gravel. A trickle of blood flowed from Harvey's left ear, as all around him the haunting chant continued – "Pick me!" "Pick mee!" "Pick meeee!"

21ˢᵗ December 2008 – 10:47am

Jack Slazenger arrived at the Qantaslink departure lounge at Sydney Airport for the morning flight to Lord Howe Island. Mid-forties, five-eight on the old imperial scale, his greying frizzy hair was pulled back in a discreet ponytail and his short-cropped beard was growing out just a little. With John Lennon glasses on his nose, a Hawaiian shirt on his back and an acoustic guitar case at his feet, you'd take him for a travelling musician, not the deputy assistant state coroner of NSW on his holiday.

Originally trained as a doctor, Jack came to coronial work later in life than most deputy assistant state coroners. But after years of working with living patients, he came to realise that he much preferred working with dead ones – for a number of reasons. One, you can't accidentally kill them, because they're already dead. Two, it's a lot easier to work out what *has* killed someone than it is to work out and prevent what *is* killing someone. And three, you don't have to talk to the dead and assure them they're going to be all right. Because they're not.

Increasingly, however, Jack was beginning to wonder if it wasn't time for another career change. A few years ago, when he first started to investigate the victims of accidents, trauma, crime and passion, he found it fascinating. He was amazed at the almost endless variety of ways that human life can be extinguished – bizarre mishaps, accidental poisonings, over-enthusiastic sex with or without partner or partners, and of course, the pharmacological pursuit of altered states of consciousness to their logical conclusion, a permanent unalterable state of unconsciousness.

But he discovered there was also a downside to death. While death is inevitable and happens to all of us, those who brought death to others for personal gain, or out of rage or malice, were a sad reminder of how we as a species are really just very slow animals. And that, after a while, greatly depressed him.

There were also the relatives of the deceased to consider. While in most cases the death of an individual was only painful and traumatic to the victim for a brief period of time, it was often a slow malingering pain for their family and loved ones that never came to an end. This was especially true for deaths that remained unsolved, despite the best efforts of the investigating officer.

All of this added to the reason Jack was standing in the departure lounge four days before Christmas, with a boarding pass to Lord Howe Island in the pocket of his Hawaiian shirt and a guitar at his feet.

He couldn't really play the particular guitar in question. But that was the point. After all the deaths he dealt with on a daily basis, Jack had to get away and take his mind off death. That was why he bought a Dobro, a handsome vintage-brown roundneck 'resophonic' acoustic guitar, and the choice of discerning blues men and women everywhere. He already knew how to play a bit of blues on a standard guitar, but he wanted to escape for a while and immerse himself in something else, such as learning how to play slide guitar, to take his mind off the constant barrage of death, death, death and more death. At that moment, his mobile phone rang.

It was his boss. "There's been a death."

Jack closed his eyes wearily.

"I want you to drop what you're doing and head for Lord Howe Island."

Minutes later Jack was sitting in his allotted seat on a Qantas Dash 8 – a plane that was ahead of its time, 40 years ago when it was built – his guitar in its case, between his knees. With its metal resonator, Jack was so worried that he might have trouble getting the Dobro through the airport's security X-ray that he completely forgot about his piercings.

There are very few things more embarrassing than having a metal detector waved in front of your private parts while it makes that high-pitched whirring noise. A quick trip to the Gents was needed to prove to the security guy that he wasn't packing heat in the pants department, just a rather impressive stainless steel 'palang' and a small 'lorum' just beneath it. For this reason alone, Jack very seldom travelled by plane.

The piercings were the net result of a broken heart he received many years ago, when the woman he believed was the love of his life went off to live with the indigenous tribes-people of the Skrang River, in the Sarawak region of northern Borneo.

After a week-long bender, he convinced himself that if he became a Dayak tribesman by adopting the preferred piercing of the region, he could win her back. Not surprisingly, the pain of the procedure sobered him up. The only consolation of now being bejewelled and abandoned was being able to tell people that his girlfriend left him to become a 'Dayak'.

It's a two-hour flight to Lord Howe on a Qantas Dash 8 – unless there's bad weather, which fortunately there wasn't.

The De Havilland-built DHC-8, or Dash 8 to its friends, seats only 36 people, or 18 really fat people, and has strict weight restrictions. On some occasions, particularly on a return flight, even the passengers are weighed. If you ate too much while you were on holidays on Lord Howe, it might take you two flights to get home.

Fortunately Jack wasn't particularly large or heavy, although as he approached his mid-forties there was some middle-age spread and he found the Hawaiian shirt the most effective way to hide it. The glare of the shirt dazzles the eye and blinds the viewer to the girth beneath it.

Being so close to Christmas, the Dash 8 was packed to the overhead lockers, with tourists leaving for a Christmas away, and island residents returning for Christmas at home.

There was another reason Jack wanted to get away over the Christmas break. It was at Christmas time 37 years ago that his mother, father and baby sister were killed in a car accident that left Jack, at age eight, the only survivor.

Although it wasn't his fault, he always felt a certain sense of guilt that he lived and they didn't. As a result, Christmas wasn't a time for celebration for him, and he didn't have anyone to celebrate it with anyway. Over the years he'd gotten quite used to it, and in a way felt lucky that unlike everybody else, he didn't have 'do Christmas'. Of course if he *did* find someone to celebrate with, that would be another thing entirely.

An attractive woman in her early thirties, carrying what appeared to be an oversized briefcase, made her way down the aisle. Jack smiled hopefully, thinking she might be sitting next to him. She returned his smile, then looked down and pulled a face of mock-horror. Jack also looked down to see what she was reacting to, only to discover the neck of his black Tolex guitar case sitting phallically between his legs, and both his hands grasping it somewhat eagerly.

Before he could recover, the woman had moved on and a scruffy looking man in his mid-twenties dressed in ripped jeans and T-shirt had taken the woman's place. He winked and nodded his approval at Jack's musical appendage, then began to stuff a seemingly enormous backpack into the overhead locker directly above Jack's seat.

Sitting next to Jack, the young man introduced himself.

"G'day, Boz Boswell."

"Jack Slazenger".

"I've played with your balls."

"I get that all the time," replied Jack with a weary smile, "but I'm not *that* Slazenger."

Boz Boswell looked at Jack's guitar, his Hawaiian shirt and then Jack himself.

"Wait a second. You look familiar. *Little River Band*, right?"

Jack looked confused.

"Oh, you think I'm a musician. No. Coroner."

"You make cigars?" queried Boz.

"No, I examine bodies to determine their cause of death."

Boz nodded his head, understandingly, and pointed to the guitar case. "So, is there a tiny little body in that?"

"No, it's a Dobro."

"What's that? A type of dog?"

"No, a type of guitar."

Boz seemed happy with Jack's reply, and the two of them put their earphones in and listened to their iPods for the next hour or so – Boz to death metal and Jack to Delta blues.

After his parents' death, Jack had been brought up by his Aunt Marion, a free-spirited feminist who instilled in him a deep respect, admiration and appreciation for women, especially during her lesbian phase.

She also instilled in him a great love of music, particularly during the time she was shagging the guy from the record shop.

Most of that record shop was now on Jack's iPod, which was where he had currently retreated to avoid his fellow passenger Boz's unusual line of questioning.

As the Dash 8 began its descent to Lord Howe Island, a flight attendant leant over Jack and Boz and pointing to their ears, mimed a request that they both turn their iPods off for landing. They complied and as they removed their earphones, Boz turned to Jack and inquired:

"You're *really* a coroner?"

"Yep – technically a coronial officer."

"Does that mean there's been a suspicious death on the island?"

Jack looked around to make sure no one else was listening. He didn't really want the other passengers to know there had been a death on the island. It could ruin their holiday, and worse, make his job a lot harder. If everyone in a community knows an investigation is going on, they tend to either get in the way, or if they're the guilty party, get their alibis in order.

Jack put his index finger to his lips, indicating with a tilt of his head in the direction of the other passengers, that this was to be kept a secret, then nodded in the affirmative.

Boz understood. He whispered, "What happened?"

Jack whispered back, "I'm not really sure at this stage. Some bloke got topped by a bird."

Boz took 'bird' to mean woman, as in a girlfriend.

"You mean, 'murder'?" he asked, whispering the word 'murder'.

"More like 'fowl play'," Jack replied, punningly.

"Let's hope you're not running a coronial inquiry on *me* soon," said Boz with a mischievous smile.

"Everybody says that," replied Jack.

"Yeah but I've got good cause," said Boz, and he leaned in a little closer. "I'm a BASE jumper."

"You mean those nut-bags who jump off really high places with tiny little parachutes?" asked Jack.

Boz nodded his head. And then for his own reasons, put **his** finger to his lips.

Jack lowered his voice. "What are you going to jump off on Lord Howe Island?"

An impish grin played across Boz's face as he pointed out the window of the plane.

The Dash 8 was now circling over Lord Howe. Below them, the majestic twin peaks of Mount Lidgbird and Mount Gower peaked majestically.

"That," said Boz.

700 kilometres northeast of Sydney, in the middle of nowhere in the middle of the Tasman Sea, Lord Howe Island is the remnant of a 6.9 million-year-old volcano. Mount Gower and Mount Lidgbird dominate the island, like two huge volcanic breasts. The rest of the island erotically curves away mermaid-like underneath them, like some kind of giant sub-tropical Gina Lollobrigida – or what a Pacific island would look like if it had been designed by the artist Brett Whiteley.

Between sheer cliffs and exposed rocks, yellow patches of sandy beach peek out like glimpses of naked golden flesh, while her nether regions are covered with a thick thatch of hot, wet and steamy jungle undergrowth. Across her midriff, instead of a piercing or an inviting tattoo, she has a huge scar in the shape of the airport landing strip, which the tiny-by-comparison Dash 8 was now directly above.

Some 20 kilometres southeast of her inviting torso, the appropriately named Ball's Pyramid stands in a state of permanent arousal, for reasons that would appear obvious. Ball's Pyramid was named by and after Lieutenant Henry Lidgbird Ball, the only officer with the gall to name Lord Howe's left breast after himself, as well.

Lord Howe Island itself was named after the first Lord of the British Admiralty, Richard Howe, the 1st Earl Howe. Howe was a naval war hero whose nickname was 'Black Dick', which would have made a far more interesting, if perhaps controversial, name for the island. Fortunately for the locals,

'Black Dick Island' was never considered as an alternative name. No one minds a few days unwinding on Lord Howe, but it would extremely difficult to relax if you were stuck on Black Dick.

None of this was going through the mind of Jack as the Dash 8 began its descent in to Lord Howe, although he was thinking about sex. Thinking about sex had become a preoccupation for Jack, and it seemed to increase in direct proportion to the rate at which having sex decreased. The only way he was ever going to stop thinking about sex, he believed, was by actually having it.

He was hoping that maybe this holiday, as opposed to the last six holidays, he might actually get to have the holiday romance he not only hoped for, but also desperately needed.

The thud of the Dash 8 landing sent the neck of Jack's guitar case slamming directly into Jack's nuts, and thoughts of sex suddenly stopped, to be replaced by thoughts of squealing and swearing, which fortunately for everyone, he managed to contain.

After the plane had finally come to a standstill, the passengers were led off and across the tarmac to a quaint white picket-fenced garden that adjoined the main airport building.

The Arrivals Gate, which was also the Departures Gate, looked more like the garden gate. Through the gate, the garden was neat and manicured like the backyard of someone's elderly retired aunt or uncle, blooming with well-cared-for hibiscus and spotted with the occasional park bench, on which sat the soon-to-be-departed passengers for the flight back to Sydney.

Beyond the garden, the entire airport facility was extremely small by airport standards. Perhaps, thought Jack, it was designed that way to make the aeroplane look bigger.

On the lawn, locals welcomed their children home for the holidays. Holidaying families greeted late arrivals; lodge and cabin owners welcomed their guests. No one welcomed Jack.

As he made his way through the glorified shed that passes itself off as Lord Howe's arrival and departure building, Jack couldn't help but notice that departing holiday-makers, and some of the locals leaving on the next flight, were being weighed along with their luggage for the flight back by a young woman in flight attendant garb. He wondered if this was a regular occurrence, or if they had all been participants on some kind of combination reality TV weight-loss show and travel program – *Lord Howe Losers* perhaps, where contestants are given a free holiday, but not allowed to put on any weight.

Jack attempted to pick up his suitcase from the back of the baggage trolley, when what appeared to be a family of wild chooks ran between his legs, closely followed by a middle-aged husband and wife, dressed in camo gear, the wife armed with an impressive set of binoculars, the husband, an extremely long telephoto lens.

"*Gallirallus sylvestris,*" confided Mr Birdwatcher to Jack.

"… Or Lord Howe Island Woodhen to you," he added, snapping off a few shots.

"It used to be the most endangered bird in the world," said Mrs Birdwatcher, almost proudly, as hubby took a few more shots.

"There were only 20 of them, but they're up to 250 now."

"Oh, what a shame," Jack replied, cryptically. "Where are they on the endangered list now?"

"Er, I'm not sure …," said a puzzled Mr Birdwatcher, his wife handing him a copy of Graham Pizzey and Frank Knight's *The Field Guide to the Birds Of Australia*, which he frantically began to flick through.

A tall, suave, middle-aged gentleman, immaculately attired in crisp khaki called out to them. "Attention all twitchers, this way. The bird bus is about to depart." And off they went.

As the other arrivals drifted away, or were mini-bused off to their accommodation, and the passengers bound for Sydney had boarded the Dash 8 and departed, Jack was seemingly left on his own. Even Boz the BASE jumper had been picked up by a boofhead on a motorbike.

It soon became apparent to Jack that nobody was going to pick him up. Looking around, the only people Jack could see were Reg, the guy who waves the ping-pong bats at the approaching planes, and Suzie, the 'flightless' flight attendant from the passenger weigh-in.

Jack took a small travel wallet from his red Swiss Army backpack, and out of it the confirmation email he'd been sent by his travel agent. He also took out his mobile phone and dialled the number for Hightide Apartments, where he had a reservation.

"Ah, that's not going work here," offered Reg, when Jack couldn't even get a signal.

"Bad reception?"

"*No* reception. Mobiles don't work here."

Jack shrugged and put away his phone. At least his boss wouldn't be bothering him for the next few days.

"They must have forgotten to pick you up. Where are you staying?" asked Reg.

"Hightide Apartments."

Reg nodded thoughtfully. "That'd be Heather. She's preggers." Reg mimed an enormous pregnant belly.

Suzie looked up from behind the check-in counter.

"Heather's in Sydney, having the baby."

"Really?" said Reg.

"Yeah, she got on the plane yesterday. Didn't you see her?"

"Oh yeah, right you are," Reg nodded thoughtfully.

"Was there a complication?" asked Jack.

Reg shook his head. "Nah, a lot of the young girls these days go to the mainland to have their babies. Not like in the old days. The women were tougher back then. Now days they want their Caesars and epidurals and what have you …"

"Oh yeah?" said Suzie. "You try squeezing something the size of watermelon out your arse, and see if you're not screaming for an epidural or a Caesar."

"I did once," cringed Reg. "And I was."

Jack smiled uneasily, as one does in the company of weirdos. "In that case, how do I contact the local police?"

Reg nodded thoughtfully. "That'd be Heather. She's in Sydney."

Just then, the woman whose frown had embarrassed Jack on the plane, came around the corner from outside the building with her mobile phone to her ear.

"Ah, that's not going work here," said Reg.

"Oh, it doesn't? Then can you tell me how I can contact the island's medical officer?"

Reg smiled. "That'd be Heather. Looks like we've got the trifecta."

In Reg's car on the way to town, they got to know each other. The woman with the briefcase was Jill Birkenstock, like the shoe – open-toed, comfortable and practical, with a light but durable bottom. It transpired that she was a visiting dentist, with a two-month contract. Apparently the islanders like to get their teeth all gussied up for what was generally regarded as the 'meeting, greeting and eating season'.

Jack was surprised they didn't ask him about his surname, Slazenger. Most people ask if he's related to the famous German sporting goods manufacturer. Unfortunately he wasn't, but the name had been a burden all his life. In school he was hassled relentlessly. Just about every day he would hear someone say "You've got fuzzy balls, Slazenger." In fact at one point that was his nickname, 'Fuzzy Balls'. He didn't appreciate it. Even his teachers got in on the act. Whenever he was caught talking in class, which was often, his English teacher would say, "You're making a racquet, Slazenger". It was this, plus an innate inability, that put him off sport for life.

Today, Jack was relieved to find himself in the company of fellow non-sporting types. He tried to explain that he was on holiday, but also investigating the recent death on behalf of the NSW Coroner's office.

"So do you always organise your holidays around a death? That'd be a good tax write-off, I suppose," asked Reg.

"No, I booked the holiday first, then the guy died," said Jack.

"That wouldn't count as a cause of death though?" asked Jill.

"I don't think he knew I was coming," said Jack. "In fact, I don't think he knew *anything* was coming."

Just then the car slowed down outside the island's medical centre. A queue of gap-toothed, foul-mouthed patients turned as one and smiled in their direction.

"Looks like someone knew you were coming," said Suzie to Jill.

Reg and Suzie made appointments to see Jill for a scrape and a polish, and dropped her off at the clinic. Reg then turned to Jack, who was watching Jill walk away, and said, "So you'll probably want to see the body next?"

For a moment Jack thought Reg was talking about Jill, but quickly realised he meant the dead body.

"Yes, definitely. Where is it?" he asked.

"That'd be at the Fish Co-op," said Suzie.

"Yeah, that's where all the dead bodies go now, since the ice cream parlour closed down," added Reg.

They dropped Suzie off at her home, which was conveniently just around the corner from the Fish Co-op. Nothing's very far away from anything else on Lord Howe Island.

Barry, the Fish Co-op guy, opened the big freezer door. Next to some frozen yellowtail kingfish and a couple of boxes of equally frozen potato scallops and prawn cutlets, lay the body of Harvey Jacob. Jack peered closely at the corpse's face, noting its receding hairline, gaunt miserly expression, tight thin lips, long pinched beak-like nose and shifty sinister eyes.

"He looks like Larry David," said Jack, name-checking the balding Jewish-American comedian, writer, producer, co-creator of *Seinfeld* and star of the HBO-TV show *Curb Your Enthusiasm*.

"Yeah, I thought that," said Barry.

Jack turned around, shocked.

"You don't get cable out here do you?"

"Off the satellite."

"Cool." Jack was impressed.

"How long have you had him here?"

"He came in first thing this morning. Norma up at the Hill Shop found him."

"So he's fresh, is he Barry?" joked Reg.

"Mate, they don't come any fresher. Cook him up with some coriander; bit of basil, some chips. Lovely."

They both laughed, but it was all a little too weird for Jack. He wondered if they'd ever practised cannibalism on the island. Come to think of it, they didn't pass a cemetery on the way in …

Lying next to Harvey Jacob was the body of a fleshfooted shearwater or Muttonbird (*Puffinus carneipes),* its neck broken, and its beak bloodied.

"And this is the murder weapon?" queried Jack.

"Yeah, apparently Norma found it sticking out of his ear, both dead."

"I'd better talk to her next." He checked the corpse's pockets for possessions, finding only a wallet, and after a quick glimpse inside, decided to look through it in detail later, and put it in his own pocket.

He noticed Reg and Barry exchanging a concerned look and attempted to explain.

"It's okay. I'm not stealing. It's Crown evidence."

Reg tapped the side of his nose and winked. "Right you are."

Jack then looked at the body once more, and noticing the Yankees tunic, the jaunty baseball cap, the track pants tucked into white socks, looked momentarily puzzled.

"Was he playing baseball when this happened?"

Because the Hill Shop doesn't open until 3:00pm, and no one knows where Norma goes the rest of the time, Reg dropped Jack off at his accommodation.

Hightide Apartments turned out to be a series of well-appointed individual cabins on top of the headland overlooking Ned's Beach, a small but perfectly formed crescent of sand on the north-eastern side of the island.

Even though Heather, who among her many other duties was also the owner and manager of Hightide Apartments, was away, Reg was able to show Jack where all the amenities were. Next to the laundry was a common room referred to as 'the library', that indeed did house a small library of orphaned books, along with snorkel gear and a small fridge stocked with beer and wine, which operated on the pay-by-honour system. If you were honest, you wrote what you took in a notebook on top of the fridge and paid Heather the total when you left.

Also in the library was a phone from which guests could only ring locally. If you wanted to make a call to the mainland, you had to go down to the phone box on Anderson Street, which was only a short walk and an even shorter ride away, on one of the rent-free bikes the apartments provided.

The bikes were kept in a carport near the main house, normally occupied by the absent Heather and her family. Guests were encouraged to help themselves to anything growing in the veggie and fruit garden.

Jack entered his apartment, put his bags down and carefully but ruefully eased his Dobro out of its case and leaned it against the wall. Its nickel-plated spider-style resonator surrounded by stripped-back hand-rubbed vintage maple, reflected a distorted view of Jack's face and he knew that sadly, he wouldn't be touching it for a while – which probably would have come as some relief to the couple staying in the next cabin, had they known he even had a guitar and that he was sometimes prone to wild bluesy freak-outs on it in the strangest of hours.

Jack was a reasonably proficient amateur guitar player, largely due to an adult blues guitar class he'd enrolled in a few years earlier. He'd always wanted to learn to play the guitar as a teenager and a young man, but it wasn't until recently that he finally got around to actually doing it, and now he felt too old to play standard rock, so determined that learning the blues might be more age appropriate, seeing as how most of the old blues guys he knew of were old. He thought that unlike rock and roll, at his age it was still possible to play the blues on a guitar and not lose your dignity.

It was learning to play blues on a standard guitar that led Jack to decide to learn how to play bottleneck blues on the resonator guitar, which was in many ways, a completely different musical animal. Resonator guitars were first built in the 1920s, and are kind of a bridge between the acoustic guitar and the electric guitar. Resonators are acoustic, but their louder metallic sound is generated by one or more metal cones embedded in the body of the guitar where the soundboard would normally be on an acoustic guitar. This construction gives them their unique sound. Resonators can be played in the standard tuning that every guitar player knows, and strummed or picked in the standard fashion. But they're probably more widely associated with slide or bottleneck playing techniques. This requires the guitar to be tuned to one of several open tunings, and notes are produced by the player sliding their finger, usually in a glass or steel tube, down the string to create the specific whiney metallic noise preferred by slide players everywhere.

The slide technique is thought to have been brought to America from Africa, in the form of a single-stringed instrument called a 'diddley bow', that was traditionally played with a slide. What they used for a slide is unclear. Certainly bottles were few and far between, as were metal tubes. Perhaps they used a monkey bone?

The term 'bottleneck' comes from the first slides used by African-American blues artists, which were literally the necks off bottles placed over one finger. Others used medicine jars. But anything that makes the strings resonate can be used. Legend has it that Jimi Hendrix famously played the guitar solo on *All Along The Watchtower* with his Zippo cigarette lighter.

These days bottleneck slides are made specifically for that purpose out of hardened glass or even steel, in a variety of sizes to fit even the chubbiest of fingers. For his venture into bottleneck blues, Jack had purchased a large Pyrex blues slide, and had taken to carrying it in his pocket, in case the urge to play came over him.

To play bottleneck blues guitar correctly, you have to learn to finger-pick, which requires the thumb of your non-sliding hand, usually the right, and anywhere from one to four other fingers to pick or pluck the strings in a fashion that makes it much harder to play than a regular guitar. Players often wear a variety of plastic or metal picks on their fingers that look like huge fake fingernails.

Jack chose to buy a Dobro brand resonator guitar because he'd often seen it listed on the credits of albums he owned and he figured it was a reliable brand. He was right. The Dobro Manufacturing Company was started by the Dopyera Brothers, Slovakian immigrants to the United States, and John Dopyera is often credited with inventing the resonator guitar. The company was later bought by Gibson Guitar Corporation, also known for its reliable guitars.

Jack changed out of his travel clothes into dark blue shorts and a maroon T-shirt. For mid-December, it was quite humid on the island. He was starving by this stage, so after a quick wash, he grabbed one of the bikes and headed up the driveway and down into the township, to get something to eat.

All of this sounds easy, but there are times in a person's life when getting on a bicycle and riding down a hill isn't quite as easy as it sounds. After a wobbly start, Jack took off, his palang pushing uncomfortably up against his lorum with each stroke of the pedals.

Fortunately it was downhill most of the way, so all he had to do was keep his balance. Unfortunately, that was the one thing about riding a bike he'd forgotten how to do. He managed all right for a while, whizzing past the kentia palms and cow paddocks until he realised he had oncoming traffic in the form of a tractor, and in swerving to avoid being ploughed or whatever it is tractors do, discovered that he was heading straight for an enormous Norfolk pine at the foot of the hill.

Barely missing the pine tree, the bike simultaneously mounted the curb and dismounted Jack, who momentarily flew, then skidded on the grassy berm, coming to an abrupt halt at one of the tables outside Humpty Micks Café – at which sat Jill the dentist, eating a muffin and drinking a latte. On seeing Jack's spectacular arrival, she laughed so hard, latte came out her nose, and she accidentally inhaled a raisin, which incited a coughing fit.

As Jack got to his feet, and wondered if he should attempt the Heimlich manoeuvre on Jill, or if it was perhaps too early in their relationship to be putting moves on her, he noticed Boz Boswell, the BASE jumper at the next table, a burger stuffed in his gob while he applauded with both hands.

"Wicked face-plant, dude," commended Boz, after extracting the burger from his mouth. "If you'd had a jumpsuit on then, you might have got some serious air."

The rest of Humpty Micks' clientele were also clapping so Jack bowed, then at Jill's beckoning, sat down at her table.

Once she'd regained her composure, Jill congratulated Jack on his spectacular arrival.

"You certainly know how to make an entrance."

"Well, in my business you need to use the element of surprise. Who knows who I'll catch off guard, besides myself, that is."

A waitress approached their table, and Jack ordered the fish and chips, then remembered who the fish and chips shared a room with earlier, so changed it to a hamburger and a chocolate milkshake.

"How's the teeth business going?"

"Good. So far I've had three fillings and a lot of plaque scraping. Nothing too exotic, thank god. How's the investigation going?"

"Well, he's definitely dead, whoever he is." Then he remembered. He'd picked up Harvey Jacob's wallet at the Fish Co-op and put it in his pocket. He took it out.

"Is that the victim's wallet?"

"Yep, one of the perks of the trade. If the ambos don't get it first."

Jill looked askance. Jack smiled. "Just joking. It's evidence."

He opened the wallet and found it stuffed with money. "And lunch is on me. Just joking again."

One by one, Jack took out Harvey's cards – American Express, Diners Club, Visa, MasterCard. His driver's licence said he was Harvey Marshall Jacob from New York City, which Jack had already kind of figured out from the baseball garb, and that he was 63 years old and an organ donor, although obviously not by trade.

There were various membership cards, and an ID card for Columbia University, history faculty.

Jack flicked through the remaining cards. "Wow, he's a qualified riverboat captain. And a card-carrying atheist." He held up a card with the bold letters AAA at the top – the initials of the American Atheist Association.

"I bet he'll be pissed off if he's in heaven right now," said Jack.

"I'm sure if there *is* a heaven, there won't be any atheists in it," quipped Jill.

"Nope, we're all going to hell," smiled Jack.

"In a hand basket," added Jill helpfully.

"The only way to fry," agreed Jack. They both laughed.

Jack continued his investigation of Harvey's wallet. He noticed a credit card receipt from the Pandanus restaurant, dated the night before, 10:40pm. Jack looked at the total. "Well, at least he had a hearty last meal."

From one compartment Jack pulled out a single condom. "Looks like he was hoping to get lucky. Poor sap."

Although she was clearly getting sucked into the investigation, Jill had to get back to work, so made her excuses. "Speaking of which – I've got a root canal at 2:30 …"

"You mean 'tooth-hurty'?" Jack joculated, recalling the ancient Scanlon's bubble-gum wrapper joke from his childhood.

Jill moaned at the appalling pun she and dentists everywhere have had to endure their entire careers. "I'd better go."

As Jill left, the waitress arrived with Jack's burger and Boz joined him from the other table.

"You work fast. You've only been here a couple of hours."

"What are you talking about? We were just chatting."

"I saw you waving that condom about. Respect."

With a mouthful of burger, Jack motioned to the twin peaks of Mounts Gower and Lidgbird. "So which one of the mighty monolithic mammaries are you going to plummet to your death off?"

"Both of them," Boz smiled.

"Ah, you can only plummet to your death from one of them," Jack pointed out.

"Yeah well, hopefully it'll be neither of them."

"Which one first?"

"Eenie, meanie, minie, moe ..."

"Don't say 'nigger'."

"That one," said Boz pointing at Gower. "But first I've got to find someone to pick me up at the bottom."

"You'll need a team of people, won't you? Especially if you splatter."

"That's not going to happen, dude. But I don't want to drown. And I'm probably going to land in the ocean …"

"You mean 'sea' in the ocean. You can't 'land' in the ocean." Jack smiled. Boz shook his head and returned the smile.

"Wow. Has anyone ever tried to kill you?"

"A couple of times," Jack shrugged.

Boz wiped his hands on a paper napkin, and stood up.

"Anyway, I'm supposed to be meeting a bloke with a boat, who reckons he can pick me up anywhere between here and Ball's Pyramid …" said Boz.

An old ute pulled up nearby. Boz looked around at the driver.

"And there he is now. See ya."

Even though Harvey Jacob's demise seemed like an open-and-shut case of death-by-incompetent-seabird, Jack wasn't entirely convinced. He still had some time to kill before Norma would re-open the Hill Shop and since he was now so full of local beef, imported buns and chocolate milk that a strenuous uphill bike ride might make him explode, he decided it would be easier on his bloated digestive system to take a leisurely cycle on some of Lord Howe's flatter, straighter roads. This led him along the lagoon side of the island on the appropriately named Lagoon Road.

As he peddled along the quiet, kentia palm-lined road, occasionally passing other tourists getting reacquainted with their bicycling skills, Jack was amazed by how little development there was on the island. Anywhere else in the world, a stretch of beach frontage like this would be lined with mega-resort Hyatts, Marriotts and Westins. But here most of the accommodation was mum-and-dad-run B & Bs or small quaint apartments and cabins. It seemed to Jack as if some tiny coastal village like Merimbula or Bermagui, back in the sixties or seventies had broken off from the mainland and floated out to sea. Or that the houses, beachside accommodation, small shops and the people who ran them had been beamed up by aliens, and deposited on an exotic tropical island.

After riding for a while, he turned back and stopped at the northern end of the beach, where Lagoon Road meets Ned's Beach Road, and walked a few steps to the beach itself.

The scene that met his eyes was spectacular. In Jack's mind, the words "picture perfect" didn't do it justice. No picture could capture the turquoise of the water, the gold of the sand, the greens of the island vegetation or the blue of the sky.

The beach stretched before him in a gentle arc for three kilometres and seemed to disappear under the twin peaks of Gower and Lidgbird. Jack could see no more than half a dozen people on it – a couple sunbaking, some children splashing at the water's edge, a lone figure just walking along the high-tide mark. The same number were in the water, engaged in a variety of non-motorised water sports. But that was all. At this time of the day, on a day like this, any comparable beach anywhere else in Australia would be teeming with people, cheek by jowl, a giant smear of swollen pink flesh and sunscreen.

Everyone seemed so happy, so calm, so relaxed. This wasn't a place for murder, and yet it wasn't a place for tragic meaningless death either. No one Jack saw seemed capable of murder or even having any need to murder. But although it appeared that a muttonbird had just fallen out of the sky and killed a man, muttonbirds don't just fall out of the sky and kill people. Jack was reasonably sure that if he checked the records he wouldn't find a single case of "death by muttonbird".

Near the beach, next to the amenities block, was a boatshed, from within which Jack heard a familiar voice as he passed.

"How's the investigation going, Inspector Slazenger?"

It was Reg, the airport ground control guy. He also appeared to be Reg, the boat and watersports gear hire guy. Still musing on the muttonbird murder, Jack walked over to the shed where Reg manned a small counter.

"You'd know most of the locals, wouldn't you?" Jack asked Reg.

"I know all of them," Reg said proudly.

"The people on Lord Howe, they're not a violent group are they?" asked Jack.

Reg shook his head.

"Wouldn't hurt an indigenous Ball's phasmid," he replied with a cheery grin.

Jack looked quizzical.

"A what?"

"One of these," replied Reg, as he produced his right hand from under the counter, on which clung a long prehistoric-looking cricket-like insect, but dark brown and slow. Jack leapt back and may have even squealed.

"What the hell is that, a spider?" asked Jack, his arachnophobia immediately kicking in, and a cold sweat forming on his skin.

"Nah, nah, nah," Reg assured him. "It's the indigenous Lord Howe Island stick insect, rare and endangered."

A dull-brown creature, about the size of a decent cigar, the phasmid looked to Jack like an alien insect from another planet. He was expecting to see its phasmid spacecraft parked not far away, and for the creature to either eat his and Reg's brain (although that might not be much of a meal, Jack mused) or demand to be taken to their leader. Jack prayed for the latter, although he suspected Lord Howe probably didn't have a leader.

"Phasmids once were common on the island, but rats ate them all," continued Reg. "We thought they were extinct, but then a breeding colony of phasmids – which is technically what these fellas are – was found on Ball's Pyramid. And now they're being slowly introduced back onto Lord Howe."

"The rats must be starving!"

"The rats are gone, thank god."

"Yes, but the phasmids are back," joked Jack.

"Don't worry. Once we get a good breeding population on the island, these phasmids are going to be a huge tourist attraction."

"Well, I can see why – I always like to go to places where they have huge ugly black insects crawling all over the place," said Jack.

Jack stared at the phasmid. The phasmid stared at Jack. To him, it looked like a breakfast sausage that had been over-barbequed, and sprouted legs.

"As you can see," said Reg, practicing his spiel for the imagined hordes of insect-loving tourists, "the phasmid is by nature a slow creature, which was why they were so easily wiped out by the rats." Jack wondered how the island's human population had survived so long, but thought it best not to ask.

Reg put the phasmid back in its living quarters, which appeared to be a Tupperware lunch box. Jack prayed there was no mix-up. It would be a tremendous shame, if Reg accidentally ate one of the last remaining phasmids, and then released into the wild an endangered breakfast sausage that was highly unlikely to breed and prosper.

The beast back in its escape-proof plastic container, Jack continued with his musings. "So, we've more or less established that the people of Lord Howe are a gentle folk, who would not even harm the ugliest insect on the planet, even though it looks like it was designed to be crushed by a size-10 work boot, or at the very least drowned in Mortein," said Jack.

Reg nodded and they both scratched their chins, and pondered.

"You'd also see most of the people that visit the island, too, wouldn't you, Reg?" Jack continued.

"As Lord Howe Island Customs And Immigration Officer, I see all of them, even the boaties," boasted Reg.

"Wow, you do wear a lot of hats, don't you?" said Jack.

"You have to out here. The UV rays are much more intense," replied Reg, oblivious to metaphor and Jack's gentle sarcasm.

Jack smiled. He wondered if Reg had already suffered from being out in the sun too long.

"Has anyone new and odd turned up on the island lately?" queried Jack.

"Beside you?" asked Reg, straight-faced.

Jack smiled. "Yes, besides me."

"We get a lot of odd types here," mused Reg.

"I don't mean locals, I mean tourists, visitors."

"Well, apart from the usual crowd who've come in on the Dash 8 …" Reg scratched the skin on his balding pate. "… There *is* that Swedish yachtie."

"A young attractive female Swedish yachtie?" asked Jack, hopefully.

"Afraid not." Reg shook his head. "An ugly old male yachtie. I had to do the customs' clearance on his boat. He's sailing around the world, single-handed."

"And what does he do with the *other* hand?" quipped Jack.

"Nothing. He's only got the one," said Reg, looking slightly alarmed.

Jack returned the look.

"I see. Is there anything *else* suspicious about him?"

Reg mused. "Besides the patch, and the wooden leg? He's got a budgie which I told him he's not allowed to bring to shore because of quarantine regulations."

"He's not a budgie smuggler is he?"

"He didn't tell me *what* he was smuggling," Reg said matter-of-factly.

"How did he get so disfigured?" asked Jack. A look of concern crept over his face. "It wasn't a shark attack, was it?"

"Combine harvester," replied Reg. Jack shuddered.

"They're even worse," Jack nodded.

Reg nodded back. "That's why he went to sea."

"Well you certainly don't see too many combine harvesters in the open waters," mused Jack.

"I think his name is Sven, or Svensen …" Reg added, scratching his head and presumably searching his memory.

"Which is it? Sven or Svensen?" asked Jack a little impatiently.

Reg looked at the customs' documents in front of him. "Sven Svensen."

"So good they named him twice," jollied Jack.

"He didn't look good to me. He looked crook," said Reg, shaking his head.

Jack was confused. "Crook or *crooked*?"

"A bit of both," said Reg.

Jack stroked his beard. Something definitely sounded fishy about this guy. He probably should talk to him at least.

"So where is this crooked Swede?" he asked.

"I think he's still out on his boat in the lagoon."

"And what's the best way to get out there?"

Reg looked at the ocean, then down at the bookings ledger open on the counter in front of him.

"At this time of the day, all the boats are out."

He ran his finger down the page.

"We've still got a windsurfer or a pedal boat. And there's plenty of snorkelling gear," he said, pointing to a plastic basket full of flippers and goggles, before adding, "there's a bit of coral out there that's worth looking at."

Jack opted for the pedal boat, but backed it up with a set of snorkel gear. He figured if time permitted, he might check out the reef on the way back – not for work purposes, but simply because it was there, and he thought the opportunity might not present itself again.

As soon as Jack was dressed in a full-body wetsuit, complete with flippers and goggles, Reg frogmarched him, literally, down to the shore where the pedal boat was waiting.

Only it wasn't exactly a pedal boat. Technically, it was an Aqua-Cycle – a floating pedal-powered sea-tricycle that could be ridden over reasonably calm water. The craft's three huge bright-yellow hollow wheels, each over a metre in diameter, were made out of polyethylene plastic, the back two ribbed, 'for your pedalling pleasure' thought Jack. These turned as you pedalled, and you steered by turning a sort of handlebar contraption connected to the front polymer wheel, as you sat on a two-man seat suspended above the water on an aluminium tube frame. Jack thought it looked like a water chopper for a clown or perhaps a member of "The Sea-Gypsy Jokers".

Reg helped Jack clamber aboard, and pushed the Aqua-Cycle out into water deep enough for its wheels to turn.

Now perched a metre and a half above the water, Jack looked out over the lagoon. There were a few small runabout-type boats anchored at various spots.

"Which one is Svensen's boat?" asked Jack.

"You can't really see it from here," replied Reg. "But it's anchored on the far side of Blackburn Island." He pointed to a low line of sand and vegetation just near the entrance to the reef. It looked to Jack to be more than three kilometres away, but in fact it was just over one.

Reluctantly, he began to pedal. The huge bright yellow back wheels of the Aqua-Cycle slowly started to turn and the peculiar-looking craft headed out over the flat expanse of turquoise water.

It was a hard slog but Jack was glad that at least it wasn't uphill. And if he lost control, at least there were no trees he could collide with.

The water beneath him was crystal clear and a kind of blue that even Miles Davis would have trouble describing. Actually Miles would have described it as 'blue as a motherfucker', which is as good a description as any, thought Jack.

Soon he was rounding the northern end of Blackburn Island and could now see the mast of the Swedish sailor's one-man-one-budgie yacht.

After a while the water started to get deeper and darker, and Jack could tell that he was now over a reef of some sort. This might be a good spot to stop for a snorkel on the way back, he thought.

Just then something long and dark glided under the Aqua-Cycle. Or maybe this *isn't* a good spot to stop for a snorkel on the way back, he re-thought.

Whatever it was beneath him, Jack didn't like the look of it, even though he hadn't had a clear look at it yet. Obligingly, 'whatever it was' turned around and slowly swam back under the Aqua-Cycle. Jack leaned over to get a clearer look at it, but the glare on the water made it hard to see exactly what 'whatever-it-was' was.

He leaned out just a little further to get around the glare. The Aqua-Cycle started to tilt, so Jack held firm onto the handlebars, calculating that the weight of the craft would counterbalance his weight as he leaned out over the side. It was a miscalculation. He'd never been very good at calculations.

The Aqua-Cycle continued to tilt more and more, until Jack was now on two wheels, the back left and the front wheel. He tried to correct it by leaning back in, but it was past the point of equilibrium and beyond the point of no return, and slowly but surely the Aqua-Cycle began to tip over and spill Jack into the 'whatever-it-was' infested waters.

As Jack slowly slid from the Aqua-Cycle, he tried desperately to hold on, but managed only to knock the skin off the knuckles of his right hand. Oh great, thought Jack, mid-fall. Blood in the water. That's all I need.

With his head now underwater, Jack pulled the goggles over his eyes so he could see – unfortunately filling them with water in the process, so he couldn't see.

41

Jack always felt more than a little uncomfortable in dark water over a few metres deep, for several reasons, all of which involved sharks in some way or another. Sharks were one of the five thousand things Jack was morbidly terrified of.

But this time it was with due cause – a rarity for Jack. He'd seen first hand the savage brutality of a shark attack, and could tell they were merciless predators, but suspected that they were somewhat fussy eaters. Most human shark casualties are really just 'tasting' victims. A hungry shark will bite a human two or three times, just to get a sense of what it is, and whether it wants to eat it. Nine times out of ten, it doesn't and buggers off – usually leaving the victim of the random 'shark tasting' to die from shock and blood loss.

The ocean to a shark is like one enormous box of chocolates which doesn't have a description list on the lid. The shark wants one with a raspberry filling, but doesn't really know what it looks likes, so it has a bite and then puts it back if it turns out to be one of those human-filled chocolates.

Jack had examined the body of a shark attack victim only recently. A wealthy businessman from Hong Kong holidaying in Sydney had hired a yacht for a few days and anchored the vessel late one afternoon in the middle harbour to spend the night. The next morning, the sun was shining and the water was warm, so he decided to swim to the nearby beach. It was a swim of only fifteen metres, and the man easily made it to shore and lay on the beach for a while. But when he waded out to begin swimming back to the boat, still standing in waist-deep water, a bull shark bit his leg off, then realised it didn't feel like Chinese, and just left him there.

And now Jack found himself in over his head and there was something large in the water with him. It could be a shark, thought Jack, or a ray of some kind. Perhaps it was the very same kind of stingray that killed Steve Irwin, a responsible, seasoned, deep-sea-killer handler.

On the other hand, thought Jack, 'whatever-it-was' might simply be a shark-shaped ball of bait fish, which unfortunately could be attractive to a shark for a number of reasons. All the more reason to get out of the water as soon as possible.

Unfortunately for Jack, the nearest way out of the water was actually getting further away from him with each passing second. It was either the Aqua-Cycle or Jack, but one of them was now in the grip of a current that was putting more and more water between them. The telescopic effect of looking at the world through a goggle full of sea water didn't help matters either.

But before Jack could empty them, he thought he saw 'whatever-it-was' swim under him again. Frantically he began to swim towards the nearest shore, which at this point was Blackburn Island. He then remembered all those nature documentaries he had seen about sharks, and how frantic swimming is one of the things that attracts them, so he ceased the frantic flaying of potentially tasty limbs, and tried to swim more nonchalantly.

Sharks are attracted to frantic swimming because they think it's a creature in distress, which it usually is if it knows a shark is heading towards it. A creature that doesn't swim frantically tells the shark it's a confident healthy creature who can obviously swim faster if it wants to, and might actually be a threat to the shark.

Unfortunately, Jack was never going to be able to pull that confidence trick off. When he tried to swim nonchalantly, he actually began to sink, which set off another panicked flounder.

Quickly regaining his composure, he tried rolling over and pretending to be relaxed by floating on his back. This seemed to work at first, although he had little idea where he was going, and unbeknownst had set off on a course away from the nearby shore of Blackburn Island, and towards his original target, the apparently gimpy Swede's yacht, the *Röda Sill*.

Yet despite this gallant attempt to look relaxed, Jack couldn't help but worry about where 'whatever-it-was' was, and kept trying to look into the water below out of the corner of his still water-filled, be-goggled eyes. While carrying out this difficult manoeuvre, Jack rotated his head a little too far to his left, and accidentally inhaled a mouthful of sea water, not enough to drown him, but just enough to encourage an enormous coughing fit – which is not an easy thing to have while floating on your back trying to swim nonchalantly. And it's a well-known fact that coughing fits attract sharks. That's why they like to isolate tuberculosis patients on islands, thought Jack. If they try to escape, their coughing will attract sharks and they'll be eaten.

His cool blown, and now coughing up a saltwater and phlegm storm, Jack gave up any pretence to aquatic nonchalance and did his best floundering, fitting, frantic food impersonation for 'whatever-it-was' somewhere below, in the direction of the *Röda Sill,* which was now about four metres away.

Fortunately for Jack, 'whatever-it-was' wasn't hungry, or possibly Jack didn't look too appetising. Perhaps 'whatever-it-was' heard the coughing and didn't want to catch whatever disease or condition Jack appeared to be suffering from.

Propelled by the desire to get onto something dry and solid so he could have a decent cough, and hopefully expel the small wave he was sure he had swallowed, Jack quickly reached the side of Svensen's yacht, only to discover that the edge of the deck was just out of his reach.

He was going to have to launch himself vertically out of the water and on to the deck somehow. Taking in a big breath of air in between wheezing and coughing, Jack closed his mouth, put his hands by his sides, and corpse-like allowed himself to sink as far as his wetsuit would let him. With his head now a metre below the surface of the water, Jack began to kick furiously with his still be-flippered feet.

The intention was to launch himself out of the water high enough to be able to grab the edge of the boat, which once grabbed he would then use to virtually vault himself onto the deck. What Jack's plan didn't take into account was the safety railing.

There were two rows of wire in the form of a safety railing around the side of the *Röda Sill*, the first row at about 20 centimetres above the deck itself. Jack's body at its widest point, his gut, was about 25 centimetres, and in a wetsuit it was closer to 30 centimetres. As he flung himself upward, Jack put his arms behind his back in a foolhardy attempt to make his body more streamlined. Mid-launch Jack saw the wire and managed to get his head under it, although it caught momentarily on his goggles, releasing a small reservoir of salty water over his face, and leaving the strap half over his ears, which made them stick out at a decidedly seal-like angle.

All in all, the launch was a success. It was the landing that was a disaster. His body had enough momentum to get him up onto the deck, but he was left high and not-very-dry halfway on and halfway off, the wire effectively hog-tying him with his hands behind his back and his black be-flippered legs hanging over the side of the boat, a tempting morsel for 'whatever-it-was', who surely must have noticed all this commotion by now.

The act itself took the wind out of him, which reduced the coughing fit he was now gratefully having on deck rather than in the ocean, to a sickening bark. He flapped his legs, desperately trying to free himself from the railing that had him pinned.

Still coughing with what seemed like half a litre of salt water in his lungs, Jack desperately waggled his body up and down to try to move it forward under the wire in an attempt to free his hands so he could hurl himself into a more upright position and at least have a decent coughing fit before he dropped dead.

Dressed from neck to toe in black rubber, with his flippers flapping over the side of the boat, coughing like an asthmatic bloodhound, the salt water glistening on his whiskers, Jack looked and sounded surprisingly like a fur seal. Especially to the semi-inebriated one-eyed man who had just stepped out of his cabin and was now advancing towards Jack, literally foaming at the mouth and carrying what appeared to be a baseball bat, or some kind of baseball-bat shaped object that crazy Swedes might use to beat fur seals to death with.

In his defence, Sven Svensen only had one eye. Where the other eye once was, he normally covered with a stylish eye patch that carried the witty motto *Take a Liking to a Viking*, a present from Karl, his prostheticist in Malmö who had fitted him out before he embarked on his voyage.

But Jack wasn't to know that. Instead he got to see what the patch normally hid, a horrible gaping hole where Svensen's Nordic blue eyeball had once been.

Apparently Svensen had a bottle of vodka in his hand when he fell into the combine harvester – indeed the bottle of vodka was the reason he fell into the combine harvester. But he didn't so much fall as he was pulled in after he deliberately put his hand into the maw of the harvester. He was so drunk he was offering it some. The bottle smashed in the harvester's whirring blades, and a large chunk of glass flew out at tremendous speed and cleanly gouged Svensen's entire right eye out.

Sadly, that had been his good eye. Svensen was short-sighted in his remaining eye, and normally wore a single contact lens, but had taken it out for the post-lunch nap he'd just taken, and having only recently woken up, hadn't had time to put it back in. Jack wasn't to know any of that either. Svensen lumbered toward Jack and angrily raised the club above his head. Jack tried to tell him that he was an Australian government official who wanted to ask Svensen a few questions. But all that came out was "Arf! Arf! Arf! Arf!"

Svensen muttered something angrily in Swedish that sounded like it might have been, "You bastard seals! I told you to stop following me!" but could have been anything, for all Jack knew.

Just before the first blow fell, Jack was sure he could see Svensen's brain pulsating within his skull-with-a-view. As the club rained down on Jack's body again and again, he marvelled at how Svensen managed to wield it so forcefully with a prosthetic device where his right hand used to be. It wasn't a fancy high-tech robotic hand, nor was it a simple old-school hook, although it had some hook-like qualities. It was an L-shaped section of hexagonal steel that Jack immediately recognised from putting together an entire houseful of IKEA furniture, as an Allen key. A huge Allen key.

Glancing around the boat Jack could now see that there were sunken hexagonal bolts on all the hatches and winches, and wondered if IKEA had branched out into nautical hardware, or whether Svensen had the yacht specially outfitted for his prosthetic attachment, when the next blow from Svensen's club woke him from his mid-beating reverie.

Fortunately for Jack, he was wearing rubber, so while the blows from Svensen's bat were uncomfortable, they were not causing any major damage. In fact, they were bouncing off. They even seemed to be actually doing some good. The last one felt like it had helped dislodge some of the ocean from his lungs. But eventually one of these blows will connect with my head, thought Jack, and he redoubled his efforts to get free, as well as his efforts to sound like a wounded harp seal.

Finally Jack managed to get his right arm and then his left arm free. Desperately he covered his head with his left arm and with his right arm tried to grab hold of the closest bit of his attacker, which turned out to be Svensen's right foot.

Jack yanked the foot forward in an attempt to sweep Svensen off his feet, but it didn't work out as he planned. Svensen was still standing there, and Jack was now holding Svensen's prosthetic leg in his hand. Amazingly the ugly Swede was still bashing Jack with the club, while perfectly balanced on his one good leg.

At least now Jack had a weapon. Using it as his own club, he whacked Svensen in the left shin, causing him to drop his weapon and fall to the ground clutching his possibly shattered shin and swearing, Jack presumed, in Swedish.

While Svensen grovelled in a semi-foetal position, Jack was able to get to his knees and then to his feet. Once upright he was pleasantly surprised to find that the barking cough had all but subsided and he could breathe relatively easily for the first time since falling off the Aqua-Cycle.

Svensen was now on his back, swearing a Nordic blue streak and rubbing his only remaining shin. Jack thought he should help the poor man up, give him back his leg, and try to explain the situation, when Svensen shouted "Mathilde! Slå ned på!"

With that, a deafening high-pitch whistle filled Jack's ears as a small yellow and green object flew out of the yacht's open cabin door, and straight at Jack's face.

It was Mathilde, Svensen's attack-budgie, and she wasn't happy.

Tiny talons lashed at Jack's nose, and he ducked as he tried to shoo the small bird away. But Mathilde didn't give up that easily, and again and again she returned, her shrill war cry filling Jack's ears, her tiny wings beating remorselessly against his unprotected forehead.

Still armed with Svensen's prosthetic leg, which Jack was now able to observe was wearing a stylishly nautical boat loafer with a special deck-gripping crepe sole, Jack waved both arms in front of his face to protect himself from the berserker budgie.

And the budgie was winning. Mathilde had put Jack on the back foot, and was slowly herding him to the pointy end of the yacht. Jack frantically swung his arms at the bird, and with more luck than intention, Svensen's faux foot connected in mid-air with the arse of the badass budgie and sent it flying into the ocean.

As Jack watched its trajectory, to see if 'whatever-it-was' that was out there was going to jump up out of the water and snatch the budgie in mid-air as it hurtled past, he heard the sound of a small outboard motor.

Somehow, while Jack was distracted defending his precious earlobes from Mathilde's millet-sharpened beak and surprisingly needle-like talons, Svensen had managed to drag himself using his Allen-key claw and corresponding bolts sunk into the decking, to the back of the boat and get in the small inflatable dinghy, untie the rope which attached it to the *Röda Sill*, and make his escape.

Jack realised this 69-year-old man with one leg, a hand missing and extremely impaired vision in his one remaining eye was more than a match for him.

But the fact that he was so readily willing to abandon his ship, made Jack assume Svensen was guilty of something, if not killing Harvey Jacob. It didn't occur to Jack that Svensen might simply be trying to get away any way that he, a severely incapacitated man, could from the barking-mad snorkeller who boarded his vessel, stole his prosthetic leg and tried to kill his budgie.

Svensen slowly started to putt away from his yacht. If he was ever going to catch him, Jack decided he'd have to act without thinking. This was not a good idea, and he would have realised that if he'd stopped to think about it for a second or two. There wasn't any point chasing after Svensen as there really wasn't anywhere that he could go. He certainly couldn't go to sea in the tiny inflatable dinghy.

But Jack wasn't thinking as, still be-flippered, he waddled to the back of the yacht, grabbed a nearby boogie board, and plunged over the side of the boat and into the water.

It was one of the few spontaneous things Jack had ever done in his adult life, and it was both exhilarating and horrifying, as he knew that 'whatever-it-was' was still out there waiting for him.

The Jack-laden boogie board hit the water, submerged briefly, then popped to the surface. In doing so, Jack felt something dragging across his face. It was the end of the nylon rope Svensen had used to tie the dinghy to the yacht, and the other end of it was still attached to the front of the dinghy.

Sensing that he shouldn't let the rope get away, but using both his hands to grip the boogie board that was supporting him, Jack did the only thing he could. As the rope slipped over his face, he grabbed it between his teeth and held on firmly.

Within a few seconds the rope tightened and jerked Jack's head forward, and then rest of him, as he and his recently acquired boogie board began to be dragged along behind the dinghy.

Holding on to the rope with his teeth, gripping the board with both hands, Jack clung on for grim death, as ahead of him the 1.5 horsepower mini-outboard motor puttered along at a mere two kilometres per hour.

Svensen was originally heading for shore, but once he realised he had an unwanted passenger in tow, he headed back out towards the reef in a zigzagging pattern in an effort to lose him. Unfortunately for Svensen, the dinghy was going so slowly, there was very little chance of Jack being shaken off.

With his teeth so far holding firm, Jack bit down and steered his boogie board out wide of the dinghy. Then using his left arm, practically hugging the top of the board, he let go with his right hand, and used it and his teeth to slowly pull himself towards the dinghy.

Soon Jack was alongside and, much to Svensen's dismay, was almost close enough to reach the rope handle that ran the length of the dinghy. But in order to grab it, he would have to let go of the rope he was currently holding and abandon the boogie board.

As Jack was just about to make his move, Svensen angrily jumped towards him and growled as he lashed out in Jack's direction with his Allen key hook. At the very same moment Jack let go of the boogie board to grab the dinghy's rope railing. The boogie board shot upwards in front of Jack just as Svensen's Allen key hook came down towards Jack's face.

Had Svensen been any quicker, Jack would more than likely have a new hexagonal-shaped nostril. As it was, he had a breather, while Svensen angrily tried to shake off the boogie board that was now skewered on his hook hand-substitute.

Jack used the opportunity to climb onto the bow of the dinghy where he collapsed, panting heavily. But within seconds, Svensen had removed the boogie board from his hook and had flung it into the ocean. He glared insanely at Jack who was now lounging, or so it seemed, on the inflated rubbery nose of the craft.

Svensen roared. Jack shook his head. "You don't understand … I just want to …" he said, between gasps for air. But before he could continue, the psycho Swede lunged at him, swinging his mean left hook at Jack's face. Jack literally pulled his head in, but Svensen's hook somehow managed to pierce the front of Jack's wetsuit.

With an almighty jerk, Svensen pulled Jack towards him. Jack noticed the deep angry scar that ran from the Swede's empty eye socket down to the point of his chin. He pulled Jack in closer, until their faces were only centimetres away. There were flecks of white foam in the ancient mariner's prickly facial hair. His nostrils flared menacingly. He opened his mouth. Svensen's breath was minty fresh. This explained why he was foaming at the mouth, thought Jack. He must have been cleaning his teeth when Jack boarded his boat.

Svensen scowled and his teeth gleamed and, in clear English with a slight Swedish accent, spat out these words.

"Get off my rubber-ducky, Seal-man!"

With one movement, the brawny disabled senior citizen Swede hurled Jack headfirst into the water.

As Jack torpedoed towards the reef below, he noticed something even worse than a crazy Swedish sailor with an IKEA-friendly hook and great dental hygiene. Directly below him, just above a ridge of coral and seaweed-encrusted rock, Jack could clearly see the dark menacing shape of 'whatever-it-was'. The creature must have heard the splash as Jack hit the water for it turned its head slowly, blew a mouthful of bubbles and made 'the sign of the devil' with its right hand. It was Boz the BASE jumper, in scuba gear.

Jack barely had time to return the time-honoured rock'n'roll greeting, before the buoyancy of his wetsuit brought him bobbing back to the surface like an ugly inflatable doll in a rubber catsuit. He gasped desperately for air even though he'd been underwater for less than ten seconds.

Floundering, Jack grabbed the side of the Swede's inflatable vessel.

"Go away!" shouted Svensen, and brought his Allen-key hook down on the spot where Jack had just placed his hand. Jack's normally sluggish reflexes surprisingly kicked in, and without thinking he quickly moved his hand from harm's way, and Svensen's Allen key punctured the side of the craft.

"I'll have to patch that now!" Svensen snarled furiously, revving the outboard and taking off at a snail's pace, but too fast for Jack, towards the *Röda Sill*.

Jack floundered for a bit, trying to avoid Svensen's propellers. The last thing he wanted was any more of his blood in the water, in case Boz the BASE jumper wasn't the only 'whatever-it-was' lurking in the depths of the lagoon.

By the time Jack had swum back to the Aqua-Cycle, righted it and negotiated his way back onto the seat, Svensen had returned to the *Röda Sill*, started up its engine and was motoring out through the opening in the reef and into the open sea, Mathilde defiantly perched on his shoulder.

Feverishly, Jack pedalled to shore, now really wishing he'd taken his flippers off this time.

Within minutes he was clambering up the beach to the boatshed where Reg was reading a copy of *Country Home Ideas* magazine he'd found in the amenities block.

"Quick! Call the authorities!" said Jack in between pants.

"I thought you *were* the authorities," quipped Reg, looking up from the editorial page that was all about how to make your shabby-chic home even shabbier.

"Then call the Coast Guard," demanded Jack. "Svensen's getting away!"

"We're not really that near the coast out here," Reg pointed out.

"You have a coast, don't you?" asked Jack. "Who defends that?"

Reg thought for a moment. "Technically, that would be the Navy."

"Then call the Navy," demanded Jack. "We have to stop him!"

Reg looked worried. "Why, what did he do?"

"He threw me off his rubber ducky, and his budgie attacked me," said Jack defensively.

"I'm not sure if that's enough to call the Navy out for," reasoned Reg, reasonably.

Jack was undeterred. "His behaviour is aggressive, suspicious and, from what I observed first hand, I'd say his psychological profile matches the type of person who wouldn't think twice about killing someone like Harvey Jacob with an innocent muttonbird."

Reg shook his head. "Not possible."

"Why not?" asked Jack.

"He didn't turn up until this morning," said Reg confidentially. "I know. I did his customs' declaration. And I told him that under the strict quarantine regulations he couldn't bring his budgie, what's its name?"

"Mathilde," Jack offered.

"That's right, Mathilde. I told him he couldn't bring Mathilde ashore. It might eat a phasmid."

Jack shook his head in disbelief.

"Why didn't you tell me that before I went out there?"

"You just asked me if anyone odd had turned up in the last few days. You didn't say *before* the murder."

"And what was so odd about him? Besides the pirate-like disfigurement?" queried Jack.

Reg glanced towards Jack with a serious, somewhat disturbed look on his face. "He asked me if there were any seals here," said Reg. "He thinks he's being followed by them for some reason. That sounded odd to me."

Jack shook his head. It all made horrible sense in a bizarre kind of way. Jack decided that Reg was right. Svensen was odd, and probably capable of killing someone with a

muttonbird, but he wasn't even present at the time the crime –
if it even was a crime – more than likely took place.

By the time Jack had de-wetsuited himself, had a shower
to wash the salt water off and re-dressed, it was after three
o'clock – time to pay Norma a visit at the Hill Shop which,
not surprisingly, was at the top of the hill he'd earlier so
recklessly ridden down.

Now, almost fully recovered from his frightening ordeal at
sea, Jack began the first of many ugly ascents by bicycle from
the low flat lagoon side of the island to the more elevated
north-eastern side of the island, where his lodgings were, and
where the Hill Shop was located. Halfway up, he began to
wonder who the department would send to investigate *his*
death if he burst a blood vessel trying to change from second
to first gear while not repeating his arse-falling display of
earlier.

Finally he made it to the top, sweat pouring down his face,
his palang and lorum tinkling with every downstroke, and
turned on to the relatively level plateau of Skyline Drive –
a long narrow road with kentia jungle on one side and a
pleasantly rural cow paddock on the other. About halfway
along on the jungle side of the road was the so-called Hill
Shop – which was more of a small shack than a shop in the
7-Eleven convenience-store-sense that he was used to on the
mainland.

The weather had changed on his ascent and now, as Jack
stopped to catch his breath, a heavy cloud loomed overhead
and began dropping fat raindrops, which to Jack was a cool

blessing indeed. The rain came faster and harder, so Jack pedalled for the shelter of the Hill Shop's awning.

Now under the expansive awning, Jack leaned his bike against an old cold-storage unit full of ice cream and frozen chickens. An assortment of fresh veggies was on display out the front, and inside groceries were stacked on the dimly-lit shelves.

The space behind the counter opened out onto a makeshift butcher shop, where Norma and her partner George butchered the local livestock and made some rather tasty gourmet sausages.

After she'd finished serving a couple of customers, Jack showed Norma his ID, and asked her to tell him about finding Harvey Jacob's body.

"I had to deliver a pig for spit roasting to the Bowls Club, so I was up here pretty early this morning."

By now the brief summer shower had moved on, so Norma took Jack down the road and around the corner into Muttonbird Drive, to the spot where she found the body.

"He was just lying there, with a muttonbird sticking out of his ear," she said, pointing to a small pool of blood and feathers on the gravel at the side of the road. The pandanus forest in front of them was riddled with muttonbird burrows.

"I wasn't sure if he was dead, so I pulled the bird out of his ear and shouted in it, 'Are you alright?' And when he didn't move, I figured he wasn't alright. So I slung him in the back of the van with the pig and dropped him off with Barry at the Fish Co-op."

"Does this sort of thing happen all the time?" asked Jack.

"What?" asked Norma.

"People being killed by suicidal muttonbirds," Jack explained.

"No, not often," said Norma, shaking her head. It almost sounded as if she was disappointed somehow.

Jack nodded almost as if he sympathised. "I see."

"Why exactly do they call them 'muttonbirds'?" asked Jack.

"Well, according to the old legend, it's because they taste like mutton," said Norma, warming to the subject. "But they don't really."

"What do they taste like?" inquired Jack.

"More like ..." she pondered this for a moment. "They taste more like seagull, actually," and smiled.

Jack nodded and sucked air in through his teeth.

"Is there anyone on the island who knows anything about *live* muttonbirds?"

"Is there ever!" said Norma with a smile.

Jack headed off to meet the island's resident bird expert. On the ride down the hill, he began to notice that his legs were now seriously aching from doing more cycling – both bi and Aqua – in one day than he'd done in the last 35 years.

He pondered the facts, and desperately tried not to jump to the wrong conclusion nearly as quickly as he had with Sven Svensen. Norma found the corpse. But did she also *create* the corpse from Harvey Jacob's once-living body? A woman of Norma's robust constitution, who was familiar with cuts of meat and the flavours of seabirds, would more than likely be able to kill a man, possibly even with a muttonbird. Or maybe she killed Harvey some other way, and the muttonbird had to go, because it 'saw too much'.

Jack felt himself jumping too soon to a wrong conclusion, so changed tack. When he rationalised the situation, he was reasonably convinced that Norma couldn't have killed Harvey. Firstly, she had no motive. She didn't even know the guy. Secondly, she had a rock-solid alibi. She was asleep in bed and her husband, and all the other people in the near vicinity that her snoring had kept awake, could testify to that.

The facts still remained the same. As unlikely as it seemed, it appeared that Harvey Jacob had been taken out by the pointy end of a poorly executed muttonbird-landing, and not by a person or persons unknown.

Before he left, Norma had filled Jack in about Brad Lawrence, the island's resident bird expert. Brad was so into the native bird life, that after coming to the island only once, five years ago, he decided to stay on permanently, and devote his life to their study and protection.

This was not an easy feat to accomplish, as non-islanders aren't generally encouraged to stay much longer than the average holiday. But a few years back, Brad married Diana Dawson, who was a good 20 years older than him, which gave him permanent residency. Sadly, Diana died a short while after the wedding in a boating accident, and her body was never found. The only thing they did find was her wedding ring, which washed up a few days later on Ned's Beach, at the exact spot where they feed the kingfish every day.

Arriving at Brad Lawrence's office and parking his bike, Jack entered the property past a sign that read 'Birders' Paradise Eco Tours,' with the word 'Eco' painted in a different colour and squished in between 'Paradise' and 'Tours'.

Jack couldn't understand how they could call them 'Eco' tours when the tours themselves involved taking a bunch of distinctly unnatural hiking-booted birdwatchers into the native birds' natural habitat, stomping around, potentially ruining the environment and even scaring off the birds with their camera shutters and gushes of twitcherly enthusiasm. Surely, he thought, if you wanted to do something 'eco-friendly' for the birds, you wouldn't allow tourists into the area in the first place. Therefore the most eco-friendly thing a birdwatcher could possibly do is stop watching birds. Leave them alone. Pretend they're not there. Go about your business.

Inside the office, the walls were covered with posters of birds and the furniture was covered with stuffed birds, many of them a bit worse for wear and tear.

Jack was looking closely and curiously at a particularly decrepit specimen when a voice at the inner-office door startled him.

"That's a Lord Howe Boobook Owl."

For a second Jack thought the stuffed bird was talking to him. He looked up to see Brad Lawrence coming through the door. Brad turned out to be the same suave khaki-clad gentleman who commandeered the twitchers back at the airport. Brad was greying and distinguished looking, except for one thing – a huge mole right in the middle of his forehead, the kind of thing you can't take your eyes off.

Brad motioned his mole towards the boobook.

"It's extinct now."

Dragging his attention away from the mole and onto the owl, Jack noted the stuffing coming out of one wing, and a glass eye hanging wonkily.

"I can see why."

Brad shook his head. "I didn't do that."

"What? Make them extinct?"

"No, stuff that owl."

"Same thing, isn't it?"

"I wasn't responsible for either. These specimens belonged to my predecessor, who is himself now stuffed." He stifled a chuckle.

"I see."

Jack showed Brad his ID.

"I'm Jack Slazenger, deputy assistant state coroner."

"What, a *bird* coroner? You're too late for these, I'm afraid," said Brad, as he attempted to straighten the boobook's eye, and pushed some of the stuffing back into its wing.

"A man was killed last night, and it appears a muttonbird was involved," Jack informed him.

"Yes, I saw the body, this morning, when Norma dropped off the bacon. Nasty." Brad pulled a face of disgust.

"The body?" asked Jack.

"No, the bacon. Still had bristles on it."

Jack pulled the same face Brad was now pulling.

"Yuck. What do you know about muttonbirds?" he inquired.

"So you *are* a bird coroner? Quite a lot actually." Brad proceeded to impart some of his apparently extensive bird knowledge. "Between September and May, approximately half of the world's population of the fleshfooted shearwater, or *Puffinus carneipes hullianus,* breeds right here on Lord Howe Island – an estimated 18,000 pairs of muttonbirds – nesting in burrows of approximately ..."

"Is it possible for a muttonbird to kill a man?" interjected Jack.

"Not in a fair fight," responded Brad thoughtfully.

"Is it possible that a muttonbird might accidentally collide with a man?"

"With half the world's muttonbird population taking off each morning and landing each evening, it's lucky we're not all being taken out by muttonbirds," Brad answered.

"What else do you know about muttonbirds?"

"Besides the taste?"

"Yes."

"They migrate here from as far away as Siberia. A graceful bird in the air and competent on water, they're crap on land, and not very good at landing. Especially when it's pitch black."

"So the probability is, the deceased – Harvey Jacob – was walking back to his accommodation late last night and a muttonbird, attempting to land, didn't see him, and flew right into his head?"

"They're not the smartest of birds. And if that bird had come all the way from Siberia, think of the velocity involved."

Jack nodded thoughtfully. He did this to make it look like he was thinking seriously about something when he wasn't really. It seemed to work this time. He thanked Brad for his time and went to leave.

As Jack was just about out the door, Brad stopped him.

"While you're on the island, if you want to come out and check out the birds with me, you're more than welcome."

"That's alright. I think I've already found one."

"You really must see the top of Mount Gower. I can take you up there, if you like," said Brad enticingly.

"I'd love to, except for one tiny thing," said Jack apologetically.

"And what's that?" queried Brad.

"I'm afraid of heights."

Jack gingerly bicycled back up the hill, concerned now that all this cycling would leave him bow-legged for life. But at the very least, his interview with Brad Lawrence had made him feel that there was no need to jump to any more wrong conclusions. It was beginning to look to him like an open-and-shut case. So, not being the most thorough of coronial investigators, Jack decided to phone it in and get back to his holiday.

He pedalled along Anderson Street to the one public telephone booth on the upper part of the island's 'residential' district. He dropped his bike, took off his helmet, and then jumped backwards about two metres when he saw that the entire ceiling of the phone booth, down to just above the top of the phone, was taken up by a high-rise spider web very visibly populated by a horde of golden orb spiders. There were a lot of things that Jack was afraid of, and spiders were most of them.

Crouching like the midget he nearly was, Jack warily entered the phone booth, cautiously picked up the handpiece from its cradle, and after inspecting both ends to make sure it was spider-free, he carefully punched the number keys to call his boss.

As was often the case, his boss was underwhelmed by Jack's report. "That's not enough. This dead guy is very well connected. The US embassy wants to know exactly what happened, who he was with, what he was doing there – the works."

Jack hung up the phone. It looked like he still wasn't on holiday. "Bugger," he muttered to himself.

Deep in thought, he stood and turned to leave the booth, forgetting completely about the spiders, and copped a face-full of golden orb, and a mouthful of dead flies and bugs.

Realising there was the very real possibility that he may actually have a huge golden orb spider somewhere on his body, Jack ran from the phone booth squealing involuntarily and randomly beating his body all over – just as Jill the dentist bicycled by, on her way home from the clinic.

"Acid flashback?" she asked with a smile.

"It's a new dance step I'm working on," replied Jack. "I call it the 'Freeform Macarena'."

Jill laughed.

"Actually, I'm just practicing the slapping dance for Oktoberfest."

She laughed even more. He still had it.

"Spiders, really," Jack admitted. "I have an irrational fear of spiders … and dentists."

"Really. That's a pity, because I was just on my way to Ned's Beach for a swim and I was going to invite you to join me."

Jack couldn't believe it. He'd only been on the island a few hours and already an attractive intelligent woman who didn't seem to mind that he was a buffoon was inviting him to get semi-naked with her. The holiday romance he'd been waiting most of his life for had finally arrived, but unfortunately he wasn't on holiday yet. Reluctantly, he had to pass up the offer. But Jill was persistent.

"How about dinner? They tell me the Bowls Club's good. And technically I'm not a dentist when I'm not working, so you've got nothing to be frightened of."

"Unless there are spiders in the Bowls Club, too."

She laughed again. This was good.

They agreed to meet at 7:00pm and Jill cycled off to the beach. Jack wearily pushed his bike up the hill, not quite sure what his next move would be in the Harvey Jacob inquiry when Suzie, the flightless flight attendant drove up in an old ute and rolled down her window. "Do you want a lift?"

Seconds later Jack was in the passenger seat of the ute and his bike was in the back.

"No more flights today?" Jack inquired.

"Nope. I'm off to my other job," replied Suzie.

"What's that?"

"Waitressing at Pandanus."

Jack remembered Harvey's credit card receipt from the Pandanus restaurant in his pocket. "Were you working last night?"

"Certainly was. It was a mad house."

"Then you were probably one of the last people to see Harvey Jacob alive."

"Me and 30 other people. It was packed."

"So you did see him?" asked Jack.

"I served him, so yeah," Suzie admitted with a smile.

"Did you notice anything unusual about him?"

"Apart from the fact he was dressed like a baseball player and he was eating with a girl who was at least 30 years his junior, no."

"What?" exclaimed Jack, looking moderately surprised. "I'd just assumed he was alone. No one mentioned he was with someone."

"You're not very good at this, are you?" she said sympathetically.

"Could it have been his daughter?" asked Jack.

"Only if his wife was Polynesian. This girl was stunningly exotic."

"Really?" Jack took out the credit card receipt from Harvey's wallet.

"That explains why there were two entrees and two mains. I thought he was just very hungry."

He looked closely at the receipt. Two bottles of wine, but only one dessert.

"Yeah, I think she left early. I was run off my feet though, so I wasn't paying that much attention."

"Did they have a fight, or an argument of some sort?"

"I honestly didn't notice," admitted Suzie. "Maybe. I did notice that one minute she was there and the next minute she was gone. Poor girl. Wait. I thought he was killed by a muttonbird."

"That is what it looks like."

"You don't think his girlfriend bludgeoned him to death with a seabird, do you?"

"Stranger things have happened," said Jack, trying hard to think of something stranger, but coming up empty. He began to seriously consider jumping to a sudden irrational conclusion about Harvey Jacob's Polynesian girlfriend, without having met her and without any corroborating evidence whatsoever that she was in any way involved in his death.

"Maybe in parts of Polynesia the muttonbird is used as some kind of traditional weapon ..." he mused.

"Does she even know he's dead yet?" Suzie interrupted, stopping Jack mid-muse.

"Holy shit in a handbag!" expleted Jack, suddenly realising that Harvey Jacob's 'significant other', for want of a better description, might still be blissfully unaware of her partner's recent tragic demise. "Do you know where they were staying?"

"Ah no. But if he was walking home along Muttonbird Drive, it was probably Hightide Apartments."

Jack told Suzie to stop the car immediately, which she was just about to do anyway as they had arrived outside the entrance to the Pandanus restaurant.

He quickly grabbed his borrowed bike from the back of Suzie's ute and biked it back to the apartments as fast as his short, hairy, exhausted legs would take him. Once back at Hightide Apartments, finding exactly where Jacob's girlfriend was staying, was a process of elimination. There were only six apartments and Jack himself was staying in one of them. He simply had to knock on the other five doors.

In one apartment, the happy twitchers were having 'fivesies' on their verandah after a hard day's birding on one of Brad Lawrence's tours. Jack asked them if they'd seen a young attractive girl in her early twenties, possibly of Polynesian persuasion. Mrs Twitcher looked at him with an air of disgust, while Mr Twitcher said that wasn't the kind of birds they were interested in, but raised his glass and gave Jack a wink.

Jack knocked on two more doors but no one answered. At the next door he got lucky. The door was opened by Jill, who'd just had a shower after her swim at Ned's Beach, and was in a white terry towelling robe drying her hair.

"You're a little early, aren't you? I thought we were meeting at seven," she said to Jack with a beguiling smile.

Jack was momentarily stunned by finding Jill in a state of relative undress, and then even more stunned when an outrageously attractive young woman, almost bursting out the skimpiest of bikinis, her warm light brown Polynesian skin still wet from the nearby ocean, strolled right past the front of Jill's apartment. She smiled politely at the dropped jaws of both Jack and Jill, and opened the door of the next apartment.

"Sorry – gotta go," said Jack to the flummoxed Jill, as he bolted after the wet nymphette.

As the extremely stunning young woman was about to open the door to her apartment, Jack cleared his throat so as not to startle her, startling her in the process.

The bikini-clad beauty simultaneously jumped, screamed and twirled around to face Jack who was now fumbling in his pocket for his official ID, so she wouldn't scream again, which only made her scream again.

Finally he whipped it out, and flashed it in her face.

"It's okay," he said as he introduced himself and asked her what her name was.

"Matahina Tetava," she replied, with a concerned look on her flawless face, before adding, "What's this about?"

As gently as he could, Jack broke the news of Harvey's death to her.

Matahina was stunned. Stunningly stunned. "Oh my god! I thought he'd just gone back to the boat. We had a bit of um, a disagreement."

"What exactly was your relationship with Mr Jacob?" asked Jack, trying his best to sound like an official investigator, yet failing spectacularly to follow up on the admission his suspect had just made.

"I was his ... employee, I guess. I'm from Aitutaki."

"That's in the Cook Islands, right?" queried Jack, now completely forgetting the investigation altogether, as his head filled with enticing images of a tropical paradise of coral lagoons lined with palm trees, where a crystal-clear ocean lapped sensuously against white hot sand, while the sound of grass-skirted Polynesian maidens singing a lilting melody to the accompaniment of ukuleles and slack-key guitars, filled the warm humid air already thick with the smell of ripe exotic fruits and fresh fish being grilled over an open fire.

"Yes, but I went to school in Sydney," replied Matahina, and Jack instantly returned from the virtual Aitutaki in his head to the actual Aitutakian before him.

"Ascham," added Matahina, which Jack took to be a sneeze, or possibly what you do if you've 'got 'em', and you've 'smoked 'em', but which was actually a prestigious private girls school in Sydney's eastern suburbs.

Matahina continued, "I recently moved back home to Aitutaki." Just the mention of Aitutaki began to send Jack back into another Aloha-shirted fantasy, which this time he valiantly resisted.

"But it wasn't going too well," confessed Matahina. "My family are very traditional, and there was this arranged marriage they wanted me to go through with …" Matahina pulled a face of utter disgust, which on a face of such sheer beauty sent a confusing subliminal message that to Jack was strangely erotic.

"But you weren't interested …" he asked, guessing that's what the message on her face was intended to convey.

"You should have seen this guy." Matahina shook her head in disbelief. "Talk about being hit with the ugly stick, this guy must have had the whole tree fall on him. And just because he was a prince and I'm a princess. No way."

"You're a princess?" asked Jack, not entirely incredulous.

"It's tribal stuff. Very 'old school'. But even if he was drop-dead gorgeous, I don't ever want to get married."

"Why not?" asked Jack, having now completely forgotten the investigation, and thoroughly sucked-in to the oceanic soap opera that appeared to be Matahina's life.

"Have you ever seen a thin married Polynesian woman? They don't exist. Every single Polynesian woman looks like me, then they get married and end up looking like Jabba the Hutt."

Jack winced at the thought. Matahina continued, "That's not going to happen to me. So anyway. Harvey turned up on his boat, sailing around the world, or whatever, and I just kind of snuck out one morning, got in an outrigger canoe and paddled out and climbed aboard."

"When he found me, which didn't take long, seeing as how it's not really that big a big boat and I kind of stick out."

"I can see that ..." added Jack earnestly.

"... he heard my story and offered me a job as deckhand and first mate. Although I didn't realise that hand would be mostly on *my* deck and exactly who the first mate had to mate with."

"Harvey put the hard word on you?"

"It was getting harder and harder, the further we went. Last night, I basically told him that was it. I was going to ring my parents in the morning, which I did …"

"In the phone booth with the spiders?" asked Jack with a look of horror.

"Yeah, it's creepy, isn't it?" agreed Matahina. "And they're organising a flight back to Sydney for me."

"The spiders?" asked a confused Jack.

"No, my parents."

"Ah …" Jack nodded thoughtfully.

By now they were both sitting on a settee outside Matahina's apartment.

"So what exactly happened last night?"

"Not much really. We had dinner, and he used every excuse in the book. He went on about how he'd bought me dinner and paid for this apartment, and he was paying me, and how he rescued me. But he isn't my type either."

"What *is* your type?" asked Jack, hopefully.

Matahina burst into tears. "If only I'd agreed to have sex with him, he wouldn't be dead now."

"That's not true," said Jack, trying to reassure her. "Harvey was in his early sixties. Sex with you could easily have killed him."

Matahina wiped tears from her cheeks and nodded in agreement.

"Or you might have stayed at the restaurant later and it might have been *you* who was killed by that muttonbird," added Jack.

"No, believe me. If I'd agreed to have sex with him, we would have been out of there immediately – if not sooner. In fact he was so desperate, we might not have even made it out of the restaurant."

Jack mused and nodded thoughtfully. "I know how he must have felt."

"So was there an argument?" he continued, trying to keep his mind focused on the investigation.

"Not really," said Matahina, looking at the ground. "He recognised some guy in the restaurant and when they started talking, I just said I was leaving, and went home. That was about 8:30pm."

"And weren't you suspicious when he didn't come home?" asked Jack.

"I slept like a log. After spending the last three nights in a narrow bunk on a boat that's constantly rocking, trying to keep half awake in case Harvey got adventurous …" she trailed off.

And then she trailed back on. "… and when he wasn't there this morning, I just figured he'd decided to sleep on the boat. In fact, I was half hoping he might have sailed off without me …"

She started to tear up again.

"If only I'd known he was lying there with a bird sticking out of his ear, I might have been able to do something".

She threw herself on Jack's shoulder and sobbed heavily. Jack tried desperately to think of the most unpleasant corpses he'd ever seen to stop from getting aroused. But it wasn't working. In desperation, he took off the bike helmet he was still wearing, and put it on his lap. This case was getting tougher and tougher.

Eventually, the sobbing and the tumescence subsided, and Jack was able to get up to leave, his helmet safely covering his other helmet. With the blood starting to flow back to his brain, he suddenly thought of something.

"You mentioned he recognised some guy. Can you describe the guy?"

"He was old, not as old as Harvey, but getting there. And he had this huge mole in the middle of his forehead."

"The bird guy?"

"Huh?"

"Brad Lawrence. He's the bird guy. How did Harvey know him?" asked Jack.

"I have no idea," replied Matahina, shaking her head.

On the way back to his apartment, Jack stopped in at Hightide's 'library', and took a VB out of the fridge, wrote his details in the book, then headed out, drinking it on his way. He liked the idea of a library you could take beers out of.

In his room, Jack picked up his Dobro guitar, slid the tempered-glass slide onto his little finger, and played a few odd-sounding yet not unpleasant notes and pseudo riffs. He smiled. Maybe this wouldn't be as hard as he thought.

But that was going to have to be it for the night, he thought, as he put down the guitar and got up to have a shower and get dressed for the Bowls Club and dinner with an actual woman. A girl, thought Jack, trumps a guitar every time.

At just after seven, he answered the door to find Jill the dentist dressed in a decidedly undentist-like fashion in a sleeveless navy and white striped top, cream three-quarter length pants and sandals. Nautical but nice, he thought to himself.

Jack was wearing his best Hawaiian shirt – a rare vintage Hale Hawaii 'Rayon Rainbow Aloha' shirt from the 1950s that he had bought online for just under a thousand dollars. The fabric featured stunning oceanfront scenes, rainbows, palm trees, coconuts, tropical flowers, and stellar blue Pacific skies. Jill blinked when she saw it.

"Wow, what a shirt. I should have brought my sunglasses."

"It's not too much is it?"

"Too much? It's everything."

Jack told her about his Aloha shirt collection on the way to the Bowls Club. Luckily one of Jill's patients from earlier in the day was also going to the club and offered to give them both a lift. Jack really didn't want to have to sweat on his best shirt while riding a bike to the club, and in fact had cycled so much in one day that at this point he would have been happy never to get on a bike again, so the offer of a pedal-free trip came as a great relief.

When they arrived at the Bowls Club, Jack was amazed. The place was packed, and for a Bowls Club, it was 'going off'. Almost before they'd walked through the door, they were offered tickets in the meat tray raffle.

Not exactly sure what he'd do with a tray of meat, and slightly concerned that it might resemble something from his day job, but still not wanting to miss out seeing how his luck was running at the moment, Jack bought three tickets.

Back on the mainland, Jack had seen bowling clubs with three patrons in them on a weeknight like this, and the greens brown and weedy and dry. Here the greens were perfectly manicured, and there must have been at least 60 people either at the bar or in the dining area. All of which made perfect sense when you realised that this was the closest thing to a pub on the island – and one of the few places you could get cold beer on tap.

Jack had felt sorry for Matahina, so they had invited her to join them. But he had no need to feel sorry for her, because as soon as she walked through the doorway, dressed in a tropical print muumuu, all eyes turned at once towards her. Blokes started lining up to buy her drinks, and she seemed to like the attention, so Jack and Jill left her to it, grabbed a beer, and went through to the dining area.

They'd both had big days and as a result were starving, which was just as well as the portions served at the Bowls Club weren't designed for those on a diet.

The meal itself was a classic – prawn cocktail with a wedge of lemon and smothered in Thousand Island dressing, followed by the roast suckling pig that Norma delivered that morning just after she dropped off Harvey Jacob's body at the Fish Co-op. All things considered, washed down with a bottle of West Australian sauvignon blanc, it didn't taste too bad.

At first the conversation was a little stilted and so they both concentrated on eating and drinking. But as Jack drank more, he started talking more.

"So how did you become an itinerant dentist?"

"It's in my family, actually."

"You come from a family of itinerant dentists?"

"No, they were all actually quite 'tinerant'. What about you, Mr Coroner?"

"Mr Deputy Assistant Coroner to you."

"Okay deputy, what's your excuse?"

"The same as yours," lied Jack. "My family were itinerant sea coroners, roaming the high seas, carrying out random inquests at the behest of grieving natives and sea captains." He closed one eye, and used a prawn as a mimic hook. "Ar! Thar she *croaks*, me hearties!"

"Really?" asked Jill after she'd stopped laughing at Jack's prawny pirate impersonation.

"No, not really," he confessed. "It's just a job for me. It's just what I'm doing until I get around to doing what I really want to do."

"What's that?"

"Blues guitarist, of course."

Jill laughed at first and then seeing the disappointed look on Jack's face, realised he was actually being serious, possibly for the first time in the entire conversation.

"So what are you waiting for?" she asked.

"Another 20 years or so," answered Jack. "You have to be really old to be a good blues guitarist."

"And black usually," smiled Jill.

"And that's another problem," Jack nodded. "But I figure if I start seriously tanning now, in 20 years I'll be getting pretty close."

"Plus you'll be able to play *The Raging Melanoma Blues*."

"Touché."

Jack was beginning to fall in love. Jill could talk nearly as much shit as he could.

It was a quality he always looked for in a potential partner and one that he always put in his Lonely Hearts ads – "Must be good at repartee, but not *too* good." He also put "Only prepared to argue if make-up sex is involved." It was no surprise that he didn't receive any replies.

After the main course plates had been taken away, they shared Jack's favourite desert of vanilla ice cream and chocolate topping – one bowl, two spoons.

"So let me get this straight …" started Jill, pointing her spoon at Jack, while she swallowed a mouthful of ice cream. "You were coming here on a holiday, when you were ordered to cut short your holiday and come here immediately?"

"Yeah, sweet isn't it?" grinned Jack. "I can write the whole thing off on my taxes, and claim overtime as well."

"So why Lord Howe Island?"

"Me, or the muttonbird that killed Harvey Jacob? I think *it* chose Lord Howe Island because it'd just flown all the way from Siberia and it just had to stop somewhere."

"And you?"

"Lord Howe Island is the only place I had enough frequent flyer points for. Which is a pretty similar reason, really."

"You only had enough points to get from Sydney to Lord Howe Island?"

"I don't fly often," admitted Jack, and came very close to explaining why but decided it might not be in his best interests at this juncture.

"So you didn't pick Lord Howe because you've always wanted to come here, and see what it has to offer?"

"I just came to play my guitar, ma'am."

"So you don't know anything about the island?" Jill was incredulous. "You haven't read anything about it?"

"Nope."

"You really should see some of the island."

"I hope to."

"I'm planning to get up early tomorrow morning and walk up to Malabar Point. Why don't you come with me? That way at least you'll get the lay of the land."

"I like the sound of that," said Jack, frowning and rubbing his chin. "Especially the *lay* bit." He smiled hopefully, called for the bill and paid.

Just as they were getting up to leave, the music that had been playing in the background over the PA suddenly stopped and Reg, the guy from the airport and the boat rental place, who apparently also worked at the Bowls Club, appeared holding a microphone.

"And the winner of the meat tray is …" announced Reg as he held up a ticket stub. "B17 … B17 …"

Jack looked at his stubs. "Damn."

"And second prize …" continued Reg, holding up another stub. "A32."

That was the number on the stub in Jack's hand. The holiday just kept getting better. He jumped to his feet and ignoring his aching legs, shouted out "Here!" – and Reg presented him with his prize, a kilo of gourmet tomato and onion sausages, from the Hill Shop.

Through the plastic wrap they looked plump and delicious. But Jack couldn't help thinking that before he cooked and ate them, he might just check to make sure Harvey Jacob was still in the Fish Co-op freezer.

Jack and Jill now made their way to the front door, Jack careful not to get his sausages too near his Aloha shirt.

Boz the BASE jumper was sitting at a table near the main bar and called out as they passed.

"Deputy Assistant State Coroner Slazenger! Over here."

"Just call me Jack, okay?"

"Sorry, Jack."

They walked over to where Boz was chatting with two similarly aged local blokes and where, sitting next to him, was Matahina.

"Let me introduce you to Mike and Mick," said Boz. "Mike's going to take me up the mountain tomorrow morning, and Mick's going to pick me up at the bottom ..."

"A few seconds later?" smiled Jack.

"Hopefully it'll be longer than that," Boz countered.

"So you don't plan to plummet?" returned Jack.

"Not exactly," said Boz, with a grin.

While Jill talked to 'Matti', as Mike and Mick had christened her, Jack took Boz to one side.

"I'm not sure you should be telling me about this insane plan of yours," said Jack in a low semi-serious tone. "I mean, technically what you're doing is illegal, and technically I'm an officer of the law."

"Oh come on," replied Boz. "You're an outsider, a rebel. I can tell. Look at that shirt. You wouldn't dob a fellow outcast in, would you?"

Jack couldn't argue with that. "Fair enough. Just don't kill yourself, okay? Or land on anyone else and kill them."

"I promise."

Jack and Jill offered Matahina a lift back to the apartments, although technically they didn't have a lift to offer her. But the Bowls Club, and many establishments on the island, offered a free bus service for drunk transportless patrons. It really was some kind of paradise. Matahina declined the offer, explaining that because she'd slept so much earlier in the day she wasn't that tired, and she had decided to stay.

Jack took her aside for a moment.

"Do you think it's okay if I have a look over Harvey's boat tomorrow?" he asked.

"Yeah, sure," she replied.

"Can you show me around it?"

"Not a problem."

They agreed to meet at 10:30 the next morning. One of the club staff collected Jack and Jill and a few others and led them outside into the cool night air where Reg was waiting in the club mini-van to drive them to their respective accommodations.

Outside the Hightide Apartments, equidistant from both their front doors, they stopped. Jack awkwardly put his hand out to shake. Jill laughed and kissed him. It was a polite kiss, but just long enough to indicate something more than just good manners.

The kiss stopped and they both yawned. Then laughed.

They agreed to meet the next morning at 7:00. Jack held up the parcel of sausages.

"Tomorrow night. Here. A BBQ at my place."

"I'm in," she smiled, waved, turned and left. Seemingly in slow motion.

Inside, Jack cleaned his teeth, had a leak, and got into his Hawaiian-print pyjamas.

In bed, all he really wanted to think about was Jill, but all he could actually think about was the investigation. What did Brad and Harvey have in common? How did they know each other? Were they old friends, or if not, were they business associates of some sort? From the wallet found on the body, Jack could tell Harvey was an academic of some sort and that his field was history. But Brad's field was ornithology, and the two fields didn't really seem to intersect in any way Jack could think of.

More suspiciously, thought Jack, why didn't Brad mention that he both knew Harvey *and* saw him last night? Brad was hiding something. But what?

Jack's mind grew wings and took off on a flight of fancy. Was this more than just another random muttonbirding? Did Brad kill Harvey? With a muttonbird? That'd be a first. What a great headline – *Man Stabbed With Endemic Seabird*. He imagined what an ideal scene it would make for a Hitchcockian *Psycho*-meets-*The Birds* movie. Harvey Jacob walking home alone in the dark, the tension mounts, and suddenly Brad Lawrence jumps out from behind with a live muttonbird in his hands and, raising it above his head like a dagger, stabs Harvey repeatedly in the ear with it, while the violins screech.

Jack decided he should return to the scene of the 'incident' and examine it a little more thoroughly than he did the first time, considering how little examining he did the first time. After that, he fell asleep imagining Jill naked in various compromising positions.

22ⁿᵈ December, 2008 – 7:00am

The next morning at seven they met outside the apartments. It was a glorious day. The early birds were in full song. The chirping of the Lord Howe Island White Eyes and the gentle cooing of the Emerald Ground Dove, joined by the local currawong and its curious call, had replaced the night time noise of the muttonbirds with a collective combo of tweeting and squawking that in some strange way resembled free jazz.

There was a light mist in the air, and also a slight chill, but conditions otherwise were good. Fortunately Jack didn't have any Hawaiian-themed hiking clothes. Instead he was wearing brown hiking boots, black socks, grey cargo pants and a green Kathmandu brand shirt made of specially-engineered polyester fibres to improve 'breathability', that had a hidden pocket for secret things! He also had a wide-brimmed hat on, Nikon Action Zoom 10-22x50 binoculars around his neck, and on his back his bright red Swiss Army backpack with many zippers. He looked, and felt, like a complete knob, but he didn't care. He wore his knobbishness with pride. It gave him a sense of purpose and identity. And a sense of security. Nobody messes with a complete knob!

Jill was wearing khaki shorts, Teva hiking sandals, a navy blue T-shirt with some Japanese writing on it, wraparound sunglasses and an orange baseball cap with *Cabelas* embroidered on it. All she was carrying was a bottle of water in a holster on her hip. She looked like Lara Croft's slightly nerdier bookish twin. More *Tome Reader* than *Tomb Raider.*

They were both pretty quiet at this time of the morning and got on with the business of walking, first through pandanus and then past a bizarre banyan tree that looked like the legs and necks of a group of dinosaurs, then along the little track that led from Hightide to Ned's Beach, all the time ducking their heads to avoid getting a face-full of the Golden Orb spiders' webs that hung across the track, most inconveniently, at face height.

They passed through a manicured picnic area and over the road leading down to the beach, where a sign announced the beginning of the Malabar Track. Beyond the sign, a wide dirt pathway tunnelled its way through a dense thatch palm forest that ended abruptly when the path came to a quaint wooden sty.

"Is this to keep some kind of farm animals in, or the really dumb tourists out?" quipped Jack, before almost tripping on the last step and landing face-first in the cow dung that littered the paddock on the other side.

A few sleepy cows in one corner of the paddock looked in their direction with an air of disinterest. Before them stood a really, *really* steep hill, with a tiny little goat trail or rather, a tourist trail, seemingly going straight up for what appeared to Jack to be hundreds of metres.

And so they began their ascent. Jill took the lead and Jack, his legs still aching from the ordeals of the day before, comforted himself with the thought that if she slipped, her bum would hit him right in the face.

And when he became breathless and thought his heart would burst, the sight of those fulsome yet firm glutes only centimetres from his eyes kept him going.

Without major mishap, they made it to the ridge. From here they could see the Hightide Apartments, Ned's Beach and the whole island, neatly set out like the Google Earth satellite version, only in glorious high-definition 3D.

They stopped here for a breather – the breather in Jack's case was a heavy breather – a drink of water and to take in the view, which was an odd mixture of rural countryside and tropical paradise. Lush green paddocks, populated by the odd cow or horse, nestled next to even lusher clusters of dark palms and pine trees.

Jill pointed out Old Settlement Beach, a strip of gold that separated the turquoise water of Hunter Bay from lush green paddocks, under a sky-blue sky, the horizon augmented with fluffy white Simpsonesque clouds.

After this brief but not unpleasant respite, the climb began in earnest. Through a forest of short windswept bushes, the goat trail followed the ridge up to the summit. The view was spectacular, and not just the one directly in front of Jack's eyes. On their left, the white cliffs of Malabar Spur curved around toward the Admiralty Islands like the white cliffs of Malabar Spur. On the other side of the ridge, the same paddock curved around and dropped steeply all the way down to Old Settlement Beach, Hunter Bay, and beyond, to

Dawson's Point. It was the type of scenery that scenery writers run out of words for.

Looking back they could see below them the perfect curve of Ned's Beach, as if some giant sea creature had taken one clean bite out of the island. Jack removed his binoculars from the padded case around his neck and put them to his eyes. He zoomed in and could make out the shapes of two people, a man and a woman, walking along the sand on the water's edge. It was a gloriously warm late-December day. The weather was perfect, the sea was calm and clear and those two people had this pristine beach entirely to themselves. Jack could not believe it.

Further up, Jack stopped to catch his breath once again and noticed some sheets of distressed metal strewn along the steep incline of the paddock above Old Settlement Beach.

"It looks like someone's shed blew down," he joked, in between wheezes.

"That's what's left of the Catalina," Jill replied, panting in a way that Jack found strangely exciting.

She could tell by his expression that he had no idea what she was talking about.

"I'm pretty sure that there's a plaque up here somewhere that should explain it better than I can," she added and took off up the path ahead of him.

A few metres along they came to the plaque erected on the spot where, in 1948, a RAAF Catalina flying boat clipped the ridge and crashed, killing seven of the nine crewmen.

They both read the plaque in silence.

ON 28TH SEPTEMBER 1948 A R.A.A.F.
CATALINA FLYING BOAT A24 381 FROM
N°.1 SQUADRON CRASHED ON THIS
SPOT AFTER DARK. SEVEN OF THE
CREW OF NINE MEN WERE KILLED.

"Shit," Jack exclaimed softly, and shook his head in despair. "That's the wreckage?" He pointed to what he'd previously presumed were the remains of a blown-down shack, and shook his head again. "Poor bastards."

The plaque listed the names of the seven men who died.

Jill explained that the aircraft was apparently attempting an emergency landing on the lagoon, which it overshot. Exactly why it was attempting an emergency landing in the middle of the night had never been discovered. The crash took place eight years before the first flight data recorder or 'black box' was produced by an Australian, Dr David Warren, of the then Aeronautical Research Laboratories of Melbourne. The locals came to the rescue and were able to save two lucky airmen before a fireball engulfed the rest of the seaplane, but the pilot and the co-pilot didn't make it.

Jack had been to plane crashes before, usually fresher than this one, but he knew escape from a tiny tin tube when it falls from the sky and bursts into flames is extremely rare.

He nodded, his brow furrowed, his bottom lip tight. It was his earnest look, but it actually made him look slightly moronic – in an endearing way, of course.

They continued on in silence for a while, which was a relief to Jack, because the path kept getting steeper, although now it was under the canopy of stringy bushes of some sort, which meant at least they didn't have the increasingly warm sun beating down on them. Occasionally there'd be a gap in the bush and they'd be presented with rare glimpses of the stunning vista of either the beach below them, or blue windswept snatches of the nearby Admiralty Islands.

Suddenly there was light at the end of the tunnel. They came to a gravel clearing, beyond which was a huge expanse of clear blue sky. But as soon they emerged from under the bush canopy, Jack hit the deck.

Jill looked down at him, astonished. "What's the matter?"

"Heights. Fear of. Really steep drop." He pointed towards the edge of the gravel, where the ground dropped away dramatically.

Jill looked down. "Wow. You've got to see this."

"No. I'm fine thank you," replied Jack, hugging the ground for all he was worth.

She smiled and got down on the ground with him.

"Why don't we just slowly crawl up to the edge …?" she coaxed.

"Don't say 'edge'." Even the thought of it filled him with dread.

"There's no way you can fall," Jill promised.

"No, but I can still jump."

When he was younger, Jack wasn't particularly afraid of heights at all. In fact, quite the opposite, he relished getting close to the edge of a variety of high places, simply for the thrill of looking down and also to possibly impress any young ladies present at the time, as all young men know this sort of behaviour does.

But as he grew older, fear of his own mortality increased, and the experience of investigating the deaths of the victims of falls — many of whom purposefully initiated the fall — combined in his brain to give Jack a fear he probably would have described as 'suicidal vertigo', although its correct medical name is *Catapedaphobia*. It's the fear of suddenly, in a split second of insanity, losing control of your reasoning faculties and throwing yourself from whatever high place you happen to find yourself. In a way, it was a fear of desiring to be momentarily truly free. In another way it was a fear of suddenly making a rash and incomprehensibly fatal decision that, now airborne, one would seriously begin to regret, coupled with the fear of hitting the ground and having one's entire body smashed like a pumpkin. Subsequently, Jack found that hugging the ground at this point made him feel less inclined to accidentally hurl himself off the edge.

"Come on," said Jill, taking his hand. They both slowly edged forward on their stomachs, until Jack could see over the edge of the cliff.

He slowly and cautiously opened his eyes and looked down to see the opalescent blue ocean, crashing white against matte black rocks, at least over two hundred metres below. Beneath them but in the air, on numerous levels, a variety of white seabirds – petrels, terns, noddies – went about their lives, like the avian residents of some geo-thermal version of Fritz Lang's *Metropolis*, or a seabird version of the city in *Blade Runner*. Both Jack and Jill's gobs were well and truly smacked.

To the north-east they could see the Admiralty Islands – Roach, South, Noddy and Sugarloaf – all looking like a bunch of small pointy islands sticking out of the sea-blue ocean, which in fact they were – and in front of them, Soldiers Cap, which only resembled a soldier's cap if soldiers took to wearing large chunks of rock covered with weeds and guano on their heads.

Only metres in front of their faces a pair of Tropicbirds elevated into view on the strong cliff-face updraft.

"Wow. Look at that!" Jack exclaimed excitedly. He put his binoculars to his eyes and looked again. "Has that bird got some red string or tape hanging out of its arse?"

"That's the Red-tailed Tropicbird or *Phaethon rubricauda*. The male has two long red tail feathers," Jill informed him.

"How do you know so much stuff about the island?"

Sneakily, Jill put the World Heritage information leaflet about Lord Howe Island bird life back in her pocket.

"I've done my research."

She blinded him with science. "In the mating season, the male does loop-the-loops to attract the female."

They watched and sure enough the male hovered, then suddenly flipped back and did a complete vertical 360 for a nearby female, who followed suit.

"Wow," said Jack, putting down his binoculars. "Don't expect anything like that from me."

She kissed him. "I'm already attracted".

"What was that for?"

"Bravery beyond the call of duty."

She kissed him again. This kiss was longer.

"You weren't looking for cavities then were you?"

"Upper left, second back molar could use a crown."

They stood up and turned to take in the view over the island. Now seemingly over his fears, or perhaps immune to them due to something in Jill's saliva or just thanks to the curative powers of her lips, Jack now eagerly headed down the gravel to the end of the spur that sloped towards Soldier's Cap and, beyond it, Roach Island.

"Careful, Jack," called Jill after him.

"Look at that!" He pointed at the huge arch cut into the side of the bigger island at sea level. "It looks like something out of a pirate movie."

Excitedly Jack spun around, his binoculars to his eyes. "Is that Ball's Pyramid?" he said, pointing to a far-off jagged spear of rock poking up from behind a small ridge at the foot of

Mount Lidgbird that neither of them knew was called Immediate Hill. "My god, it *is*. That's incredible!"

Jill grabbed Jack's hand firmly, and guided him back to relative safety. She really didn't want to lose him this soon into the relationship, or in fact at all.

As they walked off hand in hand, Jack couldn't quite understand why Jill, an intelligent, attractive, funny, successful young woman would be attracted to him, a neurotic loser with very few of the physical attributes most women find appealing. But Jill knew what she was doing. She had experienced quite a number of relationships with handsome, over-confident, accomplished men who had all – to a man – turned out to be total arseholes. After the last one had unceremoniously dumped her before she could dump him, she decided from now on to stick with ordinary-looking, neurotic men with low self-esteem, who had keen senses of humour – and Jack fitted the bill perfectly. Besides, she really liked him.

They continued along the cliff-side track to Kim's Lookout, Jack being careful not to look into the beckoning maw of oblivion on his right side, and Jill being careful not to let go of his hand.

At Kim's Lookout, they looked down over Old Settlement Beach and the two emerald-green peaks of Mount Gower and Lidgbird that dominated the view. The tops of the peaks partially shrouded with cloud, it looked like the classic stereotypical tropical paradise – like the island of the lost boys in *Peter Pan*. Jack half expected to see Captain Hook's pirate ship in the bay below, but it was a luxury powerboat, the type rich people keep moored at the Finger Wharf marina at Woolloomooloo, but never actually go anywhere in. As they sat and watched the view from Kim's Lookout, Jack couldn't help wondering who Kim was, and exactly what he, or she, had to look out for.

Around about the same time, on top of Mount Gower, BASE jumper Boz Boswell and his local guide, Mike, came out from the dense plateau jungle into a clearing right on the edge of a cliff, overlooking the lagoon 875 metres below, according to the digital altimeter strapped to Boz's wrist. His specialised BASE-jumping rig was packed and on his back. The rest of him was covered mostly in a black and grey nylon jumpsuit and a low-profile matte-black carbon-fibre helmet with a small camera aperture on one side – very little protection should the thing on his back fail to open. It had taken them four hours to hike up to this unique vantage point, so they stopped to catch their breath and get a lay of the land below them.

The plan was for Boz to get as close as he could to Blackburn Island, the small, low, cigar-shaped, sparsely vegetated spit of land adjacent to the centre of Lord Howe Island that marks the point where the edge of the reef meets the lagoon.

To the ocean side of Blackburn, they could just make out local bloke Mick, in a wetsuit on a jet ski. Mick was going to watch Boz's descent, and planned to get as close as possible to him when he hit the water, or landed, without actually ending up being the thing he landed on. It wasn't a precise science.

Boz, adrenalin pumping through both his body and brain, giving him an all-over pre-jump buzz, carefully checked all the straps on his helmet, and the harness container system on his back. He only had one parachute in his rig because he knew that if something goes wrong in a BASE jump, you simply don't have time to deploy a reserve chute before the ground comes up and flattens you.

After scanning the horizon left and right, Boz pulled his goggles over his eyes, and with a wicked smile on his face, gave Mike the thumbs-up, and literally dived off the side of the sheerest of Mt Gower's cliffs, and simply disappeared from view.

Boz's signature move was a forward somersault, performed just after jumping, followed by the release of his chute shortly after. But halfway through the somersault, as he was dropping upside-down but parallel to the side of the cliff, Boz momentarily saw one of the weirdest things he had ever seen in all his jumps.

Time slows down for the first few seconds when you jump off an 875-metre cliff with nothing but an ultra-light polymer fibre parachute on your back. As a result, the few nanoseconds that Boz was upside down seemed longer, which was why he was pretty sure he saw a medium-sized black and white seabird on a ledge, wearing a pair of black patent leather shoes.

If that wasn't bizarre enough, he also thought he saw, right next to the shoe-wearing seabird, another similar-looking seabird, sitting on a nest, inside an upturned pith helmet with a gold star insignia on it.

Then suddenly he was the right way up again, staring at the blue curve of the horizon and the rapidly approaching ground below him, and was struck with the sudden realisation that he must be getting close to terminal velocity, so he'd better deploy his chute.

Unlike skydivers, BASE jumping rigs don't have a ripcord, so Boz reached around to the bottom corner of his rig with his right hand and pulled the circular fabric disc on the apex of his pilot chute, releasing it from the container on his back.

The pilot chute rapidly filled with air, slowing his freefall and dragging the main parachute from the container. Instantly the scarlet red 'ram-air' chute flew from his back and its nine cells filled with air, jerking Boz upwards, and creating a huge rectangular airfoil-shaped canopy above his head that resembled an extremely long and slightly curved air mattress.

Boz quickly grabbed the toggles on the two steering lines and took control of the canopy. For the first time he was able to fully appreciate the awe-inspiring scene below and beyond. A huge smile took command of his face and as he directed his chute towards Blackburn Island, he shouted to no one in particular, "Woo-hoo! Fuck yeah!"

At Kim's Lookout, Jack and Jill were appropriately enough looking out, directly toward the two mountains when Boz jumped, and watched him descend, sharing Jack's binoculars. It was incredible to see this madman first plummet like a rocket and then float gracefully under what seemed to be an extra-wide, bright red surf mat, around the curve of the island, only to land on his feet on the lagoon-side sand of Blackburn Island. Once again they felt as if their gobs had been smacked.

It was a perfect landing. After quickly rolling up his chute, Boz was actually able to jump on the back of Mick's jet ski without getting his feet wet for the ride back to the main island.

Jack and Jill walked down the hill, their gobs still smarting from the visual smacking they'd received. But being gob-smacked takes it out of you, so when they eventually made it back to what passes for civilisation on the island, they both enjoyed a hearty breakfast of crispy bacon, poached eggs and hot coffee at Humpty Micks Café , after which Jill went off to her first appointment, and Jack got back on the dead-guy case.

Matahina was waiting for him down by the jetty. Wearing a light lime-green cotton dress, bare feet and a frangipani flower in her hair, she certainly looked the part of a Polynesian princess.

As they untied the inflatable dingy and headed out into the blue expanse of Hunter Bay, all either of them could talk about was the brilliant BASE jump by Boz.

"He either has no sense of fear whatsoever, or some of the biggest, ah, *cojones* this side of Pamplona," exclaimed Jack, truly in awe.

"And he's so handsome too," Matahina added.

Jack furrowed his brow and demurred. "I was further away, I didn't notice that from where I was."

"Well, he is," she confided and smiled.

"I'll take your word for it."

By now they were both in the dingy and heading out into the middle of the bay. It was then that Jack realised they were headed for the same expensive-looking luxury powerboat he and Jill had admired from Kim's Lookout.

"This is Harvey Jacob's boat?" asked Jack, as they pulled up alongside it. For some reason he was expecting another budget-sized yacht, similar to the one on which he had encountered the crazy, peg-legged, one-eyed Swedish budgie-fancier, Sven Svensen. But this enormous vessel was definitely no *Röda Sill*. Matahina tied the dinghy up to the ship's shiny chrome ladder and climbed aboard. On the bow were the words *True Love 2*.

She gave Jack a hand at the top of the ladder, and he stopped and took in the opulence. "My, she's *yar!*" he exclaimed, doing his best Katherine Hepburn, which made no sense at all to Matahina, who had never even seen *High Society*, let alone *The Philadelphia Story*.

Matahina led Jack through a low doorway, above which a sign thoughtfully read *Mind Your Head*, and proceeded to show him around below deck. It was filled with all kinds of high-tech gear, including satellite TV, LCD screens, and that was just in the galley.

She showed him her bunk, which looked quite comfortable, if a little snug. "This is where I slept …" Then she opened another door. "And this is where I *could have* slept if I had accepted one of several offers."

They entered Harvey's cabin. It was, in boat terms, huge. A queen-size bed, another TV, a DVD player and stereo. There was a surprisingly large desk with papers and books on it, and more books in a bookcase next to it.

Jack looked at the books and found they were nearly all about the Second World War, and in particular, the Pacific Conflict. A couple of them had even been written by Harvey Jacob himself.

Mounted on one wall was a series of framed photographs. One featured a younger Harvey Jacob in diving gear, a rusting wreck of a Japanese Zero fighter plane half-submerged in the ocean behind him. In another, he was smiling and shaking hands with either Jacques Cousteau or Marcel Marceau – Jack always got those two mixed up.

A framed article from a newspaper featured another photo of a smiling Harvey Jacob, with the caption *History Nut Finds War Booty*. This explained how a university professor could afford to buy the *True Love 2*, but not who he bought it for – although looking at Matahina, Jack figured it was for anyone like her that Harvey could get aboard.

Next to the newspaper clipping was a photograph of a disparate group of academic-looking men, below a banner that read *The Asia-Pacific Historical Society's WWII Treasure Hunters Symposium of 1992*. Jack looked closer and noticed that in the centre of the front row was a slightly younger Harvey Jacob, and in the back row, amidst the various nerds, geeks, dorks and misfits, a tall thin man with an all-too-familiar mole right in the centre of his forehead.

He took the photo down off its hook and showed it to Matahina. "Is this the man you saw talking to Harvey at the Pandanus restaurant that night?"

Matahina looked closely at the picture. "Yeah. That's him. I'd recognise a mole that size anywhere. It's nearly as big as his eye!"

Jack furrowed his brow and looked like he was thinking about the case, when in fact he was thinking that here he was alone on a luxury yacht with possibly the most beautiful woman on the planet, and that if this was a letter to *Penthouse*, she would have jumped on him and forced him onto the bed and had mad passionate sex with him. He wondered how that would affect his burgeoning relationship with Jill, and then the possibility of a threesome, when Matahina interrupted his idyll.

"You think 'Three Eyes' killed Harvey Jacob?"

"I do?" asked Jack, astonished that he hadn't fully realised that was what he actually was beginning to think. Then he added, "It's certainly worth consideration." But the one thing he still didn't know was why.

Jack left Matahina at the Bowls Club, where she was meeting Boz, and cycled up Middle Beach Road. Something about this wasn't right, thought Jack. Maybe ol' 'Three Eyes' really *did* kill Harvey Jacob. But with a muttonbird? He shook his head. It sounded crazy.

Halfway up the hill, he stopped at Joy's shop – which was essentially a big old house converted into a supermarket of sorts – bought a Crunchie bar and a chocolate milk, then sat outside and caught his breath while stuffing his mouth. He already knew from experience how steep the road was about to become and he was going to need all the energy that dairy products, sugar and chocolate would give him.

Halfway up the really steep bit, when he was pretty much convinced that a major coronary event was about to put him in the Fish Co-op freezer alongside Harvey Jacob, he decided it might be a better idea to visit Harvey while he, Jack that is, was still alive.

Barry opened the freezer door and allowed Jack first entry. "He's still there. I haven't had any takers yet. But Christmas is in two days, and if I run out of stock, someone's going to snap him up for sure." This guy was a card. But Jack wasn't entirely sure that he was joking.

Jack re-examined Harvey Jacob's body. He was still dead. He thought he should give it a quick once-over for entry or exit wounds, just in case. And in fact, he knew he probably should have done that the first time, but this really wasn't his field. Even though he did have a medical background, he'd normally let the autopsy guys do this sort of thing.

He pulled up Harvey Jacob's Yankees shirt and was horrified by the expanse of white scrawny dead man before him. He quickly lowered it. It was like seeing Homer Simpson's emaciated geriatric boss Monty Burns in the shower. He gently rolled the body over to look at the back, an action which caused the Yankees cap to slip from its jaunty angle on the corpse's head, and fall to the ground, revealing a large purple contusion on the back of the cranium.

Examining the injury – technically, a blunt force trauma wound to the back of the head – Jack was pretty sure that the dead muttonbird lying next to him hadn't created it. Judging by the indentation at the top of the contusion, Jack figured if a muttonbird *had* been involved in Harvey's death it must have been a really big angry muttonbird wearing steel-capped boots. He doubted this was the case, and re-covered the wound with the cap.

Now that the cap was back on, Jack noticed that the blood stains on it – that he previously and perhaps too casually had assumed were the result of the muttonbird beak penetrating Harvey's brain – directly corresponded with the contusion the cap had been covering.

Jack borrowed a small torch from Barry for a closer examination of Harvey's ear hole, and was immediately nauseated by what he found. Harvey's ear canal was full of thick, viscous earwax, matted hairs and what appeared to be seabird snot. But no blood.

Next Jack turned his attention to the muttonbird. Its beak was pristine, bar a healthy coating of Harvey's ear wax, which meant it wasn't really pristine at all, except in the sense that pristine means 'blood free' – which it doesn't really. So let's just say there wasn't any blood on the bird's beak.

Picking the feathery corpse up from the box of frozen calamari rings it had been laid out on, Jack could tell by the way its head lolled about on its stiff body, that the muttonbird's cause of death was more than likely a broken neck. Yet suffocating on Harvey's earwax could not, at this stage, be entirely ruled out. Jack desperately hoped for the bird's sake that its neck had been broken *before* its beak ended up in Harvey's ear, because asphyxiation by earwax is a horrible way for any creature to die.

The lack of blood on its beak suggested that the bird hadn't killed Harvey. If it had indeed flown into Harvey's ear at a speed fast enough to knock him to the ground and break its neck in the process, it would have definitely drawn blood from Harvey's ear canal.

This suggested to Jack that the bird's neck had been broken *before* it entered Harvey's ear. And as living people usually object to having dead muttonbirds rammed into their ears, the evidence suggested to Jack that Harvey was probably already dead before the intra-aural muttonbird insertion took place.

Jack noticed that he was still holding the muttonbird while he was thinking, and absent-mindedly flicking its loose head backwards and forwards between his finger and thumb. He gently placed it back down on the calamari box, straightened its head and smoothed out its feathers before heading back out into the sunlight.

Not long after that, he was back on Muttonbird Drive at the scene of what was increasingly beginning to look like a crime.

When he arrived at the spot that Norma had shown him the day before, he first waited for a couple and their two children to bicycle past, pretending to be just another happy tourist taking a pedalling breather, which to a certain extent he was.

He didn't want to be seen crawling around on all fours looking for evidence, and not just because of how ridiculous he knew he looked. In the past, when citizens had caught him in this position they were often *too* helpful. Sometimes they assumed he'd had a fall and would try to help him back on his feet. Other times they'd assume he'd lost something important, and would eagerly get down on the ground to help him look for it. What was even more embarrassing was that when he eventually told them that he was a coronial officer carrying out a murder investigation, they usually didn't believe him at all.

Once the coast was clear and the family had cycled away, Jack began to thoroughly scour the area – both sides of the road, the paddock to the north and the pandanus grove to the south. He was surprised by how tidy the place was. The Hill Shop was nearby but there was virtually no rubbish lying around at all. Apart from a couple of ripe, healthy-looking cow pats on the paddock side, there was no telltale anything to be seen. And the pandanus side, although it did have its share of leaf litter, was also completely devoid of vital or incriminating clues. Of course, it didn't help that he wasn't entirely sure what he was looking for.

His hands and knees now covered with plant matter, but fortunately no cow matter, Jack was just about to give up, when not very far from where the body was found, he saw out of the corner of his eye, something both vital and incriminating wedged up under the roots of a particularly old pandanus tree – it was half a house brick.

Brushing the leaf litter off his hands and onto his trousers, Jack put on a pair of rubber gloves he always carried for such an occasion, picked the half-brick up and carefully, so as not to destroy or brush off any DNA evidence, put it in an extra-large plastic zip-lock bag that he also regularly carried for the same reason, and then into his backpack.

Cycling to the phone booth on Anderson Street made Jack realise that riding a bike with half a brick in his backpack was much harder than riding a bike *without* half a brick in his backpack. By the time he arrived at the scary spider-infested phone booth, he was just grateful that whoever hit Harvey over the head hadn't used the whole brick.

Puffing and wheezing, he threw down his bike, carefully removed his backpack, and cringed as he entered the Golden Orbs' telephonic lair. He dialled the office and told his boss he was sending the guys in the lab part of a brick that may well contain a DNA clue to Harvey Jacob's killer.

"I thought the killer was a bird."

"No, I now think it's a bird guy."

"What, a guy dressed like a bird?"

Jack ran out of coins and the line went dead.

Jack then cycled to Brad Lawrence's office, but Brad wasn't there. This was something of a reprieve for Jack because he wasn't entirely sure what he'd say. He was now reasonably convinced that Harvey had definitely been murdered. It looked to Jack that someone followed Harvey from the nearby Pandanus restaurant, picked up the semi-brick and whacked Harvey over the back of the head with it. The alleged killer must have then broken the neck of a nearby muttonbird and stuck it in Harvey's ear to make it look like an accident. Just saying it in his head, it sounded ludicrous, even to Jack.

But was it Brad Lawrence? Without a motive or witnesses, short of a confession, the only way Jack could prove Brad had been Harvey's killer was if the forensic guys in Sydney could match Brad to whatever they found on the brick. And one thing Jack never liked doing was asking a full-grown man for a DNA sample.

Instead, Jack rode off to the Bowls Club where he had planned to meet Jill after work. At a table near the bar, Jack was not too surprised to find Matahina having a beer with Boz and Mick and Mike.

Boz had what could only be described as a shit-eating grin on his face, and it wasn't just because Matahina was sitting on his knee. He'd had a few beers, but he still hadn't come down from the jump.

"Hey, Jack, come and join us," he called out as Jack came through the door.

Jack looked around and could see that Jill hadn't arrived yet, so thought, why not? He grabbed a beer and sat down at the table.

"No coronial work for you here today, I'm afraid," joked the beaming Boz.

"I don't know," replied Jack, with a smile. "You look like you've died and gone to heaven."

"That's because BASE is the ultimate high," explained Boz smugly. "You know what it stands for, right?"

"Brainless Aerodynamically Stupid Endeavours? Blatantly Asinine Suicidal Exercises? Bouncing And Squashing Experiment? Brief Association of Soon-to-be Ex-persons?" Jack offered mischievously.

"Building, Antenna, Span, and Earth," Matahina piped in. "It stands for the all the things you can BASE jump from – Buildings, Antennas, Bridges and Earth."

"Why don't they say 'Bridge' then instead of 'Span'?" asked Mick.

"That would make it BABE jumping," quipped Jack, "which actually might be more appropriate!" Mike and Mick laughed, Matti blushed a little, and Boz just smiled.

"Very funny," said Boz. "Anyway, the 'E' is for Earth. And today I did an 'E' – which explains why I'm so high."

They all laughed this time.

"I don't know what's wrong with you extreme sports addicts," said Jack, shaking his head. "Why don't you just take real drugs like normal people?"

"Believe me. They're not as good," enthused Boz.

"So what was it like?" asked Jack, always intrigued by altered states of consciousness of any kind, even the plumb crazy.

"Oh man, it was fantastic," Boz gushed. "But I did see something really weird up there. I thought I was tripping." He pulled a weirded-out confused face, then went back to smiling.

"Wow," said Jack, assuming Boz was talking about some kind of adrenalin-induced hallucination, or perhaps some rainbow-like visual effect caused by the refraction of light, that only people stupid enough to jump off very tall things ever get to experience. "What did you see?"

For the first time in the conversation, Boz was a little guarded.

"I'd rather not say. I'm going to talk to a guy who knows all about it a bit later."

"Your shrink?" joked Jack.

"Ha ha. Very funny."

They were all laughing when Jill turned up from the medical centre. Jack introduced her, although she'd already met Mick and Mike because they'd had a scrape and a polish the day before. Jack gave Jill his seat, went to the bar and bought another round.

They were still talking about BASE jumping when Jack returned.

"Why don't *you* try it?" Boz asked, as Jack put the tray of beers on the table.

"What?" joked Jack, "Killing myself? I'm doing it now, just a lot, lot slower," he said raising his schooner glass. "Here's to crazy bastards like Boz. Long may they live!" They all toasted and took a synchronised slurp of their drinks. "I really mean that," Jack said to Boz.

"Come on," urged Boz. "Haven't you ever wanted to just jump off the top of a lookout or building?"

"All the time," said Jack. "I live in fear of it."

"Huh?" said Boz.

Jack tried with limited success to explain his fear of losing control and throwing himself off high places.

"You know what you need?" enthused Boz.

"The name of your therapist?" joked Jack.

"No," said Boz, "You need a *wingsuit*. That'd be perfect for your condition."

"What's a wingsuit?" asked Jill.

"It's a jumpsuit that has fabric 'wings,' or 'airfoils', technically between the legs and under the arms," explained Boz.

"Oh yeah!" said Matahina in recognition, "A squirrel suit!"

"They call them that too," admitted Boz.

Jack shook his head. "Dressing up as a squirrel isn't going to help me overcome my fear of heights. If I dress up like a squirrel, people will *know* I'm nuts."

"They don't make you look like a squirrel," added Mick, who'd seen a documentary about it on the *Nat Geo Adventure* channel. "More like a bat."

"Or a sugar glider," offered Mike, who'd watched the same documentary.

"You can basically fly in it," explained Boz. "You can do what I do, but without a parachute."

"And why would I want to do *that*?" asked Jack.

"Well," said Boz, "if you're afraid of jumping off cliffs or whatever, if you were wearing a wingsuit, you wouldn't have to be. If you've got the urge to jump off something, you could just do it."

"I don't think that's a good idea," said Jack. "I'd have to wear it all the time, just in case. And any suit that I actually wore while jumping off a cliff or a building is going to need a lot of dry-cleaning, even if I did happen to survive."

"But if the wingsuit is the way to go," continued Jack, "why don't *you* wear one?"

Boz shrugged. "I don't know. I guess I'm just 'old school'."

"I didn't think you guys lived long enough to become 'old school'," said Jack with a smile and a raise of his glass.

They both laughed and took a swig of their beers.

Boz told Jack that he and the others were going off for a meal at Arijilla, a fancy-pants resort down near Old Settlement Beach, and invited Jack and Jill to join them. But Jack told him they had other plans. Jack was going to cook Jill the gourmet sausages he'd won at last night's meat raffle.

After they cycled back up the hill to Hightide Apartments, they both decided they needed a shower, and went to their separate apartments, agreeing to meet in half an hour on Jack's balcony for the barbie.

Jill turned up wearing a red sarong-style dress with the classic tropical hibiscus motif on it. Jack was wearing another vintage Aloha shirt – this one a rayon bamboo print from the '50s, manufactured by Surfriders Sportswear, the bamboo blue with flecks of yellow on a tapa-brown background. He was a man who firmly believed in living in the moment in a Hawaiian shirt.

The barbeque itself was a very old-style affair, three walls of bricks, three rows high, with a rectangle of blackened steel plate resting on top. Primed with paper and kindling, it only took a match to turn it into the perfect sausage sizzler.

Jack brushed the sausages with olive oil and bunged them on the barbie. Earlier there had been much axe-work in preparing the wood fire. Unfortunately it was not the axe-work he had originally come to the island for. The brand-new Dobro sat in the corner forlornly pining to be played.

Once the smoke had cleared and the ceremonial pouring of the beer on the hot plate to see if it was hot enough had concluded satisfactorily, and the mince, tomato, herb and onion meat packages were sizzling on the barbie, Jack prepared a simple salad by putting a lettuce in a bowl.

He then prepared a more complicated salad from fresh veggies he'd bought earlier at the Hill Shop.

"Aren't you going to drizzle something over that?" asked Jill, sipping on a glass of 2007 Pierro chardonnay – one of Margaret River's finest – that Jack had opened earlier.

"No," replied Jack, "but I may drool a little bit over these sausages later."

The sausages and the salad both proved a success, so they moved on to Jack's signature dish – affogato – or a generous serving of Streets Blue Ribbon vanilla ice cream with espresso coffee poured over it.

It was, in Jack's opinion, the perfect end to a meal, in that it combined both dessert and coffee in the one bowl, or cup, depending on how you preferred it.

From where she was sitting on the small wooden outdoor table, Jill could see Jack's Dobro guitar leaning against the wardrobe.

"That's her, is it?" she asked, with a nod in the Dobro's direction. "The 'other woman'?"

Jack looked around at the guitar. "Yep. She's feeling a little neglected."

"Can I have a look?" asked Jill.

119

"Sure," said Jack, getting up. "But no cat fight please. I want you two to play nice."

Jack stepped inside, returned with the Dobro, brushed off a bit of the dust that had already begun to settle on it, and handed it to Jill. He thought to himself, "If she whips out a bottleneck slide and plays a blistering rendition of *Love in Vain* right now, she's seriously dumped."

Fortunately for him, she didn't. She simply looked it up and down admiringly, and said "My she's *yar.*" That was it. He was gone.

Then she said, "Play something." She handed it to him.

The horror. Performance. Jack shook his head. "No, I couldn't do that. Not drunk enough."

But it turned out he *was* drunk enough. He slipped his hand into his pocket and pulled out his now ever-present bottleneck slide. It was as long as his index finger and about twice as wide.

Jill couldn't let the joke go by. "So *that's* what that bulge was."

Jack smiled, raised his left pinkie, and in way of reply, slipped the Pyrex slide over it, semi-suggestively.

He then put plastic picks on his right thumb and first two fingers and resting the Dobro on his knee, surprised even himself by pulling out a fairly convincing slow blues in G, complete with a wicked solo in the middle.

Jill clapped. Jack shook his head. "Wow. I've got to drink more often."

"That was fantastic," Jill said, and kissed him. "What a great evening."

"Ah, yeah." He kissed her back.

"And it's not over yet." They kissed again, then she grabbed his hand and led him inside.

Seconds later as they grappled eagerly at each other's clothing, Jill slipped her hand into Jack's boxer shorts, and let out a squeal.

"Oh my god! What is that?"

"It's nothing to worry about. Really."

She pulled down his boxers and inspected his chrome-plated palang.

"*What* possessed you to do *that*?"

Jack shrugged and smiled sheepishly. "You know what it's like when you're a medical practitioner. You're home alone, with access to powerful painkillers and surgical equipment. But it's all right. It doesn't hurt or anything, in fact …"

She smiled, took his hand and guided it inside her dress, where he soon felt something smooth, round and metal.

"You're bejewelled as well!" She smiled again as he felt it. "There's a stone of some sort on it. What's that?"

"You'll find out," she laughed. And in a few minutes he did. It was a pearl. After a while he came up for air, and said "I've decided to give up being a coroner and become a pearl diver."

"Be careful. You don't want to get the bends."

They were on the bed now, naked, and Jill gently guided his palang, to the spot directly beneath her pearl, and soon they were humping like creatures that hump a lot.

The entire enterprise was a complete success, except for one moment when their metal clashed and his piercing caught in hers, and they both screamed in horror.

Once it was established that nothing had been damaged, they continued, and were soon both trying to suppress any loud cries of ecstasy, although by this stage the muttonbirds had arrived home and any noise Jack and Jill made would have been drowned out by the haunting chorus of "Pick mee! Pick meee!"

Jack hadn't wanted to talk about the Harvey Jacob case before dinner in case it somehow put a dampener on the proceedings. But now, as they lay in a warm and slightly damp post-coital embrace, he figured a dampener wouldn't make much difference, and began describing his most recent findings to Jill.

"So *you* think 'Three Eyes' killed Larry David?" she asked after he'd finished.

"Harvey Jacob," he corrected her. "Something like that. It's a possibility. Somebody killed him, unless that half a house brick I found fell from the sky, and then a muttonbird nose-dived into his ear …"

"*Nose*-dived into his *ear?*"

"Seems unlikely, doesn't it?"

"What if the muttonbird was carrying the half a house brick, dropped it, killing Harvey Jacob, then dived to retrieve it, overshot and wound up beak-deep in Jewish-American grey matter?"

"You should stick to dentistry."

But Jill wasn't giving up. "And what's so fishy about Brad Lawrence, besides the weird third eye?"

"You've met him?" asked Jack, surprised.

"I replaced a filling for him this morning. You can't keep your eyes off it."

"I know. It follows you around the room. It's like the eyes of the *Mona Lisa.*"

"Surely he could get it frozen off?"

"Maybe he hasn't noticed it?"

"Maybe he likes it."

"Maybe Harvey called him 'Mole Face' or 'Three Eyes', and Brad got angry and killed him."

"It's a possibility, I suppose," admitted Jack, "but what's weird is he knew Harvey Jacob. They'd met at least once. At a *history* convention, not an ornithological convention. If only I could get some background on him."

"On 'Three Eyes'?" asked Jill.

"Yeah. 'Mole Face.' If only I had a computer."

"There's a brand new iMac in Heather's office."

"Pity she's away."

"The office is unlocked. I checked my email this morning."

Two minutes later they were sitting in front of the thin, anodised-aluminium 24-inch screen, finding out all about Brad Lawrence.

"He's got tertiary qualifications in history and languages, but nothing in ornithology," said Jack, scanning the information on the screen.

"Can you actually *get* a degree in ornithology?" asked Jill.

"A Bachelor of Birds?"

"From Big Bird University?"

"I guess so. But whatever it is, Brad doesn't have one."

"You'd better be careful," warned Jill. "If you're right and the bird guy did kill the old guy with half a brick, that means he's still got the other half of the brick."

Jack scratched his beard and nodded his head semi-thoughtfully.

23rd December, 2008 – 7:00am

Jack woke up from a deep comfortable sleep to find Jill creeping out through the apartment door.

"Got an early patient. Catch up later," she whispered, blowing him a kiss, and crept out.

He rubbed the sleep out of his eyes and looked at his watch – 7:03am – time for a swim, he thought.

Putting on his Billabong board shorts with the black and white hibiscus pattern, a grey T-shirt featuring the skull of a longhorn steer wearing sunglasses and the slogan 'Riscky's BBQ, Fort Worth Texas', his Keen's Bison Newport sandals and his prescription Ray-Ban wrap-around sunglasses, he grabbed his brown Maui Surf Co. baseball cap with the yin and yang surfing lizards logo, and headed down the small winding track to Ned's Beach, looking like a walking billboard.

Walking over the grass embankment at the beach's edge, Jack looked both ways along the stretch of sand. Unbelievably, he had the entire beach to himself. The water was crystal clear and more or less flat, but with just enough swell to be refreshing.

He dropped his towel near the water's edge. He took off his shirt, cap, and sandals but kept on his sunnies. Then he looked around once more, and definitely seeing no one at all in the near vicinity, dropped his board shorts with the black and white hibiscus pattern, and ran bare-arsed into the water. It was the prefect temperature – not too cold, not too hot. He dived under the water, resurfaced, and then sank gently backwards into the warm, clear liquid.

Wiping the water out of his eyes, he thought he saw a flash of silver in the shallows not far from where he was now standing. It must have just been the sun reflecting on the water, he decided. Then there was another flash of silver. He furrowed up his brow in the thinking position, and suddenly something brushed his leg, as directly in front of him a fin briefly cut through the surface of the water.

Jack looked down to see the water seething with dozens of kingfish, each about a metre long, their backs the same colour blue as the sky.

Suppressing a yelp, Jack protected his private parts with his hands, for fear the fish might take his palang for some kind of lure. Like this, he sprinted from the water and soon was sitting naked on his towel, panting heavily. He heard an odd noise, like a dud note played on a piano accordion. The same noise again. He looked around to see at least 10 ducks heading towards him, their tails wagging as they waddled.

Soon they were all around him, and as one duck peered curiously over his knees to see what he had to offer them, another duck pecked, or rather billed, him on the upper thigh.

Jack jumped to his feet and hurriedly re-pantsed himself, for fear his tackle might now be mistaken for a worm with two be-studded eyes. And just in time too, as a small car was now parking near the shelter/amenities block that housed the honour-system rental snorkelling equipment. Two bicycles had just arrived and soon there were a small group of people following an old bloke with a bucket straight towards where Jack was standing.

"You're just in time," said the old bloke who proceeded to scatter by hand the contents of the bucket, which appeared to be stale bread mixed with a little water. The ocean where the gluggy concoction landed boiled with activity as the kingfish went into a stale-bread frenzy, cruising back and forth impatiently and jumping out of the water, their huge mouths gaping, swallowing down each and every chunk of stale bread.

"I was just swimming in there," said Jack.

"Good thing you're not bread-flavoured," the old bloke quipped.

Around the onlookers' feet, the ducks desperately and defiantly picked any crumbs the old bloke dropped, occasionally getting into a squabble with the marauding kingfish, who were quite willing to beach themselves in pursuit of the precious stale bread.

"What kind of fish are these?" asked Jack.

"Mostly kingfish," said the old bloke, "although you see that black one up the back ..." he added, pointing to a dark shape a few metres from the shore.

Jack nodded.

"That's a young grey nurse shark."

As he walked back up the beach, Jack reminded himself never to swim alone at Ned's Beach while eating a day-old sandwich.

Twenty minutes later, Jack was sitting at a table at Humpty Micks Café deciding whether or not to order a day-old sandwich or freshly-made bacon and eggs, when he noticed something at another table. It was Boz, talking animatedly to Brad Lawrence. It appeared that Brad was shaking his hand and putting a finger to his mouth, in the classic 'hush-hush' mode. Boz nodded, as if he understood, and then left to go back to the table where he had been sitting with Mick, Mike and Matahina.

Jack thought now was as good a time as ever to have a word with Brad Lawrence, so he went over to Brad's table and sat down.

"Mind if I join you?" he asked.

"Not at all," said Brad. "Just trying out the new filling your lady friend gave me. And it works." Jack was tempted to mention the filling *he'd* given his lady friend the night before, but not being one to boast, thought better of it, and sat down. He pointed to Boz.

"What was that about?" asked Jack. "He wasn't trying to get you dressed up in a squirrel suit, was he?"

Brad looked momentarily confused, then dismissed it with a wave of his hand. "Oh, he saw some unusual bird behaviour.

I told him it was just normal behaviour for this time of the year."

"Oh yeah, I saw that the other day," said Jack enthusiastically.

"You did?" Brad looked puzzled.

"Yeah, the loop-the-loop. Pretty amazing."

A waitress took Jack's order, and when she left he leaned towards Brad and smiled. "Why didn't you mention that you knew Harvey Jacob when I spoke to you the other day?"

"I thought that's *why* you wanted to talk to me. I thought you already knew. Everyone saw me talking to him in the restaurant."

"And you thought I was just being very cryptic when I didn't ask you how you knew him?" queried Jack.

"Not at all," smiled Brad, "just a little incompetent."

"So how *did* you know him?" Jack persisted.

"In another life I was a history teacher, and he was someone I met at a conference," said Brad, dismissively.

"Not just someone. He was kind of famous in those circles," added Jack.

"Was he? I don't travel in those circles any more. Not since I discovered the wonder of birds, and the amazing avian life that abounds here on Lord Howe Island," Brad said, quoting one of his brochures.

"Despite having no ornithological qualifications whatsoever?" asked Jack.

"How do you know that?"

"I Googled you."

"You don't need qualifications to have a deep and very real love of seabirds. Besides, I *am* a member of Birds Australia."

"So you didn't kill him because you thought he was on to some kind of treasure that you were also after on Lord Howe Island?"

Brad laughed.

"Treasure? *On* the island? If there's any treasure it'll be *off* the island, not *on* the island. If I was after treasure, I'd be looking in the ocean. More than 250 ships have sunk off Lord Howe over the last 250 years."

Jack did the maths.

"That's one ship a year!"

"Yes, flying is much safer."

"Are muttonbirds ever known to use house bricks as nesting material?"

"Not usually."

Jack nodded, knowingly.

"Can I get a DNA sample?"

"Certainly."

Brad picked up a napkin, blew his nose in it, handed it to Jack and walked off.

"Ta."

A short while later – after he'd bagged the napkin and thoroughly washed his hands – Jack was replacing the bacon grease and egg yolk in his moustache with the froth of a latte as he considered what to do next. Some clouds had rolled in, and it looked as if it might rain shortly. He walked to the nearby phone booth and called his boss.

"I'm sending you some more DNA. It could be the murderer's."

"Okay. But it could take a while to get a result. Forensics has closed down for the holidays. And another thing. The US embassy is pestering us to confirm the identity of the victim. What have you got?"

"Well, I've seen his driver's licence and he looks just like the guy in the photo, only deader," answered Jack.

"That's not good enough. I'm emailing you Harvey Jacob's dental records. I want you to get onto the local dentist as soon as possible."

"I'm way ahead of you on that score."

"Good. Get them to check the corpse's teeth and match them against his dental records, so at least we can confirm to the Yanks that he is definitely one of theirs."

Jack left the phone booth and walked over to where Boz and his posse were sitting.

"Hi Boz. I hear you saw the same freaky bird behaviour that I saw."

"You saw that too?" asked Boz, quizzically. "How did *you* see that?"

"Oh, I get around," answered Jack.

Boz wondered how Jack could possibly have seen the jackbooted, hat-nesting birds on a ledge 875 metres above sea level. But then, if what Brad Lawrence had told him – that it was a rare seabird breeding program using old shoes and hats that he was secretly conducting on the island – was true, then perhaps Jack had seen something similar at some other more accessible location.

"Weird, isn't it?" said Boz.

"A little," said Jack, thinking that a bird doing a loop-the-loop wasn't really that weird, if that's what Boz had indeed seen.

"You probably see some pretty weird things, don't you?" asked Boz, who had a healthy interest in pretty weird things.

"I certainly do," said Jack. "But then, even the normal things look weird to me."

Boz laughed and invited Jack to join him, and Jack took up the invitation. He had begun to take quite a liking to Boz, in a strictly non-sexual blokey kind of way. And the feeling was mutual. There was something of a 'bromance' developing between them. In many ways they were complete opposites, and perhaps that was the attraction. Boz thought Jack was hilarious, a real card. Jack envied Boz's cavalier attitude towards most of the things Jack was petrified of – life, injury and gravity, just to name a few. But Jack was genuinely concerned for Boz's safety, and couldn't shake the feeling that it was all going to end badly. But that didn't stop him making light of the matter.

"So are you going to try to kill yourself again, since your last effort failed so spectacularly?" he asked with a broad smile.

Boz looked up at the clouds. "As soon as this storm passes."

It was spitting rain, but further out to sea, the sun was shining.

"Are you going to go off K2 this time?" queried Jack, pointing at Mount Lidgbird.

"Nope. All that climbing is a drag. I'm going to go off Malabar Hill." He pointed in the opposite direction.

"It's not as big a drop, but I'm going to try to make it out to Roach Island."

Jack shook his head and laughed. "You must have a death wish."

An hour or so later, Jack and Jill were on their way to the Fish Co-op to check the corpse's dental records.

"I can't believe you just pulled me out of my surgery for a bike ride," said Jill when they were halfway there.

"It's official state business. And how can you talk while we're cycling up a bloody great hill?" wheezed Jack phlegmatically.

"I can talk underwater," replied Jill, boastfully.

"I don't doubt it."

Minutes later they were in the Fish Co-op freezer. While Jill checked the corpse's teeth against Harvey Jacob's dental records, Jack sat behind her on the steps and checked out Harvey Jacob online, on Barry's laptop.

"This guy is amazing …" said Jack.

"*Was* amazing," Jill corrected him.

Jack smiled in agreement, and continued. "He's found more than one 'modern war treasure' has old Harvey, if it is Harvey."

"Yep, his dental records check out," said Jill turning from the corpse to where Jack was sitting. "And his breath, or lack of it, is appalling."

"Sadly, he didn't get the opportunity to brush his teeth after his last meal," replied Jack.

Jack turned his attention back to the online biography of Harvey Jacob he'd found on the computer. "He's a veritable geriatric Indiana Jones. He's found war booty in Malaysia, Saipan, Vanuatu and Guam."

Leaning over the body to get a better look at his choppers, something caught the attention of Jill's eyes. "Hang on, what's this?" She reached down over the body and picked up a folded piece of paper.

Jack jumped to his feet. "Where did you find that?"

"It was down the back of the gurney, between the boxes of spring rolls." She handed it to Jack. He unfolded it and scanned his eyes over the page.

"It's in Japanese. Or possibly Chinese," mused Jack, who had little knowledge of Oriental penmanship.

"Perhaps it's cooking instructions …" said Jill, "for the spring rolls."

Jack looked at Jill askance, then looked closely at the paper. "This is a scan of the original. I wonder if it's a clue." He tried to look serious and thoughtful, but only managed to look constipated.

Just then, Barry came in from his office. He actually looked serious and thoughtful.

"Guys, I just got a call from Mike on the two-way. There's been an accident."

They all jumped in Barry's fish van and drove as fast as possible down to the jetty. By now the sun was shining again and there was no sign of the earlier threatening weather. Just as they got out of the van, a fishing boat came around the Dawson's Point headland and within minutes it was pulling up alongside the jetty.

From the jetty they could see Boz's broken and bloodied body lying in the back of the boat. Next to it, an extremely agitated and ashen-faced Mike threw them a rope – which Barry tied off – and Jack jumped on board.

"He's gone. Something bad happened. He's gone," said Mike in a tone that sounded almost apologetic.

It was hard for Jack to see just how much blood there was because of the red parachute canopy partially wrapped around Boz's body.

He managed to free Boz's limp left arm from the tangle of suspension lines, and tried to take his pulse, but there was nothing.

"He just fell like a stone and hit the rocks. The chute came out, but it didn't open," Mike explained, in a desperate tearful voice.

Despite the horrific injuries to his face and body the impact had caused, Jack loosened Boz's clothing and administered cardiopulmonary resuscitation. First he tilted Boz's head back and listened for breathing. Hearing nothing, he placed his hands on Boz's chest and began a series of 30 chest compressions followed by two breaths into Boz's open mouth over and over, all the time talking to Boz, exhorting him to breathe and telling him what an idiot he was. It was all to no avail, and eventually Jack had to admit what his medical training had already told him. Boz was no longer in there. At this point Jack looked at the others and slowly shook his head. Jill, who'd been assisting him, burst into tears. Mike was still shaking. "Mick's still up the top of Malabar Hill. And Matti's with him. Shit."

Both Jack and Jill had been noticing that Boz and Matahina had become increasingly friendly towards each other over the last two days. They knew she wasn't going to take it well.

They wrapped the body in the semi-unfurled canopy and put it in the back of the Barry's van.

"Better take him back to the freezer, Barry," instructed Jack, stoically wiping tears from his eyes and the sweat from his brow.

"Yep," agreed Barry, shaking his head. "Jesus, if this keeps up, I'm gonna run out of room for my fish."

Barry dropped Jack and Jill off near Ned's Beach where they hoped to catch up with Matahina and help her cope. They didn't pick Mick for being much of an empathic crisis counsellor.

By the time they got up to the sty on the track to Malabar Hill, Matahina was coming down the hill towards them. Her eyes were streaked with tears, and sweat. Wailing and panting, she headed determinedly forward.

Between intermittent bouts of stoicism and uncontrollable tears, she called out, "I want to see him. He's alright isn't he?" But she could tell by the looks on Jack and Jill's faces that he wasn't alright.

She shook her head. "I don't believe you. He's alright. I know he is."

Clambering down the steep section of the hill behind her, Mick, almost as distressed, was frantically trying to catch up.

After Boz had jumped and plummeted instead of floating and flying, Matahina had totally freaked out on the lip of the ledge, and at one point Mick had to hold her back to stop her plunging off after Boz. So she stormed off in the other direction. What was normally a forty-five minute hike, she did in twenty-five.

Now that she had met up with Jack and Jill, her tears came tumbling down as they both tried to comfort her the best they could.

"I'm sorry, Matti," Jack said softly, "we tried, but ..." he trailed off. Matahina burst into tears once more.

As the three of them hugged, both Matahina and Jill were in tears, and Jack could not help but think that this may be as close as he ever gets to that threesome he was thinking about the other day. He wondered if he was becoming desensitised to death.

Once more they returned to the Fish Co-op freezer. Now it was beginning to resemble a morgue with a body on either side, the latest one laying on a makeshift gurney comprising of a sheet of plywood on top of a stack of rock-solid frozen yellowfin tuna.

Once she had accepted the truth of Boz's death, Matahina demanded to see his body, and nothing would stop her.

She sobbed, and Jack and Jill put their hands on her shoulders to comfort her as they gazed down on the young man's broken body.

Matahina thought his face looked quite serene and peaceful, although one eye was missing and his right arm was bent back and up over his head in an angle that made you wince just to look at it, and that would have been impossible were it not broken in so many places.

She looked from Boz's body to Harvey's opposite, and back again, then gasped and turned to Jack and Jill.

"My parents," she exclaimed.

"They're coming to get you?" asked Jack.

"No, they've put a *curse* on me."

"What?" queried Jill.

"Because I ran out on an arranged marriage, they're killing any man who gets too close to me."

Jack instinctively took his hand off Matahina's shoulder and took one step back.

"You don't really believe in that, do you?"

"It doesn't matter what I believe. *They* believe, and that's enough. I'm bad news. I've got to get out of here, before I kill again." She started to cry and, as Jill led her outside for some fresh air, Jack had a look at the new body.

From what Mike and Mick had told them, the parachute opened but the canopy didn't 'engage', or fill with air. It just flapped behind Boz like a big red flag as he plummeted straight down.

Jack checked the suspension lines on the canopy one by one. On the third line he hit pay dirt – the line that broke. He carefully examined both sides of the break. About 20 percent of the nylon fibres looked torn, but the other 80 percent was a clean cut – a razor cut. Fuck a duck, he thought to himself, and briefly looked serious, even though there was no one there to see him looking it, except for the two dead guys, the stiff bird and a whole bunch of equally dead seafood.

Sabotage. Another fucking murder. He'd had a premonition that Boz was going to end up dead, but from his own stupidity, not by someone else's doing. BASE jumping is deadly enough without some bastard cutting your lines for you, he thought to himself. He was angry now. It wasn't so bad when the corpses he dealt with were complete strangers, but he was just getting to know this kid, and he really liked him. Someone was going to pay for this, and he had a pretty good idea who that someone was.

Jack slammed the freezer door shut and walked up to Mike and Mick who were still hanging around, Mick puffing nervously on a cigarette.

"What the *fuck* happened up there?" asked Jack in their general direction.

"I dunno mate. I dunno," replied a worried Mick.

"He packed his own chute?" Jack asked Mick.

"I don't know about that, but *I* packed *my* chute when he went down like a stone," said Mick, taking another desperate drag on his durry.

Mike stepped forward. "We both saw him pack it this morning before we went to breakfast."

"And he took it with him?" asked Jack.

"Yeah," recollected Mick. "Not to breakfast though. It was back in his room at Pinetrees."

"Which would have been locked?" assumed Jack.

"Mate, you don't have to lock your room on Lord Howe." replied Mick.

Jack nodded and furrowed his brow.

"Well, now maybe you do."

Jack made the call to his boss to report the latest Lord Howe fatality, then he caught up with Mick and Mike at the Bowls Club, where they were trying to take the edge off their shock with a couple of beers.

Jack sat down with a schooner of Toohey's Old. He looked pissed off.

"This was sabotage." He tilted his glass to Boz's memory and took a drink. He wiped the froth off his mouth with the back of his hand. "Some bastard is trying to ruin my holiday."

He took another big gulp of beer and turned to Mike and Mick.

"Did Boz piss anybody off in the, what, *two* days he's been here?"

"No one," said Mick.

"He's hardly talked to anyone, except us, and you," said Mike.

"You don't think *I* did it, do you?" asked Jack.

"He did talk to Brad Lawrence about the bird thing," said Mick. "About whatever it was he saw up there."

Jack shook his head. "I saw that bird thing. It wasn't that odd." He paused for a thought. "Unless he saw something *else*."

"We could look at the video," offered Mike.

"What video?" asked Jack.

"Boz had a camera on his helmet."

The three men drove back up to the Fish Co-op, schooners still in hand, to retrieve the video. The lipstick lens fitted onto Boz's battered helmet was attached via a cable to a small high-definition digi-cam in his bum bag.

They rewound the video and played it back on the small fold-out screen. It began with a Boz-eye view of the island from on top of Mount Gower. He turned to Mick, who gave him the thumbs up. The continual shot panned back towards the cliff's edge and then, as Boz screamed "Geronimo!" the screen filled with sky.

Next on the screen, they briefly saw the view directly beneath Boz just after he jumped – a huge drop down to the steep rocky bottom of Mount Gower, and the ocean beyond it. Then suddenly the image tilted down until the shot was completely upside down, as Boz began his signature somersault, and the screen filled with the basalt wall of the cliff.

Then, extremely briefly, only for a few frames at most, something strange flashed onto the screen – the upside down, almost subliminal appearance of two seabirds. Boz could be heard uttering "What the fuck?" before the weird image was just as quickly replaced by blue sky and fluffy white clouds as he completed the somersault, followed by the view of the island over the lagoon as he began his slow and more steady descent.

"What the bloody hell was *that*?" said Mike, almost spilling his beer.

"Let's look at it again," said Jack, hitting the rewind button.

This time they slowed the footage down and turned the screen upside down. At the appropriate moment, Jack paused the footage. On the screen was a deep almost cave-like ledge carved by nature into the rock, and on the ledge a black and white seabird with each of its feet in a black leather shoe. The shoes were small but on the bird they looked enormous. Next to the shoe-wearing bird was an identical seabird, nesting in an upturned pith helmet adorned with a tarnished gold star.

Jack stroked his beard. Mick scratched his head. Mike shook his head, then belched.

Jack looked around. "Neither of you guys read Japanese do you?"

Mick and Mike shook their heads. "I know a bit of Kanji, but that's all," said Mick, disparagingly.

Jack hit the play button and the vision continued at the normal speed. They flipped the screen around and watched the rest of the footage the right way up.

After he'd completed the somersault, Boz glided for a few seconds then reached around and released his pilot chute and they watched, from his point of view, his beautiful slow descent over the lagoon, the camera barely shuddering as he landed on Blackburn Island. After that, the footage went to black. There was a brief interval of pixilation, then more video images appeared on the small screen.

"Hang on, what's this?" said Jack picking up the camera. Mick and Mike looked over Jack's shoulders as all three watched the ensuing footage. It was Boz's second – and last – jump and began with Mick on top of Malabar Hill, giving Boz the thumbs up again. Next Matti appeared in the screen blowing Boz a kiss, waving and giggling. Then the view off the cliff at Malabar Hill – the one Jack could only look at by crawling to the edge. The now familiar "Geronimo!" followed by the somersault, and then Boz yelling "Shit!" followed by "Fuuuuuuuuuck!" – the desperate seconds when he must have known there was nothing he could do to save himself – as the ground beneath him came thundering into view until it filled the screen and with a sickening crunch, Boz connected with the rocks and the vision went to black.

All three skulled their beers in silence.

That night Jack had dinner with Jill again. Sadly it wasn't quite as romantic as the previous night's – frozen Lean Cuisine popped in the microwave, a salad made from some fresh veggies picked from Heather's garden and a bottle of Richmond Grove French Cask chardonnay from the honesty-system fridge in the library room.

Just as Jack had unscrewed the lid and poured two glasses, a slightly bedraggled Jill came in from Matahina's apartment.

"How is she?" asked Jack.

"She's very upset, but she's young and resilient. She'll be alright. I gave her a sedative, and she's going to go to sleep."

"You can do that?" queried Jack.

"For toothache. I figure death of the guy you bonked last night is at least as painful, if not more."

The microwave pinged and they sat down to eat. Jack had the Lean Cuisine beef lasagne and Jill had the Lean Cuisine vegetable cannelloni. As they ate, the conversation turned to Boz's death.

"Maybe it wasn't sabotage," argued Jill. "Maybe Boz's death was just another freak BASE jumping accident."

"There's no such thing as a freak BASE jumping accident," grumbled Jack. "It's a freak accident when you survive."

They went to bed early and despite the grim circumstances, or perhaps because of them, had wild post-mortem sex – so loud it would have woken Matahina in the next apartment, had she not been completely sedated.

Afterwards, while Jill snored quietly in the background, Jack almost wished *he* had access to some potent sedatives. He couldn't get to sleep and he couldn't stop thinking about the case, or cases, as the case may or may not have been. What was the common link between what Boz *saw* and what Harvey Jacob *knew?*

Jack knew the gold star insignia on the pith helmet in the video was Japanese from war movies he'd seen, like Terence Malick's *The Thin Red Line,* and Nagisa Oshima's *Merry Christmas Mr Lawrence*. And with the scanned page they'd found near Harvey's body, he knew that somehow Japan, or something or someone from Japan, was involved, but *who*, and *why?* But there was one thing he knew for sure – if he was ever going to be able to get back to his holiday and play slide on his precious Dobro, he was going to have to find out.

24ᵗʰ **December, 2008 – 6:25am**

The next morning, Jack and Jill walked down to Ned's Beach for an early morning dip. Jill showed Jack that if they walked along the beach to the north, there were plenty of spots where they could happily swim without being mobbed by hungry kingfish.

They dropped their towels, took off their shirts and plunged into the gently undulating ocean. Jack decided this was a far better way to start the day than his usual morning regimen, which consisted of a scratch, a fart and a cup of coffee.

He sat submerged to his shoulders in the lukewarm water, a look of utter contentment on his face, as a series of decent-sized bubbles broke on the surface around him.

Jill joined him from a couple of metres to his left.

"Don't swim over there," she warned. "I've just created a warm patch." She smiled coyly.

"And I've just let out a depth charge," reposted Jack. "That should keep those man-eaters away," he added, referring to the kingfish.

Now that they'd refreshed themselves and despoiled the pristine waters of a World Heritage-listed natural wonder, they headed back to the beach.

"I don't know why you're worried about them. They're only interested in bread," Jill added as she majestically strode back to shore through the knee-deep shallows in her black one-piece costume, the crystal clear water cascading from her Lycra-covered buttocks.

Jack happily followed her ashore. "I'm not so sure," he replied, confidently.

After drying off on their beach towels, Jack began fumbling through the multiple compartments of his backpack. He joked that the backpack had so many compartments there was even one for putting things you'd taken out of a horse's hoof with your Swiss Army knife. Eventually he found the compartment he was looking for and pulled out a white plastic shopping bag.

"I've devised a little experiment," he said, as he took out of the bag two tomato and onion sausages left over from the barbeque two nights ago, and dangled one from each hand.

He held aloft the sausage in his right hand. "The sausage on *this* side has been coated with breadcrumbs …" He jiggled the bread-coated sausage for emphasis, shaking loose a few of its crumbs, before turning to the sausage in his left hand. "… whereas the sausage on *this* side has not." He shook the pristine sausage to prove his point.

Still holding the bangers aloft, Jack proceeded to lead Jill along the beach to the spot where the kingfish were regularly fed. "We shall now test the sausage that has *not* been breaded," he declared melodramatically.

Jack flung the naked sausage into the ocean, to the left, where it floated lazily on the surface.

"As you can see, the fish aren't touching it. Now for the breaded sausage."

He threw the breaded sausage into the ocean on his right. Immediately a swarm of kingfish appeared from nowhere and began fighting over the breaded sausage until, with a few swift gulps, it was gone.

Jack turned to Jill, his audience of one, and took a small bow. "As you can see, the fish are only interested in the *breaded* sausage," he proudly proclaimed, with more than a little Professor Julius Sumner Miller in his voice.

"Ah, they're eating the other one now." Jill pointed over Jack's shoulder.

He turned to see the water boiling with fishy activity around the spot where the breadless sausage had once been.

"Okay …" he said nervously. "That clearly doesn't prove anything …" He frowned, thinkingly. "… except that they *did* go for the *breaded* sausage first."

Jill tried to interpret his conclusions. "So what you're saying is as long as one of us isn't covered with breadcrumbs, we're not going to be eaten by ravenous kingfish?"

Jack nodded. "I think that's what I'm saying."

On the way back up the road from the beach they noticed a pair of white terns nesting on the open branch of a tree. They looked like the avian equivalent of baby harp seals, snowy white with large round dark eyes and a bluish-black pointy beak, as if a seabird had been designed by a Japanese schoolgirl. Jill pointed out that the terns nest on the bare branch of the tree, with nothing but their own bodies to hatch their eggs. Jack wondered why they hadn't been eaten into extinction like many of the extinct native birds no longer on the island. Perhaps they were just too cute to kill?

After a breakfast consisting of a bowl of cereal, followed by a bowl of raspberry yoghurt, a glass of pineapple and orange juice and a cup of freshly-made drip-filter Papua New Guinea coffee, Jack and Jill decided they had to find more crockery so they wouldn't have to share everything – and headed off for their day's business.

Jack's first port of call was the Lord Howe Museum and Visitors' Centre, as it was officially known, although Jack was really only interested in the museum part of it. Fortunately for him, the museum was situated at the bottom of the hill, an easy bike ride – although by now Jack was beginning to get his 'bike legs' in the same way as had he been on a boat all this time, he would have begun to get his 'sea legs'.

He zoomed down the hill like a bat out of hell in a Hawaiian shirt, and right outside the Lord Howe Museum and Visitors Centre he hit the brake, leaned his weight to the right, did a big screechie and skidded around 180 degrees, almost right into the bike rack at the foot of the steps.

A family having breakfast at one of the outdoor tables of the centre's coffee shop gave Jack a polite round of applause as he took his helmet off, hung it on his handlebars and casually sauntered up the steps past them.

Once inside, Jack had a look around. Most of the building's modern interior was taken up with racks of magazines, publications and pamphlets on accommodation, activities and places to eat, as well as the usual high-quality souvenirs one is always bound to find in this sort of establishment.

On one side, a doorway led to another room, with a sign proclaiming it the *Lord Howe Island Museum*. By now Jack was only mildly surprised to see Reg, the guy from the airport, the boat hire shed *and* the Bowls Club sitting behind a table set up in front of the doorway.

"G'day mate," said Reg, looking up from a copy of a *Modern Home* magazine someone had left on the Dash 8. "How's the investigation going?"

"Which one?" smiled Jack.

"Jesus, you're right," said Reg. "If this keeps up we'll have to add a serial murder display to the museum."

"How did you know about the other murder?" queried Jack.

Reg winked. "Word travels fast on Lord Howe, mate."

Reg showed Jack around the modest yet fascinating museum. Like Lord Howe itself, it was compact but impressive, with historical displays going back to 1788 when the island was discovered by *HMS Supply* of the First Fleet, and covering the 174 years of continuous settlement since 1834.

With artefacts, replicas and photographs, the museum documented the mostly maritime, then later aviation history of the island – from the time of whaling ships, to flying boats and more recently, the airstrip as the island's fledgling tourist industry developed and flourished, becoming the main source of income for the islanders that it is today.

"What specifically is it that you'd like to know?" Reg asked Jack.

"Was Lord Howe used by the military in World War II as an internment or prisoner-of-war camp?"

"Nah mate," Reg shook his head. "During the war, although I wasn't born myself until '51, the island was mostly off the radar, if you know what I mean. The government basically kept us quiet in case the other side ..."

"Which would be Japan in this case?" injected Jack.

"Yeah, Japan," nodded Reg. "They didn't want to draw attention to the place for fear the Japs might decide to invade and use it as a base for attacks on mainland Australia. So we were really cut off."

"And there wasn't ever any kind of invasion attempt?" asked Jack.

Reg laughed. "Nah mate. We didn't even get the Yanks. Our blokes used the island for communications and weather information for the war effort," continued Reg, "and of course, coast watch in case the Japanese Imperial Navy decided to drop in for a visit, which thank Christ they didn't. But the only war 'action' we saw was the RAAF Catalinas that used to fly in supplies once in a blue moon."

"And one of them crashed, didn't it?"

"Yeah but that was *after* the war, in '48."

"There were a couple of survivors of that crash weren't there?"

"Two out of the nine. A couple of local blokes at the time dragged them out of the wreckage. They got a British Empire Medal and a George Medal for that."

"Are those blokes still alive?" asked Jack.

"Sadly, they've gone," replied Reg, with a regretful shake of his head.

"What about the two blokes they rescued?"

"I wouldn't know mate. They weren't locals. If they're still alive they'd be real old blokes, somewhere on the mainland."

Jack rubbed his beard thoughtfully and nodded.

"But that's a really old tragedy. Shouldn't you be concentrating on the more recent ones?" suggested Reg.

Jack rubbed his beard thoughtfully and nodded.

Back on his bike, Jack headed around the corner to the local administration offices. The Lord Howe Island Board usually employs about 22 officers and administrators to deal with the island's management, but because it was Christmas Eve, the offices were closed. However, Jack was able to get the key from the ladies at the official Lord Howe Island Liquor Store, just around the corner.

Inside, he quickly found what he was looking for – the *Deaths Register*. It was a thin volume, because most elderly residents of Lord Howe Island eventually end up on the mainland due to insufficient population to support an aged-care facility. As a result, most natural deaths are registered on the mainland.

This made finding what he was looking for a lot easier. And there it was:

Dawson-Lawrence, Diana – 77 years of age. Missing at sea, presumed dead. Officially declared dead – Nov 21ˢᵗ 2005.

And a bit further down, he found this:

Gimbell, Norman – 65 years of age. Died from multiple head wounds sustained in fall off Fishy Point – June 23ʳᵈ 2004.

Gimbell was Brad Lawrence's predecessor and former boss, back when it was 'Birders' Paradise Tours' and not 'Birders' Paradise *Eco* Tours'. Brad put the 'Eco' in after he took over the business, which apparently he and Norman were in negotiations over at the time of Norman's death. The main difference between Norman and Brad was that Norman actually had a degree in ornithology, and *not* from Big Bird University either. Also it didn't look like Norman was a serial killer, but it was looking increasingly like Brad *was*.

Attached to the entry was a statement from Brad Lawrence at the time of the accident. Apparently the pair had been booby-watching out on Fishy Point, when Norman saw an impressive pair of boobies close to the edge. Unfortunately, it was mating season, and the male booby flew at Norman's booby-shaped beanie. He ducked the booby, but lost his footing and fell about thirty metres.

This could easily be one of Brad's, thought Jack. People obviously didn't even consider it at the time because Brad was a person of considerable character, and there was nothing to be suspicious about. Everyone around here's probably had a booby fly at them at one time or another, Jack figured.

There was no way to prove that Brad had killed Norman. But Jack thought there might just be some indicators to Brad's involvement in his temporary wife Diana's mysterious 'disappearance'.

First stop was the local Food Co-op where the scrupulous records kept by the co-op members were able to show that the day before his wife disappeared in a boating accident, Brad

Lawrence bought three kilos of white flour and a dozen free-range eggs.

The next stop was the bakery, where both the baker and the butcher remembered Brad coming in that day and buying three loaves of old bread, but then he did that regularly anyway, because he often took birdwatching tour groups down to Ned's Beach to show them the sooty terns, and they usually stopped and fed the fish as well.

Down at the jetty, Jack had a couple of facts to check out. Mike was there today and showed Jack the logbook that recorded all parcels from the mainland. The delivery that coincided with the week of Diana Dawson-Lawrence's death included a parcel to Brad Lawrence from Bunnings Warehouse, that contained a Black & Decker circular saw.

Jack asked Mike about the boat Brad and Diana had gone out in on the day of her disappearance.

"That heap of shit? I told him when I sold it to him a couple of weeks before, that it needed a lot of work. It was riddled with …"

"Holes?"

"Concrete cancer."

Jack nodded. He knew nothing about boats.

"But Brad just joked and said it didn't matter because he was a pretty good swimmer," continued Mike, "which I guess is why he didn't bother to pick up the two life jackets that came with it."

Jack paced up and down and chewed on his nails like a man desperately trying to figure out what to ask next, which he was.

"Did anyone see Brad and Diana go out in the boat on the day of the accident?"

"I doubt it," answered Mike. "They went out really early, about 4:00am. Apparently that's the best time to catch the Wedge-tailed Shearwaters taking off from the Admiralty Islets. Although why you'd bother, I don't know. We've got a breeding colony right here at Lovers Bay," he said, pointing in what must have been the right direction.

This time Jack was nodding about something he knew something about. Murder. Brad Lawrence must have been planning this for some time. He bought a boat that was unseaworthy and very likely to sink. He bought a circular saw to chop his wife's body into bite-size chunks, which he then coated in flour, beaten eggs and bread crumbs and fed to the kingfish at Ned's Beach, which explains why her wedding ring was found there.

Unfortunately, this was all circumstantial evidence, and he couldn't at this point charge Brad with Diana Dawson's murder, especially with there being no body to speak of. However, it was good to know the calibre of the killer Jack was dealing with. The guy was both very clever and extremely disturbed, possibly the worst combination in a rampant serial killer.

As Jack cycled to his next destination, his mind was spinning almost as fast as his flywheel. So far, it appeared that

Brad Lawrence may have killed Norman Gimbell, Diana Dawson, Harvey Jacob *and* Boz Boswell. But what did they all have in common? And what did it have to do with Japan?

He stopped the bike, and turned it around. Against his better judgement he decided he was going to have to confront Brad Lawrence. He pedalled off in the direction of the Birders' Paradise Eco Tours' office.

This time he was genuinely surprised to see Matahina working behind the counter.

"Matti, what are you doing here? I thought you were …"

"An emotional wreck?" she smiled shyly. "I was. I still am." She gave Jack a fragile smile. "Brad saw me this morning crying at breakfast …"

"Wow, you got up for breakfast?"

Jack took his bike helmet off and held it in his hands.

"I hadn't eaten anything for about 32 hours and I was starving."

"That's a good sign."

"Anyway, he offered me this job to keep my mind off the deaths. It's only for a couple of days."

"I thought your parents were organising you a ticket back to Sydney?"

"They did. But all the flights to and from are booked out for the next three days. Christmas, you know?"

"Is Brad here, by the way?" asked Jack, looking around in case Brad was lurking somewhere.

"No. He's taking a group of twitchers from Wollongong up Mount Gower. He won't be back until about 6:00pm, I think …" she said, looking at the schedule on the counter in front of her.

"Did you say "*Witches* from Wollongong?" queried Jack.

"No, *twitchers*. You know, birdwatchers." Matahina corrected him.

Jack nodded and stroked his beard. He furrowed his brow and winced. "You're not involved with him in some way, are you?"

Matahina was outraged. "No! I am not! What do you think I am, some kind of sea-slut?"

Jack apologised. "Of course not. Just … be careful okay?"

"Why? What have I got to worry about?" She looked a little concerned.

"Yesterday you said you were responsible for Harvey and Boz's deaths. But you know who else spoke to both of them just before they died? Your new boss."

"Three Eyes?" Matahina shook her head. "He wouldn't do anything like that, would he?"

"I'm not sure. But if you feel you're in any kind of danger, let me know, okay?"

"Sure."

Jack beat a hasty retreat, coming within millimetres of knocking the stuffing out of the last remaining Lord Howe Boobook with his bicycle helmet.

Over kingfish burgers and chips at Humpty Micks Café , Jack shared his latest findings with Jill.

"It has something to do with Japan, and I think it has something to do with the Catalina crash."

"But that took place *after* the war. Japan were our friends, or at least our subjugated lackeys," Jill said popping a chip in her mouth.

"I can't fully explain it yet, but it's the only connection I can make between a World War II Japanese Imperial Army pith helmet, the letter we found on Harvey's body, and Lord Howe Island itself," said Jack.

"I just wish I was on the mainland so I could check out the survivors of the crash," he added.

"Why is that?"

"To see what was *really* on that plane."

"Well, we have access to a computer. You might be able to find them online."

"I don't even know their names," said Jack, putting the last mouth-watering morsel of fish burger in his mouth.

Jill smiled. "I can help you out there."

Minutes later they were both on their bikes, peddling past the jetty to Old Settlement Beach. Being Christmas Eve, Jill had no appointments that afternoon, and she was more than happy to join Jack in his investigation.

"This is like being in an Enid Blyton book," she called out to Jack.

"What? *Noddy and Big Ears?*" he called back.

"No. *The Famous Five* or *The Secret Seven.*"

"So what are we?"

"The Terrific Two?"

A short time later they arrived at the end of the road where there was parking, a convenient bike rack and a picnic area. As they put their bikes in the rack, Jack noticed what looked like part of one of the engine blocks of the crashed plane.

Dominating the picnic area was a huge three-bladed propeller mounted on a steel beam. At its base was a small brass plaque set in a concrete block. They both knelt to read the inscription:

"DEDICATED TO THE MEN AND WOMEN OF AUSTRALIA'S DEFENCE FORCES WHO HAVE SERVED THIS ISLAND AND THEIR COUNTRY: ESPECIALLY THE CREW OF RAAF CATALINA FLYING BOAT A24-381 WHICH CRASHED AT LORD HOWE ISLAND ON SEPTEMBER 28TH, 1948."

Beneath the inscription, and next to a side-view relief of the flying boat, was a short list:

DIED

F/LT Malcolm. D. Smith

F/LT James McCoy

F/LT William D. Keller

F/LT Alex McKenzie

PLT 111 Sydney L. Piercy

W/O Sydney H. Bacon

W/O Donald E. Salis

SURVIVED

F/LT John R. Tout

W/O Bert D. Slater

Jack nodded solemnly. "Wow."

He looked at Jill. She was crying.

"Sorry," she sniffed. "It just makes me sad."

"Yep," agreed Jack, and wiped his nose of what he pretended was a tear, but was in reality just sweat.

"Well, we've got our names," said Jack, getting to his feet. "But that was over sixty years ago. Even if the survivors were in their early twenties in 1948, they'd be in their eighties now, if they're still alive."

"There's only one way to find out," smiled Jill. "Let's hit the computer."

They hopped back on their pushbikes and began the heartbreaking bike ride up the hill to Hightide Apartments.

Stopping for a breather halfway up at the Fish Co-op, Jack bought a kilo of cooked king prawns, some dipping sauce and a couple of marlin fillets for Christmas lunch, in case they couldn't get a booking at one of the few restaurants actually open for Christmas on the island.

Soon they were back in Heather's office in front of the computer. They found it much easier to find information about the plane, from aviation enthusiast websites, and the crewmen who *didn't* survive, than information about the two who *did* survive.

Because of his coronial security clearance, Jack was able to get into the government records, and soon traced the two missing men. Flight Lieutenant John Tout left the RAAF shortly after the incident, but died 10 years later in a water-skiing accident on the Myall Lakes, just south of Forster, where he worked as a semi-professional waterskier.

Warrant Officer Bert Slater stayed on in the RAAF for another five years, then left to become a fitter and turner at the Newcastle steelworks. He retired in the early '80s, but while they couldn't find any record of his death, they did find his address and shortly after that, a telephone number.

Minutes later, Jack and Jill arrived at the spider-filled phone booth on the corner of Anderson Street. After several calls from this booth to his boss, Jack found the best approach was to crouch close to the floor of the booth, thus putting the greatest distance between the spiders and the top of his head.

Jill handed him the Post-it note that she had written down the number on, and Jack gingerly dialled it.

An elderly woman answered the phone. "Thelma speaking."

"Oh hello, my name's Jack Slazenger. I'm a representative of the state coroner's office. Is Bert there?"

"You've missed him, love."

"Oh, has he gone out?"

"No, he's been dead for two years."

"Oh dear."

"That's what everyone said. He was so full of life, until he died. You're not investigating his death are you?"

"No. I'm investigating something that happened when he was with the RAAF. Did he ever talk about the Catalina crash on Lord Howe Island?"

"No, love. He didn't talk to me about *any* of his crashes. The only time I think he ever talked about the Catalina crash was just before he died, when that nice man came to visit."

"And what nice man was that?"

"I can't remember his name. But he was very nice. That was just a few days before Bert had his fall."

"Off a cliff?"

"No, off his stool at the club. It was a terrible tragedy. He broke his hip and never really recovered, poor thing. That was his favourite stool too. We buried it with him you know."

"That's nice," said Jack, but thinking it was actually sort of weird. "Do you remember anything about the man who came to visit?"

"Well, he was tall and quite distinguished looking …"

"Yes …?"

"And he had a huge mole in the middle of his forehead."

"Really?"

"Yes, you think he'd get it removed, but he must have liked it for some reason."

"And what did they talk about?"

"Ooh, I don't know, love. I went to the kitchen to make a cuppa."

"That's a shame."

"Yes, but it's probably all on the documentary the chap said he was making."

"Documentary?"

"Yes, about the old flying boat days. He filmed the whole conversation."

When he hung up, Jack was thinking so hard, he forgot about the spiders, stood up and nearly ended up with a web hairnet, if Jill hadn't grabbed him and yanked him out of the phone booth.

"What is it?" she inquired, inquisitively.

Jack rubbed his beard extra hard. "I think we're going to have to break into Brad Lawrence's house."

Brad Lawrence's house was only about half a kilometre from where they were, but on Lord Howe island, just about everybody's house was only about a half a kilometre from where they were. When they arrived, they hid their bicycles in the bushes so they wouldn't be seen.

"Oh this is *so Famous Five*," said Jill, girlishly.

Jack stopped and looked Jill in the face. It was a pretty face. He made a mental note to look at it more often.

"Look, you don't have to be here if you don't want to," he said, deftly indicating with his eyebrows that she may want to leave.

"No, I'm enjoying it." Jill's eyebrows indicated that she'd very much like to stay, to which his eyebrows reacted with a display of mild alarm.

"But I mean, in official terms, I'm a coronial officer authorised to investigate a suspicious death by whatever means I consider worthwhile. And you're a dentist."

"Are you saying you outrank me?" asked Jill, looking slightly offended.

"That's not what I'm saying."

"Are you saying I'm not allowed to be here?"

"No, I'm saying you don't have to be here if you don't want to. It could be dangerous."

"I spend most of my time with my hand in strange people's mouths," said Jill. "I'm not afraid of anything."

"Fair enough." They both nodded in agreement and snuck towards Brad Lawrence's back door.

It was extremely fortunate for their purposes that the back door to Brad Lawrence's house was unlocked, but extremely unfortunate that they couldn't find anything pertaining to the murder inside. There was a TV and a DVD player, but no video player and no videos.

There was however an abundance of World War II memorabilia – stacks of it. Most of it pertained to the Asia-Pacific conflict. The walls were adorned with flags of regiments on both sides.

There were displays of medals, uniforms on manikins, helmets, hats, caps and even a variety of weapons, including machetes and bayonets. It was clear that Brad was a serious collector. But they couldn't find the so-called video they were looking for.

After a while, they gave up.

"There might not even be a video," Jill pointed out. "The whole documentary thing was obviously a charade. If he just wanted information about the Catalina crash from Bert, he didn't really need to videotape it."

"Good point," agreed Jack. "But, if you went to the trouble of that charade and you had a camera there, you might just record it anyway, just in case you missed something."

"Equally good point," conceded Jill.

"There's only one place we haven't searched," continued Jack. "The shed."

They raced into the backyard to discover that unlike the house, the shed – an impressive aluminium building closer to the size of a small warehouse – *was* locked. Then Jill remembered seeing some keys in the kitchen and ran back into the house. Moments later she returned with a big wad of keys.

She handed the keys to Jack, and on his third go he found the match and unlocked the door.

Jill looked a little apprehensive as Jack opened the door.

"What if Brad comes home?" she inquired nervously.

"It's only 4:00pm. He's halfway up Mount Gower with a bunch of twits from Wollongong. Matahina said he wouldn't be back until at least six."

But Jill wasn't convinced. "Okay," said Jack. "We'll leave the shed door open, so we can beat a hasty retreat."

This seemed to work, and they went inside. If the war memorabilia in the house was impressive, this was the British Museum.

"Woah! This guy must have spent a fortune on eBay!" exclaimed Jack, as he looked around, impressed with Lawrence's mighty collection.

As well as more uniforms and flags, there were documents in large plastic storage boxes, each labelled with the name of the conflict they pertained to. There were models of famous battleships and famous aircraft. On the wall was a signed portrait of US Field Marshall Douglas MacArthur, along with a corncob pipe and a peaked military cap, which presumably once belonged to the so-called American Caesar – all sealed in a glass display cabinet.

This time, they hit pay dirt. At the very end of the shed, almost hidden behind the boxes of wartime paraphernalia, was a space that Brad had clearly set up as his work area. There was a workbench set up as a desk, a computer, a TV monitor, a primitive videotape machine and an even more primitive video camera plugged into it – the old kind that used to take full-sized VHS tapes. It was on a tripod.

Jill looked through a stack of tapes. "These are all porn." Obviously, war memorabilia wasn't the only thing Brad got off on.

"Maybe it's still in the camera?"

Jack started looking at the camera to see if he could get it to work, as Jill was distracted by what she'd discovered on the bench.

"You were right about something," she said. "It *is* to do with Japan. Look at this."

On the bench were several sheets of yellowing rice paper with Japanese writing on them. And behind these, also on the bench, an antique-looking Japanese lacquered box was open, revealing its contents – several more similar-looking rice paper letters. Next to them were a magnifying glass and a few textbooks on Japanese language and Japanese text.

"Are these letters like the photocopied one we found on Harvey Jacob?" Jill asked, as Jack came over to the table for a closer look.

They pored through the letters but had no idea what they were about, who they were addressed to, or who or where they were sent from.

Jill admired the lacquered box. "This looks like it could be an antique."

Jack looked at the textbooks. "He's translating them," he said, referring to the letters.

On the wall behind the desk was a large surveyor's map of the island, with a grid drawn over it. Many of the squares of the grid had been 'X'ed out with a marking pen.

Jack peered at the map. "I knew it. He's searching for something."

On a corkboard next to the map were a couple of photographs of RAAF Catalinas.

"And there's the Catalina connection," said Jack. He went back to the map and noticed that most of the squares that had been 'X'ed were radiating out from around the site of the 1948 Catalina crash.

Jill called from the table, "I've found his translations." She held up a data disk freshly ejected from on Brad's computer.

Jack nodded and furiously rubbed his beard. "Let's watch this tape. It's in the machine."

"You mean take it and watch it somewhere else?"

"No, watch it here. It's already in the machine."

He turned the camera and the monitor on.

"What are you, *Little Red Riding-Beard?*"

"I think you mean, *Beardilocks.*"

Jack turned the sound up on the monitor.

The video started. It was a locked-off shot of an old man sitting in what must have been his favourite armchair. He still had a thin covering of grey hair on top of his head, although it was wispy, and you could see a lot of skin under it. His face was wrinkled, pockmarked and weather-beaten, like old leather. His hands were big, broad, rugged stumps of fingers, the hands of a man who did, or had done, a lot of manual labour. He was wearing a mostly blue checked flannelette shirt, the type you buy from a supermarket like Woolworths or Target. He wore navy blue track pants, and grey socks and checked brown slippers on his feet, which he had up on a small footstool.

On a small side table next to him were his reading glasses and the form guide. This was former warrant officer and Catalina crash survivor, Bert Slater, now an old man.

Old Bert squinted his eyes and peered towards the camera. "Are you rolling yet?" He flicked his false teeth forward and briefly out of his mouth with his tongue, then sucked them back into place and smiled.

"Yes we are rolling, Bert." The disembodied voice of Brad Lawrence could be heard from behind the camera. "So it's probably best you keep your teeth in your mouth, if that's okay."

Jack wondered why Brad was so concerned about what his footage looked like. The whole 'documentary' story was surely just a ruse to get information out of this old codger. Then again, the sight of old Bert's false teeth slowly peeping out of his cracked pale lips, like some alien parasite living in his mouth, then slowly disappearing back inside, *was* a little disconcerting.

Old Bert jokingly took the whole set of dentures out with his huge right hand. His lips collapsed into the cavity left behind, as he looked toward the camera and asked, "Wou wore wou won't want we woo woo wip wipe whis, woo-woo?" – spraying enough saliva for Brad to have to wipe the lens before he began.

Old Bert laughed and put his dentures back in. Jack was beginning to like this old bloke.

Brad's voice interrupted Bert's reverie. "Have you ever spoken to anyone about the crash on Lord Howe Island before?"

Bert looked angry for a second. "Is that what you want to talk about? I thought you wanted to know about what I did in the war, in New Guinea. That's the interesting stuff."

Brad's voice replied, "I want to know about the Lord Howe crash, because you're the last surviving member of the crew, and no one's ever heard the full story of what happened that night."

"There was a reason for that. It was a top-secret mission. We weren't allowed to tell anybody. I've never even told the missus."

"It's been over fifty years, Bert. Let's talk about the Lord Howe crash first, and then we'll talk about New Guinea."

"Why, in case I drop off in the meantime?" He laughed. "Yeah alright. What do ya want to know?"

"Why were you on that flight, Bert?"

"After the war I stayed on for a few years in the RAAF. I was made a warrant officer in the RAAF Provost Unit ..."

"You mean the military police?"

"Yeah. They call 'em the Service Police these days."

"So you were looking after security?"

"Security, law enforcement on RAAF bases, street patrols to ensure good conduct by our troops when they were on leave, and general guard duties. On this particular occasion, our orders were to escort a prisoner."

"What kind of prisoner, Bert?"

"A Jap POW."

"A Japanese prisoner of war? But this was three years *after* the war?"

"I know. Jap POWs were pretty rare on the ground even during the war."

"Why was that?"

"Well, a number of reasons. One, they didn't like to surrender much. It was a loss of face. A personal disgrace to them, their country and their family. So they used to fight pretty fucken hard, pardon my French. And number two, our blokes didn't really like to take Jap prisoners."

"Why was that?"

"There were some rumours on the front line about Jap soldiers surrendering, and then doing a 'Kamikaze' and pulling the pin on hidden grenades, and blowing up themselves and the Aussies who they surrendered to."

Bert wiped his face with a handkerchief. It looked like he might have shed a tear or two. "It was a bloody horrible situation, mate."

"I know, I know," Brad said, sounding genuinely empathic.

Bert continued. "And when we found out about some of the atrocities their blokes had done to our blokes, most Aussies on the front line were more than happy to shoot any Jap prisoners they ended up with. And the Japs seemed to prefer that too. So it was a win-win situation. Except we won in the end."

"And of course when Japan surrendered, we had more Jap POWs than we knew what to do with, although that was mostly up in New Guinea and New Britain. But even by '48 they'd all been long-ago repatriated, except for the ones that were charged with war crimes."

"So where did *this* POW come from?"

"That's what we wanted to know. I was stationed at Rathmines Base on Lake Macquarie at the time. They brought him in from Townsville."

"You might recognise these ordinance papers," said Brad, his hand coming into shot, and handing a couple of yellowing sheets of paper to Bert, who took them, and put his reading glasses up to his eyes, without actually putting them on.

"These are the ordinance papers for that prisoner transfer," said Bert, a bit confused. "How did you get them?"

"You'd be surprised what you can buy on the Internet these days," replied Brad, sounding more than a little pleased with himself.

"Bloody hell. There's his name. I can't even pronounce it."

"Tsukasa Kobayashi," Brad told him, as Bert handed the papers back.

"So where did the Queensland blokes get him?" asked Brad.

Bert put down his glasses. "Apparently a couple of months before we got him, he just walked out of the jungle in Port Moresby one day, plain as you like. He was picked up by the authorities there and shipped to Townsville, where they interrogated him. Turns out he was a Japanese army surveyor or scientist or something, and he'd been on his own in jungle up there, living on nuts and berries and still thinking the war was still going."

Bert laughed hard. And farted. "Whoops. Pardon."

Jack and Jill laughed and continued watching the video.

Off camera, Brad added, "I've heard stories of other Japanese soldiers doing that."

"What, farting?"

"No, being unaware that the war had ended."

Bert nodded. "Well, somehow this bloke found out it was over, and he wanted to go home."

Bert shifted in his seat, scratched his arse, and continued.

"So after they were finished with him in Townsville, and everyone was satisfied that he was harmless, it was decided that he should be repatriated. Only problem was, we didn't want to have to take him all the way back to Japan. In 1948 there weren't commercial flights to Tokyo like there are today. We couldn't just bung him on QF whatever it is. So some genius in intelligence, what limited intelligence they had back then, came up with this plan to give him back to the Yanks."

"On Lord Howe Island?"

"No, *off* Lord Howe Island. They knew that the American warship *USS Agerholm* – which was assigned to Destroyer Division 12, or DesDiv 12 as they called it – was in the area at the time. It was heading out of Auckland for Korea, and the Yanks agreed to take him on board, if we met them halfway. But there wasn't much time, so our blokes had to get him there fairly fast. The plan was to land the flying boat close enough to the *Agerholm* to transfer the prisoner."

"In the dead of night?"

"It was all hush-hush. Even though it was three years after the war, there were still real hard feelings towards the Japs, so it was decided to do it on the 'Q.T.' as they used to say."

At this point, Bert's wife Thelma entered the frame, carrying a tray with two cups of tea and two small plates with biscuits.

"Cuppa Time," she sing-songed to the camera, and placed one cup and one plate on Bert's side table, which he grabbed with some glee.

"Thanks, love," said Bert, as he took a big slurp form his cup.

Thelma turned towards the camera and proffered the tray with the remaining tea and bikkies.

"Would you like a cuppa, dear?" she said, and they could see her looking quizzically at the mole on Brad's forehead, and then pruning her face up when she realised what it was and how unfortunate it looked.

A hand came into shot and took the cup and saucer. Thelma peered down the lens again, her nose so close they could count the hairs. Fifteen.

"Like a bikkie, love?" she asked, filling the screen, the lens momentarily frosting over with granny-breath.

The same hand reluctantly reappeared to snatch the plate of bikkies, and satisfied, Thelma toddled off, allowing the interview to resume. But Jack could tell that Brad was beginning to get frustrated.

"So what happened on the plane?" he asked, and took a crunch of a Monte Carlo off-camera.

Bert slurped his tea and continued. "Well, the Queensland MPs – that's military police, not members of parliament – brought him down to Rathmines in the afternoon, and we put him in the brig because there wasn't anywhere else really. I mean, we couldn't put him in the barracks or the officers' quarters, even though, technically he *was* an officer, I suppose. Because we were worried that if we did, he might run away, and then we'd never catch the bugger."

"So what happened *on the plane*?" Brad asked again, a little louder this time in case old Bert was a bit deaf and hadn't heard the question the first time.

"Around 8:00pm, or 20.00 hours, as we used to call it back then, we went to the brig to collect the little chap. Or Jap. Jap chap, I suppose."

"Yes … *and* …?" Brad snapped.

"He had no idea what was going on when we put him on the plane. There was three of us from the Air Force Police, and six flight crew."

"Why so much crew?"

"Buggered if I know. You know what the military is like, the public bloody service, mate. There had to be a pilot, co-pilot, navigator, and because there was three of us from the Provost Unit, they had to match it for some protocol reason. In the end it didn't help, and it just meant more blokes got killed."

"Why? What happened?"

"Like I said, this poor bugger had no idea what was going on. He couldn't speak English, and we no-speakie-Japanee," said Bert, half-closing his eyes and affecting a politically incorrect Asian facial stereotype.

"And another thing," added Bert, leaning forward. "I don't reckon he'd ever been on a plane before. And definitely not a seaplane."

"So what happened when you got in the air?"

"Well, it was about 8:30pm when we finally took off ..."

"Thank god, we're finally in the air!" interjected Brad.

"And it was basically a two to three hour flight, and six of us had nothing to do, really. Just sit there watching this little Japanese bloke."

Bert put down his now-empty cup, and continued. "Now you've got to remember that this was still only just after the war, and most of us were still a bit sore with the Japs, and a couple of these young fly-boys on the flight were teasing him a bit, in a kind of a friendly way. But he wasn't to know that."

"And was it a smooth flight?" asked Brad, as if he already knew, which when Jack thought about it, he figured that super-efficient Brad probably had already checked the meteorological records for that night.

"As soon as we took off, the weather started to close in. It was a bit rough, a fair bit of turbulence. And those Catalinas were noisy bastards at the best of times. All of us were used to it, but the little Jappy chappy, he jumped every time we hit a bump. And every time he did, all the young blokes on the flight would laugh at him."

"Was the prisoner handcuffed or restrained in any way when you put him on the Catalina?"

"Well no, you see. He was such a little fella, and there was three big burly MPs, as well as the fly-boys. There didn't seem any point."

"So what actually caused the crash?"

"Well, finally we hit this really big air pocket and the whole thing just dropped about twenty feet, and he just lost it completely. He jumps out of his seat, and tries to get into the cockpit."

"What did you do?"

"None of us were prepared for that. But we all jumped up, and wrestled him back to the bench we were all sitting on."

"What do you think he was trying to do?"

"I don't know what he thought was going on. Maybe he thought we were going to kill him, or he was being taken somewhere to be executed. But for all I know, he could have thought that the war was still on, and he was going to try to take us out, like his mates with the hidden hand grenades had taken out some of our mates in New Guinea."

"We were all trying to get him to calm down, but then a couple of seconds later he jumped back up again. I was sitting directly opposite him, so I jump up and grab him by the shoulders."

Bert puts his hand out in front of him, miming a big burly military police officer grabbing the shoulders of a tiny Japanese prisoner.

"And I'm shaking him, shouting "Calm down, mate. Take it easy". And the little bugger grabs my pistol out of its holster and fires off a shot. On the plane."

By now Bert had dropped the imaginary prisoner and was staring straight ahead, into the mists of time, as if is watching it replay on a screen just behind the cameraman's shoulder.

"I couldn't believe it. The bullet went through the fuselage of the plane and straight through the fuel tank in the wing, and fuel started spurting out. And here we are on a top-secret flight that officially doesn't exist, in the middle of the Tasman Sea, with a bloody great hole in the fuel tank."

"And an armed Japanese soldier in front of you," added Brad.

"And an armed Japanese soldier in front of me," repeated Bert. "Immediately the pilot starts bringing her down, because at the very least she's a seaplane, so we can land anywhere. But if we don't land soon, we'll either run out of fuel, or even worse, a spark from the engine or another bloody gunshot could hit that fuel pissing out of the wing, and the lot of us will go boom!"

As if to add effect to the statement, Bert took a big bite out of a Scotch Finger biscuit. Crumbs exploded all over his lap.

"Fortunately, we were only minutes away from Lord Howe, so the captain's now trying to get the plane down and turn it around so we can land in the lagoon."

"In the middle of the night."

"Mate, it wasn't going to be easy, but at least there were some lights out there to help us land."

"The houses, you mean?"

"That's right. It wasn't much light, but it was more light than anywhere else out there. And of course we're losing altitude fast now as we run out of fuel."

"And what's the prisoner doing?"

"He's aiming a RAAF service revolver at all of us, and shouting at us in Japanese. And none of us are moving."

"Then what happened?"

"The captain banks the plane over the island and the Jap goes flying backwards, against the cabin door, and drops the gun. We all jump up to try and grab him, but the crazy bastard just opens the door, and jumps out."

"What?"

"Mate, I could not believe it. But I didn't have much time to think about it, because about two seconds later we hit the ridge, didn't we."

Bert put his now-empty biscuit plate back on the side table and looked back at the camera.

"And all hell broke loose. All I remember is the plane being ripped apart. Metal engine parts, everything flying down that hill in flames. It was like a fireball. They pulled me and one of the fly-boys out, but how they did it, I do not know. And we had burns all over our bodies."

He lifted up his right arm as if to show the scars, but his skin was so blotched with age that it was hard to tell what were burn marks and what weren't.

"And the other seven?" asked Brad.

"Well, you know the story. They all died."

"What about the Japanese prisoner?"

"What about him? We never mentioned it again. Neither did the Yanks. The whole thing was covered up. But as far as we were concerned, he was gone. Problem solved. He either fell in the ocean and drowned, or died when he hit the island. Either way it didn't matter."

"Did they ever find the body?"

"Well there was no search by the RAAF as far as I know."

"Is it possible that because you were coming in so low that when he jumped, he might have survived?"

"I suppose it's possible. But they would have found him, wouldn't they? On Lord Howe? I mean, eventually. It's not that big an island."

Off-camera, they could hear Brad standing up.

"Thanks for all your help Bert. It's been a pleasure."

Bert looked up at him, confused. "What do you mean? I haven't even told you about New Guinea yet."

"Unfortunately we've run out of tape," replied Brad, and the picture went to static, then black.

Jack nodded and stroked his beard thoughtfully, as Jill studied the translation document on Brad's computer.

"We should make a copy of this," she said, taking what Jack thought was a pen knife out of her pocket, but was in fact a four-gigabyte flash drive, and inserting it into the USB port of the computer.

"I carry it for dental records," she explained to a quizzical-looking Jack.

"I think we'd better go," said Jack.

"Why's that?" asked Jill.

"Because I think I hear a car approaching," replied Jack.

They both stopped and listened. There was indeed a car approaching, or to be more precise, Brad Lawrence's mini-van.

"Shit-shit-shit. Let's go!" exclaimed Jack.

"But my drive's just loaded up!" said Jill, frantically trying to copy the file onto the flash drive.

"Hurry up!" whispered Jack, as they both heard the sound of mini-van tyres on gravel as Brad pulled into his own driveway.

"It's nearly finished," cried Jill, willing the computer to work faster. Suddenly it went 'ding'.

"Got it!" said Jill, grabbing the flash drive, just as Jack grabbed her hand and led her to the open doorway.

They both peered out. The van had now stopped in the driveway, and Brad was walking up the steps to his house.

They listened intently to his footsteps on the wooden floor. Then they heard the sound of a toilet seat going up, and the familiar tinkling of a stream of urine.

"He's taking a leak. Let's go," urged Jack. Almost bent over double they snuck out of the shed, Jack careful to quietly close the door behind them. Then, using the mini-van for cover, they made their way to the side fence, which they were able to duck behind and scurry to where they'd hidden their bicycles earlier.

Back at Hightide Apartments, Jill plugged the flash drive into Heather's computer.

"He's done a very thorough job of translating these letters, by the looks of things," said Jill on opening the recently-pirated file, and scanning the pages of the translation document.

"Well, that *is* his area of expertise," quipped Jack, looking over her shoulder, "or at least one of them."

"They all seem to be letters from Tsukasa Kobayashi to a Noburo Kobayashi, the abbot of the Koan-ji Zen monastery on the outskirts of Tokyo," said Jill. "The first one is dated December 7th 1941."

"That's the day the Japanese attacked Pearl Harbour," said Jack, stroking his beard. If only he'd been on *Millionaire Hotseat* and said that.

"It doesn't mention it anywhere here," Jill said peering closer at the on-screen translation. "This letter was sent from Hanoi."

"The Japanese invaded Vietnam, then part of what was known as French Indochina, in 1940."

"He's apologising to his brother for leaving the monastery without telling him." Jill read on, "… 'but there had been no time.' He had to leave in a hurry, apparently."

"He expresses great sorrow in having to leave the monastery and his duties and training there … he's a monk."

"A 'Zen' monk," added Jack, who nodded approvingly.

"But he felt a greater duty to his country in such troubled and troubling times." Jill scanned the next line. "And if his skills and knowledge of geology can help Japan become a great world leader, then he must accept that his place is in the Imperial Japanese Army."

"So he's run away from monk school and joined the army?" interpolated Jack.

"As a geologist apparently."

At that point the phone rang, and they both nearly jumped out of their seats.

Jack picked up the phone. It was Matahina, calling from the Birders' Paradise Eco Tours office. She sounded nervous when she asked Jack, "You know what you said to me about Brad Lawrence?"

"Yes," said Jack.

"Well, I think you're right."

"Why do you say that?" Jack asked.

"He just called me from his house. He accused me of watching some video."

Jack suddenly remembered that they had left Brad's monitor on, and didn't rewind the tape.

"There's also something I didn't tell you …" she added apologetically.

There wasn't time to hear Matahina's confession. Jack was worried what Brad might do to Matahina, but didn't want to let on. So calmly and carefully, he said to her "Okay, I think you should leave there *now*."

"Where should I go?"

"Um, somewhere public, like, um … the Bowls Club. We'll meet you there in ten minutes. And be careful."

"Okay."

Jack hung up the phone and turned to Jill.

"Fancy a fast downhill bike ride and drink at the Bowlo?" he smiled invitingly.

"I'm taking my laptop so I can read more of these letters," said Jill, as she got up and ran off to her apartment like a big girl.

Minutes later they were in the Bowls Club, Jill plugging the flash drive into her laptop, while Jack brought drinks over from the bar. Matahina was nowhere to be seen.

"How could we have beaten her here?" Jill asked as Jack returned from the bar and handed her a glass of white wine.

"I really don't know," he replied, with a concerned look on his face as he sat down next to her.

"What do you think has happened to her?" asked Jill, taking a sip.

"I hate to think. I really hate to think," muttered Jack as he took a big gulp of his beer. "Let's give her five more minutes, and then we'd better go looking for her."

He pointed to Jill's laptop computer, which she had fired up on the table and open at one of the translated Japanese letters.

"What's your boy Kobayashi up to now?"

It's six months later and he's just returned from Vientiane."

"That's in Laos," Jack buzzed in.

"… I know that. His job seems to be scouting out geological deposits for the Japanese military. It's quite bizarre. So far he's found a tin deposit in Laos, an iron ore deposit in Cambodia and a bauxite deposit on the northern Thai border."

"How does that work, exactly, army geologist?" inquired Jack.

"Well, he finds them, informs his superiors, then they move in and either use locals or bring in their own people to set up a mine."

"Well, as you know, being so small, Japan has always been natural resource poor …" Jack was just showing off now.

"The other thing is, he's going out into the field, all on his own," added Jill.

"You mean he's 'out standing in his own field'?" quipped Jack.

"No, he's like some kind of survivalist. He goes right up into the jungle or the mountains, all on his own, with virtually nothing but a compass. In one letter he credits his monastic discipline as helping him survive alone in whatever wilderness he finds himself."

Just then Matahina walked briskly into the Bowls Club, looking more than a little frazzled.

She explained that she been about to leave the office when an elderly couple driving a rental car pulled up outside, came in and wanted to book a guided walk. Then Brad Lawrence had turned up, but fortunately Matahina was able to get out of a difficult situation and make her way out of the office by asking the couple if they could give her a lift.

"What would you fancy?" asked Jack.

"Beer please," said Matti.

While Matahina made herself comfortable and caught her breath, Jack popped back to the bar, got another round of drinks and a big packet of sea salt and balsamic vinegar kettle chips, and sat back down.

"I'm frightened now. I'm *really* frightened," said Matti, in between gulps of beer.

"What happened? Did he hurt you?" asked Jill.

"No, he was just … menacing, and a little weird. In a bad way." Matti took another slurp and, turning to Jack, said "But I think you were right. Brad Lawrence did kill Boz and Harvey."

"Why is that?" asked Jack.

"There's something I didn't tell you," confessed Matti, staring into her half-empty beer. "When I implied I didn't know Brad Lawrence, I wasn't exactly telling the truth." She put her beer glass down.

"How did you know him?" asked Jill.

"When I was at school, at Ascham, he was a teacher there. History and languages. Anyway, we sort of got on, not in a sexual way, just a good teacher/student thing. He really helped me prepare for the HSC. That sort of thing."

Jill was listening, but still reading the translated Japanese letters on her laptop at the same time. Jack just kept nodding and beard stroking, seemingly trying to massage it into growing longer.

Matti continued, "But that was five or six years ago, and I really hadn't thought about him for years, when he contacted me, and offered me this job."

"Working behind the counter at Birders' Paradise 'Eco' Tours?" asked Jack incredulously.

"Not *this* job, this other job. He described it as a kind of friendly prank. Mock-espionage. He said he was living on Lord Howe Island now, and he knew that I was back on Aitutaki. He said this 'old mate' of his, an American guy, was on his way from Hawaii to Lord Howe in his boat, and that he was stopping in Aitutaki. And my job was to get friendly with this guy and maybe even get on the boat with him."

"So you're not really a Polynesian princess running away from a loveless arranged marriage?" asked Jill, sounding slightly disappointed.

"No, I'm still that. But then most single girls on Aitutaki are Polynesian princesses running away from a loveless arranged marriage. That's why his idea sounded so appealing. I got to get out of the marriage *and* off Aitutaki, which, you know, is fine for a couple of weeks but after that it gets a bit boring. Plus he was going to pay me $5,000. Or $10,000 if I found the letter."

"Exactly which letter was that? I've got 17 at least," asked Jill, poring over the transcripts of several letters on her laptop.

"Letter 18," Matahina replied dramatically.

"What do you know about these letters, Matahina?" inquired Jack.

"You'd better get us all another drink," said Matti, polishing off the last of her middy. Jack was up and back from the bar in a flash, and Matti continued her story.

"The way he explained it to me, he met Harvey at a history conference in the US about seven years ago when Brad was still a teacher. When Harvey learned that Brad collected World War II stuff, and was also into languages, he told him about this box of Japanese letters that was about to come up for auction."

"Apparently the box was found by a US marine after Japan surrendered and the US occupied the country. The marine found it in the ruins of a monastery that burned down after the US Air Force fire-bombed Tokyo. Somehow, the box had survived intact …"

"Wait a second," interrupted Jill at the computer. "There are some pictures of it here and it looks like the back of the box is singed a bit."

They all looked at the jpegs of the box Brad had included in the transcript document. The bottom of the box was burnt black, and the lacquer on the back of the box had bubbled and cracked. But miraculously, the rest of the box was okay.

Matti continued. "There were 18 letters in there, all of them unopened. The marine 'liberated' it from the monastery ruins, if you know what I mean."

"You mean he nicked it," said Jack.

"Yeah," agreed Matti, "and took it home as a souvenir. Maybe he thought his girlfriend would like it, or whatever."

"And he left the letters in it?" asked Jill.

"They were in Japanese and he just didn't care about them. Anyway when he left Japan and the army and went back to the US, he took the box home, and the girlfriend loved it. They got engaged, and married, and lived happily ever after until they eventually got old and sick and died."

"Bummer," nodded Jack.

"Exactly," agreed Matti.

"Where is this story going?" asked Jill, confused at the oddly domestic direction Matti's tale had recently taken.

"Well," continued Matti, "the box survived in the US for 60 years, and then the marine's son has inherited it, and gone 'What do I want a box of Japanese letters for?'"

"Exactly," nodded Jack. "You want a box of *French* letters."

"The Japanese ones aren't big enough, eh?" quipped Jill, while nudging Jack playfully with her elbow.

"Are you guys taking this seriously?" asked Matti.

"Of course, go on," said Jack, trying to look serious.

"So anyway, the son decides to sell the thing online," continued Matti.

"Antique Unopened Japanese Letters, Still In Original Box," joked Jack.

"So Brad bid on the box, and won it. But someone else was bidding on it, and when the box arrived, it was one letter short. Brad reckoned he knew who had the missing letter, and who was bidding against him."

"Harvey Jacob ..." said Jack.

"One and the same," nodded Matti. "And it was my job to find that letter. Which was why I had to convince Harvey to give me a job on his boat when he turned up at Aitutaki."

"Well, to be fair," interjected Jack, "if I'd just sailed single-handed from Hawaii to the Cook Islands, I'd offer you a job too," smiled Jack.

Jill and Matti looked at Jack blankly.

"And did you find it?" Jill asked Matti.

"Find what?" asked Matti.

"The letter," both Jack and Jill said in unison.

"Oh, the letter. Um, I *thought* I did. I found a letter on the desk in his cabin one day while he was up on the poop deck or whatever it's called. It was in Japanese, so I thought it was the letter Brad wanted. The envelope was already opened of course, so I just took the letter out, and I scanned it and I

197

printed it, and put it back. Now all I had to do was deliver it to Brad and get my $10,000."

"And that's what you were doing at the restaurant on the night Harvey died? Planning to meet up with Brad and slip him the letter?" surmised Jack.

"That's right. When I found out Harvey had made reservations at Pandanus, I called Brad and he booked a table as well."

"This is all a bit confusing," interjected Jill.

"Hey, it wasn't my plan. I was just following orders," Matti said defensively.

"'Befehl ist Befehl,'" muttered Jack. "*The Nuremberg Defence.*"

"What?" asked Matti.

"Nothing. Go on," said Jill, glaring at Jack.

"The idea was to put the letter in my napkin and when Brad came over to say hello to Harvey, I'd drop my napkin on the floor, Brad would pick it up and swap it for the one with the cash in it."

"That really *is* espionage stuff. Who does this guy think he is, Daniel Craig?" said Jack, wide-eyed and slack-jawed.

"Anyway, unfortunately it all went horribly wrong. And now Harvey is dead."

"Why? What happened?" asked Jack.

"Harvey was on to me from the beginning. He knew that I was working for Brad, and he said he planted that letter for me to find and that it's not the missing letter at all. He said that he managed to track down the son of the marine while Brad was bidding on the box and convince him, with the aid of a financial inducement of course, to sell him – Harvey – the last letter, as well as make copies of all other letters."

"That's why he *is* the master treasure finder," said Jack.

"*Was*, you mean," corrected Jill.

"I stand corrected," said Jack.

"You're sitting," said Jill.

Then I *sit* corrected," corrected Jack.

"Just sit correctly, thank you," said Jill, pointing out Jack's appalling posture.

"Why are you two being so goofy?" inquired Matti.

"Hey, it's Christmas Eve, remember? You're allowed to be goofy on Christmas Eve," said Jack.

"You're in love, aren't you?" smiled Matti.

"Of course not," grumbled Jack.

"A little," admitted Jill.

"Come on everyone, back to the main story," Jack clapped his hands. "The love interest can wait."

"*Love interest?*" said Jill in mock outrage. "*Leading Lady* thank you very much, *Boy Toy*."

"Fine, as long as we both know our place," said Jack, turning back to Matahina. "Now please continue, Miss Matahina ..." He smiled, and she did.

"That's it really. Before Brad could come over to our table and he and I could do the 'swap-aroo', Harvey called me on it. Said he knew what I was doing, and that I'd better go. So I left. But I didn't think Brad would kill Harvey just for a stupid letter." She gulped on her beer.

"So the letter that we found on Harvey's body …" Jack trailed off.

"Is the letter that I copied, the fake final letter …" added Matahina.

"Which explains why Brad left it there I suppose," guessed Jill.

"If he even knew at that time that Harvey had it on him," added Matti.

"So Harvey must have known all along that Brad Lawrence was living on Lord Howe Island now," said Jack. "Much the same way that Brad was clearly keeping an eye out for Harvey Jacob's every move across the Pacific."

Jack stroked his beard more fondly than ever before. He used both hands this time. Then he spoke.

"He must have known Brad would seek him out. It's almost like he was trying to set it up himself. I wonder what they talked about that night at the restaurant before Brad followed Harvey out and killed him? Do you think one of them suggested a deal? I guess that would be Brad. If Harvey had all the letters, which I imagine are the keys to a treasure of some sort, he didn't need Brad's partnership. Maybe that's what happened. Brad offered to share his 17 letters with

Harvey in exchange for Harvey sharing his one final letter, the most important letter one presumes, with Brad. And Harvey must have said 'No thanks sucker. See you in the funny papers'."

"Or something like that," interjected Jill.

"Brad went into a seething rage, as you do," said Jack "and followed Harvey out of the restaurant, down the road and ..."

"... Killed him with a muttonbird," added Matahina

"A brick, then a muttonbird," corrected Jack, to her horror.

"Ew!" she ewwed.

"Exactly," added Jack. "The one thing I'd really like to know is what's in that final letter." He scratched his head and stroked his beard simultaneously.

Jill looked up from the laptop computer screen. "I think I may be able to help you on that one."

"The 17th letter. August 1944. New Guinea. He hints at an 'important find' and what a 'man of morals' would do with the information. Apparently by now he says he's seen things during the war 'done by our people' that he feels cannot be justified. He doesn't like the fact that his field work, or the results of his field work, are funding a military exercise that in his opinion is out of control, and not in keeping with his Buddhist beliefs."

"He must have had an epiphany," said Matti.

"He must have seen an atrocity. Or several," said Jack.

201

"He's also concerned that the Japanese authorities might be reading and censoring his mail," said Jill.

"He's getting paranoid," said Matti.

"Well, that's understandable. They've got some wicked weed up there in PNG. It's easy to get extremely paranoid," said Jack.

Jill rolled her eyes and continued. "So he tells his brother that he's going to send him another letter, in the form of a series of poems." Jill furrowed her brow. Matti screwed up her nose. Jack stroked his beard.

"Finally, a chance to use my three-unit HSC English," said Jack. "But what does he mean by 'important find?'"

"He does mention the Kinkaju-ji Temple in Kyoto," said Jill as if Jack should know what that is.

"Er … yes?" replied Jack, clearly without a clue as to what that is.

"Also known as *The Golden Pavilion*," Jill added.

"Okay …" he nodded.

"So named because it appears to be made entirely out of gold," she added.

"I get it. But what context is it mentioned in?" he queried.

"The rough translation is that the 'important find' would make Kinkaju-ji Temple look 'like a brick shithouse'."

"So there *is* a treasure!" Jack concluded. "Where do we think this final letter is?"

Jill pulled a horrified face. "Please don't say it's on Harvey Jacob's body somewhere. I've already had to look in a dead man's mouth this week, and they're the only kind of cavities that I'm prepared to search."

"Where else could it be?" pondered Jack.

"It's got to be on the boat somewhere," said Matti, as if declaring the obvious.

"I've already searched the boat," Jack pointed out.

"Not very well," giggled Matti. Jack acted affronted, despite knowing how poor his investigative skills were.

"Thanks, great. I'm a coroner, okay? I'm not a detective," said Jack defensively. "My job is to work out how people died and whether there should be an inquiry. I've worked that out, and I'm going to recommend that there *be* an inquiry as soon as I get back to the mainland." He skulled the rest of his beer.

Jill and Matti looked at him as if he was being a spoilsport. Finally, he gave in.

"Oh alright," Jack conceded. "Let's search the boat again," he said reluctantly.

Jill and Matti both clapped their hands in anticipation.

By now the sun was beginning to set over the lagoon.

"Isn't it romantic?" said Jill as they bicycled along the shoreline.

"It would be, if we weren't playing *Famous Five*," grumbled Jack.

When they arrived at the jetty, Harvey's dinghy was gone.

"That's odd," said Jack.

"Someone's probably just borrowed it," said Jill innocently.

"Oh well, let's 'borrow' someone else's," said Jack as he proceeded to 'liberate' a small wooden rowboat. "After all, this is official government business."

Jill and Matti climbed in the front and then Jack hopped in the back of the boat and began rowing.

"Arr, there be nuthin' I's likes better than t'have me hands 'round a couple o' rough old oars," Jack said in fluent pirate.

"What are you calling us? How dare you!" mocked Jill.

Jack was still speaking fluent pirate when they reached the *True Love 2* and tied up their 'liberated' rowboat. He was still speaking fluent pirate when they climbed up the ladder and onto the deck. And he was still speaking fluent pirate when they entered Harvey's cabin, where his Long John Silver impersonation came to an abrupt end when he felt the sudden painful impact of something very hard on the front of his head and everything went black.

When he regained consciousness, Jack was lying on the padded bench that ran along one wall of Harvey's cabin. Jill and Matti were kneeling beside him, and Brad Lawrence was standing over them.

"Are you alright?" asked Jill.

"What happened?" mumbled Jack, rubbing the raised lump in the middle of his forehead.

"You forgot to duck," said Matti.

"What?" asked Jack. Confused, he couldn't work out what Brad Lawrence was doing here.

"You knocked yourself out on the top of the cabin doorway," said Jill.

"You actually hit your head on the sign that says *Mind Your Head*." added Matti, as she suppressed a giggle.

"Saved me doing it for you," said Brad, smiling.

"What?" said Jack, even more confused.

Brad showed Jack the vintage .32-calibre Iver Johnson 'Double Action' model 1900 five-shot safety automatic revolver, chrome plated with a black handle, that he now held in his hand. It was made by Iver Johnson's Arms & Cycle Works, a company who specialised in shotguns, revolvers and bicycles, thus potentially facilitating the world's first pedal-by shooting.

In fact, this was the same model gun that would-be anarchist and presidential assassin Leon Czolgosz shot and killed 25th US President William McKinley with in Buffalo, New York on September 6th 1901. It was also the same *brand* – an eight-shot .22-calibre Iver Johnson – which was used by Sirhan Sirhan to shoot and kill presidential candidate and US Senator Robert F. Kennedy in Los Angeles, California on June 5th 1968. If Jack had known this, he would have felt slightly safer in the knowledge that he wasn't presidential in any manner, and therefore perhaps less likely to be shot.

Brad laughed. "I was waiting behind the door to coldcock you when you walked in, and you did it for me. Funniest thing I've seen in my life," said Lawrence.

The others nodded in agreement.

"He's right, it was pretty funny," admitted Jill.

"And just as well too," continued Brad. "I've never knocked anyone out with the butt of a gun before, and I didn't know exactly how hard to hit you. I might have killed you."

"Well that's probably the only way you haven't killed anyone yet," said Jack, rubbing his head and sitting up. "You've killed people just about every other way so far."

"That's up to a court of law to decide – if they ever indict me," smiled Brad.

"They never bloody will if *I* end up dead!" said Jack angrily, before seeing the obvious mistake he made. "I mean, I haven't made my final recommendations yet," he said with a conciliatory tone. "Who knows, you could be completely innocent of all the allegations, although that gun in your hand is a bit of a giveaway."

"Anyway, I'm going to have to tie you all up now," said Lawrence. Still brandishing the gun, Brad picked up a length of nylon rope in his free hand.

"How are you going to do that without putting down the gun?" asked Matti.

"I'm not, *you* are," said Brad, throwing the rope at her.

Matti caught the rope, but remained defiant. "And what if I refuse?"

"Then I'll have to kill you," said Brad, calmly.

"You're going to have to kill us anyway," said Jack, rubbing his sore head.

"True," conceded Brad. "So would you rather be dead now or dead later? It's your choice."

"Later," they all said in unison.

"Then tie them up," said Brad to Matti.

Matti unfurled the rope and, apologising first to Jill, reluctantly began to tie the slim, attractive female dentist's hands together with the nylon rope.

Jill was extremely nervous. "Please don't kill us," she pleaded with Brad.

"I promise I won't kill you until I've found what I'm looking for," said Brad, beginning to poke around Jacob's desk, while keeping the gun trained on Jack and Matti.

"Here it is!" he said, picking up a piece of paper. Jack, Jill and Matti's jaws dropped in unison. "Just kidding," said Brad. "You should have seen the look on your faces. Priceless." He laughed. Then more seriously, added, "Keep tying, and tighter."

Jack timidly raised his hand. "Ah, Brad," he said, to get Brad's attention. "Before Matti ties me up – I've just drunk three schooners of Hahn Premium – can I, ah, use the, ah, 'head' I believe is the correct nautical term."

"No," said Brad, point-blank.

"Wow, you *are* evil!" said Jill.

"I don't care if he has to piss himself," said Brad from behind the desk.

"It's not just that. I have to do the *other* thing, too," said Jack delicately.

"So?" retorted Brad.

"So I don't mind shitting myself either, but if it takes you a while to find whatever it is you're looking for, it might get a little stinky in here," said Jack apologetically.

"Okay then, maybe I'll make an exception and shoot you right now." Brad aimed the gun at Jack's head.

"Believe me," said Jack desperately, "as an officer of the state coroner's court, I would advise strongly against that action, on the grounds that it's very common for murder victims to evacuate their bowels at the moment of death, which would again make it rather stinky in here."

Brad furrowed his brow. He looked in the direction of the extremely small nautical ensuite. He opened the door and looked inside. There was a tiny porthole window, way too small for Jack to get out of, and no other exit.

"Very well then," said Brad, signalling with the revolver for Jack to go into the bathroom. "But no funny business."

A thousand retorts went through Jack's mind, but he resisted every one. All he said was "Thanks," and raced for the 'head', shutting and locking the door behind him.

He really did need to take a leak, but he'd made up the story about needing to take a crap, just so he could get into the bathroom. He had an ulterior motive. He wasn't quite sure what it was at this point, but it was better than just waiting to be tied up and killed.

He lifted the lid and dropped his pants as loudly as possible for effect. Due to the limited space in the tiny bathroom, he sat down on the toilet seat – and started to think.

What he needed was a weapon of some sort. He looked around the tiny room. There were a couple of hooks on the wall in front of him. But without a screwdriver, they'd be impossible to get off the wall without raising the suspicions of Brad Lawrence. And of course if he *did* have a screwdriver, he wouldn't need to remove one of the hooks. He could just use the screwdriver as a weapon.

On his right, next to the tiny porthole, was an equally tiny washbasin. The one tap, a mixer, was securely fastened. If only he had a wrench, he thought, before realising that it fitted into the same category of obsolescent logic as the previously discussed screwdriver theory.

He carefully stood up, trousers still around his ankles, and looked around. Above the basin, a small mirrored cabinet was built into the ship's hull. To cover the sound of opening it, he grunted loudly and made a 'raspberry' sound with his tongue and lips. He blew a couple more choice raspberries as he ratted around inside the cabinet.

Outside, Matti had finished tying up Jill, and Brad had finished tying up Matti and was continuing his search for the missing letter.

Jack was getting the hang of the grunting and raspberrying and was really going for it now.

On the other side of the door, as the barrage of obscene noises continued unabated, Jill screwed up her eyes and called out to Brad.

"Could you put the stereo on so we don't have to listen to that?" she pleaded.

Brad shrugged, picked up a remote control and aimed it at the Bang & Olufsen system built into the opposite wall. Immediately the cabin filled with the sound of Harvey's favourite album – the soundtrack to the '50s film *High Society* featuring Bing Crosby, Frank Sinatra, and of course, the great 'Satchelmouth' himself, Louis Armstrong.

Now it was Matti's turn to wince. "Oh God, I've heard this so many times!"

Inside the toilet, Jack was relieved not to have to faux-fart anymore. And the soundtrack to *High Society* was one of his favourites as well. Sadly though, he wasn't having much luck on the weapons hunt. Harvey used an electric razor to shave, and that was no good as a weapon, even though it did have a battery. Threatening someone with razor-rash was about the most that could be hoped for.

There was a toothbrush which Jack took, just in case, as it was the only even remotely knife-shaped object he could find. There was a roll-on hypo-allergenic scent-free deodorant, which would really only harm the most feeble being in the universe.

He briefly contemplated pocketing Harvey's electric nose-hair trimmer, thinking if correctly placed in the right orifice, it could at least startle its victim. And, of course, applied directly to the eyeball it might actually do some damage. But he couldn't see Brad standing or lying still for it, unless he was tied down, and then there wouldn't be much point, except for the sheer pleasure of torturing someone with an electric nose-hair trimmer.

Harvey was just about bald so there was only a rather blunt comb, and some sunscreen and a tube of toothpaste. Jack took them all and put them in his pockets.

The only place he hadn't looked by now – besides the bowl, and he pretty much knew what was in there – was the cistern itself. Maybe Harvey was a *Godfather* fan like Jack was, and kept a pistol in the cistern like Jack didn't, but would like to. And maybe Jack would find it there like Al Pacino as

Michael Corleone did in the toilet of Louis' Restaurant in the Bronx, when he volunteered to kill Virgil 'The Turk' Sollozzo and his crooked-cop bodyguard, Captain Mark McCluskey, played respectively by Al Lettieri and Sterling Hayden.

And to paraphrase Michael's brother Sonny – played by James Caan – Jack didn't want to be coming out of that toilet with just his dick in his hand.

All this was running through Jack's mind as he carefully unscrewed the ring that secured the chrome plunger, delicately removed the plastic cover of the cistern and silently put it down on top of the toilet seat.

Outside, while Bing Crosby and Louis Armstrong were dueting on *Now You Have Jazz* – Bing singing the lines while Satchmo translates it into fluent scat – Brad was ripping up the cabin's carpet with a Stanley knife, and Jill and Matti were both sitting trussed-up like good-lookin' turkeys, and both wishing they'd asked if they could use the toilet first as well.

Inside the bathroom, Jack peered into the half-sized cistern. There was no pistol taped to the back wall like Clemenza had promised Sonny there would be. Nor were there any bits of cistern, such as an old ballcock, that Jack might be able to use as a weapon should he attempt to overpower Brad Lawrence. He half-hoped he might find a half-brick, like some people put in large cisterns in old houses to use less water, simply for the irony of being able to kill Brad Lawrence with the same weapon he used to kill Harvey Jacob. But sadly, the cistern was brickless.

There was however an extra-strength zip-lock baggie taped to the front wall of the cistern. Jack carefully peeled back the tape that was holding the top of the baggie just above the water line, and slowly pulled it out of the water.

Perhaps Harvey was smuggling drugs, thought Jack, and the baggie would be full of enough crystal meth ice to send Jack into the kind of drug-induced psychotic rage he was going to need to overpower Brad Lawrence – enough for him to be able to take a bullet or two in the process and not even know it, until later of course. But by that time, help would have arrived and Jack would be transported back to the mainland for urgent medical treatment as a hero.

He dried the plastic baggie off on a hand towel, and could not believe what he could clearly see through the plastic. It was an unsealed envelope, with Japanese characters on it. It was the missing letter, for sure.

Jack thought to himself, "he said he wouldn't kill us until he found the letter. If I take it, he won't find it, hence, he won't kill us."

Not exactly sure what to do with it, but sure that he wasn't going to hand it over to Brad, Jack pulled up his trousers and put the letter in the baggie down the front of his underpants, and zipped and re-belted the outer garment.

Next, he carefully and quietly put the top back on the cistern and tightened up the chrome plunger. He pressed the flush button and washed his hands in the basin, before finally opening the bathroom door and coming back out.

"Geeze, you were in there long enough," said Jill.

"Yeah, sorry about that. You can tie me up now, Brad," said Jack, proffering his arms to Brad, who had stopped looking under the desk top and was now training his Iver Johnson back on Jack.

Brad proceeded to tie Jack up with the remaining length of nylon twine. Now that all three of them – Jack, Jill and Matti – were sitting in a row like extras in a bondage flick, Brad returned to turning the place upside down in pursuit of what, in reality, was now hidden in Jack's jocks.

"Just one question, Brad," asked Jack. "If you knew the letter was here somewhere, why didn't you check the boat earlier?"

"Quite simple," said Brad, taking the photos off the wall and smashing the glass on the corner of the table. "I thought Princess 'Lei'-er here had it on her. I was just killing Harvey Jacob …" He ripped a photo of Harvey meeting the Dalai Lama out of its frame, and screwed it up in his hand. "… for the fun of it, I suppose," he added, pulling the entire frame apart and finding nothing.

"Then *you* turned up, and I half expected you to be competent." He ripped another photo of Harvey standing next to a life-size cut-out of John Wayne out of its frame. "And since then of course, I've had my hands full."

"That's right. Killing Boz," added Jack, helpfully. The thought made Matti angry. She added, "You prick," less helpfully.

"Poor old Boz. He had to go," said Brad, finally taking the picture that featured himself carefully out of its frame.

"I might keep this one," he said, putting it down on a portion of the table not covered with shattered glass.

"Why exactly did Boz 'have to go'?" asked Jack.

"He'd seen too much."

"I've seen what he saw," said Jack.

"I don't mean the Tropicbirds' loop-the-loop," sneered Brad as he continued to trash the room.

"No," replied Jack. "You mean the Japanese Imperial Army pith helmet, with matching boots and birdlife."

Brad stopped smashing things momentarily and looked at Jack with astonishment.

"Oh well, you're going to have to go anyway," Brad continued. "But how did *you* see that?"

"Helmet-cam," said Jack.

"Oh … I forgot about that," said Brad, nodding thoughtfully.

"Me too," said Jack. "Mike pointed it out to me. Whoops."

"Then he's going to have to go as well," said Brad, now cutting open the padding on the desk chair.

Jack laughed. "The way news spreads around this island, I reckon you're going to have to kill just about everyone." Then he was serious for a moment. "You're *not* planning to kill just about everyone, are you?"

"No, I'll be out of here in 24 hours, I'd say."

"So what's so important about what Boz saw, anyway? I mean, the shoe-wearing bird was pretty weird, but the bird nesting in the hat, I'm sure that happens wherever hats are left on ledges," asked Jack.

"Why should I tell you anything?" queried Brad.

"Well, you're going to have to kill me anyway, so why not?" pointed out Jack.

Brad thought about this for a moment, and then said "Fair enough. That pith helmet and shoes belong to the man who wrote the letters."

"Tsukasa san," said Jill.

"How do you know?" Jack asked Brad. "It could be any old Japanese pith helmet and shoes."

"You think there's more than one dead Japanese geologist on the island?" asked Brad.

"Hmm, probably not, come to think of it. But what's the significance?" asked Jack.

"I think it pretty much verifies my long-held belief that Captain Kobayashi didn't jump out of the Catalina into the ocean and die, and that his body is more than likely on this island somewhere. And more than likely somewhere near where Boz saw that hat and shoes."

"That begs another question, I'm afraid," said Jack.

"Shoot," said Brad, now ripping the wood panelling off the wall where the destroyed photos had previously hung.

"I wish I could," Jack muttered under his breath. "You've been on this island for, what, five years now?"

"Yes, roughly," agreed Brad.

"In fact, you came here specifically to find the body or remains or some possession of this Japanese geologist who jumped out of the Catalina …"

"Yes …" said Brad.

"How come you haven't found it by now?"

"Yeah?" chimed in Jill and Matti.

"It was a little more involved than that," said Brad, as he continued his search-and-destroy mission on Harvey's cabin. "Life has a habit of getting in the way of one's …"

"Evil schemes?" asked Jill.

"I was going to say dreams, but that'll do," smiled Brad.

"You must have translated the letters first," posited Jack. "Then traced Tsukasa to Rathmines RAAF base, right?"

"He was transported there from Townsville the day before the Catalina crashed on Lord Howe," admitted Brad. "Rathmines was an RAAF Catalina base. It all made sense."

"That led you to Bert Slater, who confirmed that Tsukasa was on the plane, and why he was never heard of again. Then you moved to the island to find his body, or whatever it was that was on his body that you seem to think you need to find. And when at first you couldn't find it, you convinced Norman Gimbell that you were the potential successor to his birdwatching business, and you convinced Diana Dawson that you wanted to marry her, thus giving you permanent residency on the island, and more time to find whatever it is you're looking for. And when they were no longer useful, you got rid of them."

"I'm impressed. You're not half as incompetent as I thought you were," said Brad, now approaching the padded seat where Jack, Jill and Matti were tied up, the Stanley knife in his hand.

They all flinched as he approached.

"I'm going to have to ask you all to stand up now," he said, smiling, and popping out the blade on the Stanley knife so it protruded a couple of centimetres further from the handle.

The three captives reluctantly stood up, allowing Brad to slice open the vinyl cover of the padded seat they had been sitting on.

Together they shuffled quietly to an already-slashed bench on the adjoining wall and sat back down.

"Couldn't you have better spent that time trying to find the last letter instead?" asked Jack.

"Why bother?" replied Brad, rummaging inside the now slashed seat cover to no avail. "I knew who had it. I just had to wait for it to come to me, which it almost has."

"How do you know Harvey even brought the letter with him?" asked Jack, knowing full well that the letter was rubbing up against his palang as he spoke.

"Oh he brought it with him, alright," said Brad, now slashing the back of the seat in the same manner. "He told me so on the night he died. Which is one of the reasons he died. He shouldn't have tried to rub my nose in it." As Brad spoke, he slashed another seat-back, with some pent-up anger.

Angry and frustrated at finding nothing, Brad threw the Stanley knife across the room, where it hit the wall and fell to the floor.

"This is ridiculous!" he shouted. "Where the fuck is it?"

"Maybe he took it with him to the apartment at Hightide?" suggested Matti. "I mean, he probably wouldn't have wanted to leave it here on the boat while he was onshore, knowing that you were after it."

"Fuck," exclaimed Brad. "I didn't think about that. Finally, my investment in you is beginning to pay off."

He picked up the Stanley knife and cut the rope around Matti's ankles. Angrily throwing the knife back behind the desk, he then dragged her to her feet and said "Get up, you're coming with me."

He turned to look at Jack and Jill and said, "You two can stay here until we come back. I may need you yet, and if not, well …" he smiled menacingly, "… we still have some business to attend to."

With that, Brad pushed Matti, whose hands were still tied, through the doorway and closed and locked the door behind him.

"I thought they'd *never* leave!" exclaimed Jill to Jack, like a woman to her husband after a pair of particularly boring dinner guests had departed.

She jumped to her feet and said "Quick! Undo my pants."

"You're kidding?" said Jack. "What? Here? Tied up? Kinky."

"I need to pee!" Jill said pointedly.

"Even kinkier," said Jack, as he too jumped up and began to fumble with the button of her fawn cotton cargo pants. Even though his hands were firmly tied to the point of almost cutting off the blood flow, Jack was eventually able to undo the button and pull down the zip, and now they both were pulling at her waistband, which allowed her to jiggle the pants to her knees.

"Now the knickers, hurry!" she ordered impatiently.

Jack obeyed, and soon her camo-print undies were around her ankles, and she was bunny-hopping bare-arsed to the bathroom.

While Jill sought blessed bladder relief, Jack busied himself with the business of escape. At first he tried to pick up a shard of glass from one of the picture frames Brad had demolished, but was concerned about the possibility of doing more damage to his fingers than to the rope, and as a result of being still tied up, bleeding to death.

Then he remembered the Stanley knife that Brad had thrown across the room in a fit of pique. Hopping over to the desk like a hairy kangaroo in a Hawaiian shirt, Jack quickly found the yellow and black plastic-handled Stanley knife, and managed to pick it up without cutting the tips off any of his fingers with its razor-sharp blade.

"Who's incompetent now, eh Brad Lawrence?" sneered Jack as he picked it up.

Next, after considering the degree of difficulty involved in using the knife on himself, he quickly hopped over to the open bathroom cubicle where Jill was still seated on the toilet.

"Put out your hands," ordered Jack enthusiastically. Jill obeyed and Jack used his thumb to push the lever on the side of the Stanley knife to extend the blade several centimetres. Then, slowly and with a great deal of care, he used the knife to saw through the orange nylon rope that the still-enthroned Jill held tight with her wrists.

One by one, the sliced ropes popped until Jill was able to get her hands free.

"Great, now do me," said Jack.

"What, here in the toilet? Who's kinky now?" mocked Jill.

She took the Stanley knife Jack was proffering and repeated the cutting task on the ropes around his wrists.

Jill then handed the blade back to Jack, who hopped back into the main cabin to cut the ropes around his ankles, while Jill began hitching up her pants and knickers. With his hands and legs now free, it was easier for Jack to untie the rope around Jill's ankles.

Now they were both untied, but still locked up in the cabin of Harvey Jacob's luxury cruiser.

"What shall we do now?" asked Jill.

"We could watch a DVD and have a glass of champagne," Jack replied, looking in the mini bar. Then going over to the pile of DVDs that Brad had taken out of a drawer in the entertainment centre and systematically removed from their boxes, Jack picked one up, and showed it to Jill.

"It's Christmas Eve, and he's got *It's a Wonderful Life*," said Jack.

"You don't take anything seriously, do you?" said Jill. She was a little upset, and understandably.

"We've just been tied up and threatened by a mad man who has clearly stated that he plans to come back here and chop us into little bits and feed us to the fishes at Ned's Beach," she said, exasperated.

"He more kind of hinted at something like that," replied Jack.

"So, what do we do now?" Jill repeated.

"Well, I suggest that we get out of here as soon as possible so that we're not here when he comes back to kill us," said Jack. "That way, he'll have to kill us somewhere else."

"And that's it?"

"That's as far as I've got."

"Okay …"

"Oh …" added Jack, as if remembering something. "There is *one* thing."

"What?"

"Give me a kiss."

She rolled her eyes, then smiled and puckered up. They shared a short hot passionate kiss and then simultaneously disengaged.

"Okay, that's going to have to hold you until we get this thing sorted out," said Jack looking around the room. "Now we have to find a way out of here."

Jack paced over to the locked door and shook it by the handle.

"Do that 'bargey' thing they do in the movies," offered Jill.

Jack looked at her quizzically, then looked at the door, steeled himself, and then shoulder-rammed the door, which didn't budge an inch.

Jack recoiled and walked in a tight circle, rubbing the part of his upper arm that took the impact.

"Ow!" he whined, pathetically.

"Do it again!" enthused Jill.

"No. *You* do it!" said Jack, still rubbing his sore arm.

Jill shrugged, and charged at the door, recoiling just as Jack did. Now rubbing her arm, she agreed. "I see what you mean."

Jack looked around the cabin again, stroking his beard like a pro. "Hang on …" he said, and walked over to one of two reasonably large windows on the opposite side of the cabin, and slid it open.

"My god, you're a *genius*!" enthused Jill, enthusing for the second time in so many minutes.

"There's only one problem," she said looking out the window. "This drops straight into the ocean," she added looking down in the dark watery abyss below her.

Jack joined her in leaning out the window. "Hmm … not if we go … *up*!" he said pointing in an upwardly direction.

"Did I mention you are a genius, already?" said Jill, as Jack began to clamber through the window and up onto the top of the boat.

Jack reached his hand down and pulled Jill up onto the upper deck. The sun had well and truly gone down by now, and although they could see the lights on the shoreline, they were too far from land to call for help.

From their vantage point on the cabin roof, they were able to see that Brad had taken not only Harvey's inflatable dingy, but also the little wooden one Jack had purloined to get himself, Jill and Matti to the *True Love 2* in the first place. Both boats were now tied up alongside each other on the jetty.

"How are we going to get to shore?" asked Jill.

"Hmm …" ruminated Jack, and pulled delicately on just two or three hairs right at the centre of his chin. "Swim?"

Jill gave him the 'you must be joking' look, and shook her head. "All that way in the dark? I don't think so."

"Hmm …" said Jack and went back to the hair-pulling thing. "If only we had a boat."

"We do have a boat," said Jill.

"Where?" said Jack, looking around fore and aft for something he might have missed. The *True Love 2* was so big and decked-out, it was quite possible there was another dingy or maybe even a helicopter onboard. He wouldn't have been surprised.

"We're standing on it," said Jill pointing to the flybridge deck they now found themselves on.

"Oh yeah, *that* boat," twigged Jack. "I can't see why not. I've already stolen, or rather 'commandeered' one boat tonight. This one's just a little bit bigger."

"And look," said Jill, pointing to the flybridge itself. "It's even got one of those upstairs helm thingies."

Jack reluctantly approached the sophisticated instrument panel positioned in front of a white vinyl padded swivel chair. "Oh yeah. If only Harvey had left ..."

"... The key in the ignition?" She jingled a set of keys that were sticking out of the ignition. "He did."

"Ah ... great," muttered Jack, reluctantly taking the captain's seat, and running his gaze over the instruments.

"It shouldn't be that difficult, should it?" queried Jill.

"It shouldn't be," agreed Jack. "But that doesn't mean it *won't* be."

"All you have to do is turn the key, push that throttle thingy forward and steer us to shore with that steering wheely thing," Jill tried to assure him.

"Okay ..." said Jack cautiously. He reached for the key and turned it. Immediately the powerboat's twin inboard 1000-

horsepower engines sprang into thunderous life, scaring Jack, but making Jill jump for joy and clap her hands gleefully.

Jack felt a little more confident now. He smiled. Maybe it was easier than he thought it would be. But he was still sure he was missing something. He put his hand cautiously on what he thought might be the throttle.

"Push it! Push it!" urged Jill, a little too over-enthusiastically in Jack's opinion. He stopped.

"Don't we have to weigh-anchor or something?" he asked.

"Yeah, yeah," said Jill. "This button." She pointed to a yellow button on the instrument panel with a picture of an anchor on it.

"How are you sure this is the right button?" queried Jack.

"Because," said Jill, pressing the button recklessly. Instantly an electric winch in the pointy end of the boat sprang to life, and the sound of a wet chain being dragged from the depths of the ocean made them realise that the button Jill pressed was indeed the 'weigh anchor' button.

Within a few seconds the anchor appeared at the front of the boat and locked into a special anchor-enclosure in the side of the hull, and the winch turned itself off.

Jack started to think that maybe Jill did indeed know what she was talking about, and again returned his guitar-pickin' hand to the throttle stick.

"Okay, so all I have to do is push *this* forward." He applied pressure to the throttle and slowly pushed it all the way forward. Instantly, the two engines roared, white water churned at the ship's aft and both Jack and Jill were flung backwards, Jill nearly going off the back of the flybridge as the boat lurched forward – unfortunately in the wrong direction – and out to sea.

"Oh-my-god-oh-my-god!" squealed Jill, getting to her feet, and by crouching and clinging to the bridge's chrome railing, made her way to a seat next to Jack, and sat down. "Isn't there a point of land just out there? Turn it around. Turn it around!" she shouted urgently over the noise of the engine and the water it was churning through.

"I'm trying to!" screamed Jack, his knuckles turning to alabaster as he grimly held on to the steering wheel, trying to turn the monstrously powerful boat to the left as it headed, pointy-end first into some dark watery oblivion.

The boat began to turn at its full speed of 32 knots, but it was completely apparent to both Jack and Jill that they were overshooting the jetty.

"Fucken shit piece of crap boat!" Jack shouted about the million-dollar vessel, and he put all his weight into turning the ship's wheel.

"Why don't you slow it down?" Jill shouted at Jack over the roar of the engines and water.

"Oh … Yeah." nodded Jack, only now realising he had the option of deceleration, so concentrated had he been on trying to steer the 66-foot behemoth at full speed. He put his hand on the throttle and pulled it all the way back. The boat began to ease up, but it was too late. They had already overshot the jetty and were now approaching an outcropping of razor-sharp semi-submerged rocks just off the headland at the north end of Lagoon Beach.

"Is there a handbrake on this thing?" asked Jack, looking around in vain.

"Watch out!" shouted Jill, and pulled on Jack's shoulder, gesturing towards a large pointy shard of ancient volcano jutting out of the water on their left.

His hands deftly grasping the wheel, Jack compensated to avoid the rock, only to find the boat now heading for a dark patch of rock-coloured water on their immediate right.

Jack eased the wheel back to the left, but now the boat was drifting directly over the dark patch. The boat let out a sickening scraping noise as it barely glided over the rocky outcropping directly below them.

"We're going to get stuck!" Jill yelled, the panic in her voice palpable.

"No we're not!" said Jack with determination as he pushed the throttle all the way forward again, and held tight to the wheel.

The boat lifted off, with an even more horrifying crunching noise, knocking Jill on her arse once more.

"Fuck this!" said Jack determinedly, holding the wheel firm as the powerboat headed at full throttle directly towards the beach.

As the shore rapidly approached, Jack aimed the boat carefully between an anchored swimming platform and a glass-bottomed coral-viewing vessel, and calling out to the stillbeseated, now wet-bottomed Jill to hold on, drove the boat straight up and onto the dry sand, where it slowly ground to a sandy halt, until the pointy-end was wedged deep into the beach, and at the blunt end both propellers were completely out of the water.

The engines came to a shuddering halt, Jill got to her feet, and both she and Jack looked at where they were – right in the middle of the main part of Lagoon Beach, just at the end of the main street.

A group of teenagers who were hanging around on the grass at the edge of the beach clapped their hands and whistled. Jack and Jill took a bow.

They then climbed down the stairs to the main deck, descended the ladder on the side, and jumped onto the sand, managing to get ashore without even getting their feet wet.

"Now *that's* how you park a boat," said Jack confidently as the walked up the sand to the grass.

"I think you might have done a bit of damage to Harvey's boat," said Jill, looking over her shoulder at the *True Love 2*'s scratched and torn hull.

"Well, Harvey won't be needing it anymore," said Jack. "And after what Brad did to the inside and we did to the outside, I've got a feeling that after this is all over, I might be able to pick up the *True Love 2* for a song."

25th December 2008 – 12:01am

When they reached the road, they stopped and faced each other. Jill put her hands around Jack's neck and gave him a long passionate kiss.

"Thanks for a wonderful evening, but I think I might go home now," she said after disengaging her lips from his.

"What? You're giving up now, just when it's started getting interesting?" mocked Jack.

"Yes, but what do we do now?" asked Jill.

"I don't know," said Jack. "But there's something I've got to show you." He put his hand into his underpants and rummaged around.

"I've already seen it, and as much as I admire it, I'm a little tired right now …" said Jill, stopping only when Jack produced from his pants a plastic zip-lock baggie with a yellowing envelope in it.

"I found this in the toilet," boasted Jack, handing it to Jill, who grabbed it extremely cautiously by one corner of the plastic bag.

"How nice of Harvey to provide you with some reading material, while you were in there."

"No, I found it actually *in* the toilet," enthused Jack.

"Ew!" said Jill holding it away from her face. "I hope you found it *before* you went."

"I didn't actually go. I was just pretending," confided Jack. "I was looking for a weapon, but all I could find was the missing letter."

"The one letter that solves everything?" asked Jill.

"That's the one."

"And …?" Jill prompted.

"And of course it is in Japanese and I haven't got a clue what it says," said Jack. "But at least Brad Lawrence doesn't have it, which hopefully means he won't be coming to kill us immediately."

"Although when he doesn't find it in Harvey's apartment at Hightide, he may decide to kill Matahina." added Jill.

"Unless Matahina is actually still in cahoots with him and she's been lying to us all along."

"Do you really think that?"

"I don't know. Let's go and find out," said Jack. He headed to a nearby public bike rack, planning to appropriate two bikes for their uphill journey to the Hightide Apartments.

"Wait," said Jill, clearly not looking forward to the prospect of another uphill bike ride. "What about this?" She pointed to a golf cart with *Capella Lodge* on it and the key in the ignition.

"What is wrong with these people?" asked Jack, getting in the driver's seat and turning the key in the ignition. "Don't they have *pockets*?"

While the golf cart ride up to the Hightide Apartments wasn't any faster than the bicycle ride, it was much easier on the legs and hearts of our heroes, and it was also much quieter, as the silence was not being regularly broken by the grunts of two adults who really should only ride bicycles on flat terrain.

On arrival at Hightide Apartments, they piled out of the golf cart at the top of the drive. They crept as quietly as they could down the gravel driveway and into Matahina's apartment – although technically it was Harvey's apartment, because he was the one who had booked it and had paid for it in advance.

In the dark of what was now the very early morning, they opened the door to the even darker apartment to find Matahina once again tied up, and sitting on the sofa, this time with a tea towel tied around her mouth as a gag.

At first Jack thought that she might be dead, but then her eyes sprang open, nearly scaring the crap out of both Jack and Jill, and she made the kind of grunting noises that people with a tea towel in their mouth usually make, as Jack examined the chaos of the apartment. Brad had turned the place upside down looking for the missing letter.

As Jill quickly untied the gag, Jack asked Matahina where Brad Lawrence was.

Breathlessly Matahina replied, "He's not here. He's gone. He didn't find the letter."

"Well he wouldn't," said Jill as she started working on the nylon rope that was still around Matahina's wrists from the boat. "Jack found it in the boat's toilet and put it down the front of his pants."

Jack turned around and gave Jill a look, which was basically meant to say, "What did you say that for?" But Jill wasn't looking, so Jack had to actually say it.

"What did you say that for?" he said, repeating the look at the same time.

"What do you mean?" asked Jill innocently.

"Well – and no offence, Matahina …" said Jack. He gave Matahina a nod, then looked back at Jill, "but we still don't know if Matahina is on our side or Brad's side".

"I think I can answer that," came a male voice from the darkened kitchen annex. The lights suddenly came on, and they could see the devastation that Brad's fruitless search had caused, and they could also see Brad Lawrence, now standing behind them brandishing his Iver Johnson again. "You've finally earned your ten grand my dear," he smiled slimily in Matti's direction.

Jack rolled his eyes. "Okay, well at least we know whose side she's on now," he added.

Matti objected. "No, it's not true. He made me say that. He said he'd kill me if I didn't make whoever it was go away."

"Shut up and hand over the letter!" snapped Lawrence.

233

Jack shrugged apologetically. "I haven't got it. I had it, but then I felt this compulsion to post it, so I put it in the letter box outside the museum."

Brad pistol-whipped Jack with the butt of the Iver Johnson. "Don't be a prick," said Brad, thrusting his hand down the front of Jack's pants, only to suddenly withdraw it.

"What the hell is *that*?" he asked.

"A palang," chimed in Jill. "It's a type of tribal piercing favoured by the tribesmen of Borneo."

"And the odd coronial investigator," added Jack, rubbing his freshly whipped chin from where, unbeknownst to everyone, a red mark was slowly developing under his beard.

"Where's the letter?" demanded Brad thrusting the Iver Johnson into Jill's neck.

Jack reached around behind his back and pulled the letter out of his trouser waistband. "Here's your stinkin' letter."

Brad turned the gun back on Jack as he carefully took possession of the zip-lock baggie that contained the letter.

"What is it with that antique gun, anyway? Is that part of your Pacific War collection?" asked Jack.

"No, it's from World War I actually," said Brad, with more than a modicum of pride. "My great-grandfather gave it to my great-grandmother before he went off to the trenches. He left her just three bullets and instructions for her to kill her two daughters and herself if the Germans ever invaded."

Jack shook his head. "Let down by the Germans again."

Brad threw a roll of gaffer tape at Jack who caught it just in front of his face.

"Okay, it's your turn to tie someone up," said Brad.

"Oh goody," said Jack, "Is it you? Because we've all had a turn and it's lots of fun and we'd hate for you to miss out."

"No, tape up your lady-friend here," ordered Brad. "And no funny business this time."

Reluctantly Jack taped up Jill's wrists and ankles, and then held his own hands out while Matti taped first them, then his ankles.

"Sorry. I really don't want to be doing this," whispered Matti.

"And I'm sorry, because I really don't believe you anymore," replied Jack.

"Put some tape around that goose's mouth too," ordered Brad. "I'm sick of his smart-arse comments."

"Oh come on," pleaded Jack. "Don't tape the beard, I beg you." But it was too late. Matti stuck a big piece of tape right over his mouth and around the back of his head. Jack knew that was going to hurt when, and if, he took it off.

Just to be sure, Brad re-tied Matti, and left all three of them on the sofa, just like they were on the boat. He even took the extra precaution of gagging Jill and Matti as well.

"Okay now you're all going to sit there nicely and behave," he told them, as he finished tying up Matti. "I want no moaning, no grunting, gargling, farting or having to go to the toilet," he said, turning his attention to the zip-lock baggie in his hand. "I'm going to need some peace and quiet to translate this."

While Jack, Jill and Matti watched like the silent witnesses they indeed were, Brad went about the task at hand. He sat at the dining table, with a notepad and a Sharpie extra-fine point permanent marker – the preferred pen of letter translators and psychotic mastermind killers, although Brad wasn't quite of that ilk yet.

Carefully, Brad took the yellowing rice paper envelope out of the zip-lock baggie. It didn't look like an envelope. With a simple Japanese ink brush stroke for an address, a red cancellation above it and a black arrival mark beneath, it looked more like a piece of ancient Japanese calligraphy than a relatively modern letter addressed to a monk from his brother.

There were also some minor brown stains along one corner, which had probably occurred after it was posted in Japanese-occupied Singapore, on one of Tsukasa's rare returns to civilisation from his jungle geologising – not that you could actually call a bombed-out demoralised and occupied city, 'civilisation'.

Brad opened the envelope, took out its contents and unfolded them to reveal three sheets of even finer rice paper, each graced with lines of black ink that made the calligraphy on front of the envelope look like the graffiti of a talent-challenged vandal.

Brad held each sheet up to the light. You could see right through them. From where they were trussed up on the sofa bed, Jack, Jill and Matti could clearly make out the thick black lines of ink. Sadly, unlike Lawrence, none of them had any knowledge of how to decipher Japanese calligraphy the right way around, let alone back-to-front.

Brad spread out the three sheets on the table in front of him and carefully examined them. The first thing that he noticed was that each sheet was numbered, so they were obviously meant to be read in a certain order. He swapped 'three' with 'one', and was ready to proceed.

Each sheet of rice paper had three descending lines of calligraphy on it. The letters were a mix of the three main Japanese scripts – Kanji, Hiragana, and Katakana. To help with the process, Brad had brought with him three big textbooks, and referred to them on a number of occasions while translating the documents.

Halfway through translating the second line of the first page, Brad laughed and said to himself "Oh this is Haiku!" – referring to the traditional Japanese three-line poem, consisting of only seventeen syllables, five in the first and last lines and seven in the middle line.

Brad finished translating the first poem, and read it out to his speechless audience.

"A mountain of gold

Hides from the world above it

In a simple smile"

Jill and Matti nodded politely, as if Brad had written it himself, or as if they really did admire its poetic sentiments.

Jack made an urgent moaning noise under his gaffer-tape mask, and rocked back and forward with some enthusiasm. Brad ignored him and continued working on the next sheet of rice paper.

Soon, with the aid of his reference books, Brad had completed the second translation. He read it out to his captive audience.

"The mouth of the mine
Shares its hidden secret with
Sixteen stalactites"

This time Matti shrugged her shoulders as if to say she preferred the first one to the second one. But Jill frowned and glared at Jack, as if to say, "I think I know what you're on about." And Jack jumped up and down in his seat like a smartypants schoolboy shouting, "Sir! Pick me!" to his teacher. Brad continued to ignore him. On completion of the third translation, he read it aloud.

"A gold compass points
To wealth beyond expression
Under ivory"

Now both Jack and Jill were champing at their gaffer-tape bits. This was beginning to get on Brad's nerves. He got up from the table and walked to the sofa bed where they both bobbed and nodded and attempted to speak through their gags.

Brad pulled Jill's gaffer-tape gag off carefully, but ripped Jack's gaffer-tape gag off with some force causing Jack to wail like a banshee and swear like a trooper.

"What the hell is the matter with you two?" shouted Brad.

"It's in his mouth!" said Jack.

"His teeth, something to do with his teeth," agreed a gasping Jill.

"What is?" shouted a clearly disturbed Brad.

"Whatever the hell you're looking for," said Jack. "The clue, the map reference."

"The location to the 'mountain of gold'," added Jill.

Now Brad was annoyed. "I know!" he whined like a spoiled teenager. "I can work out my own puzzles."

"Fine. Just trying to be helpful," grumbled Jack.

"I got all this way without your help," snapped Brad.

"Which way?" queried Jack, "On your way to being sent to jail for the rest of your life for the murder of, how many people so far?" he continued, "Harvey, Boz, Diana Dawson – your temporary wife, your predecessor, what was his name?"

"Gimbell," helped Brad.

"That's right," continued Jack. "Norman Gimbell. And let's not forget Bert Slater, the warrant officer who survived the Catalina crash, but not a bar stool at the Cessnock RSL."

"That wasn't me. He just fell of his perch. Honestly."

"Either way it's four murders, plus the three of us, that makes seven."

"You're not going to kill *me* are you?" asked Matti.

"Of course not," said Brad politely.

"Yeah, like we're going to believe *you*," said Jill spitefully.

"Anyway, I'd really love to stay and chat," said Brad, gathering up the pages of the letter. "But I've got a corpse that I definitely *wasn't* responsible for, to find." It didn't sound quite as good as he thought it would.

"You're not going to kill us now, are you?" asked Jill.

"I wouldn't dream of it. There'll be plenty of time for that when I'm on Harvey's luxury powerboat making my escape," said Brad.

He picked up the roll of gaffer tape and approached Jack, pulling off a length of tape.

"Um yeah, *about* the boat ..." Jack chimed in apologetically.

Brad wrapped the tape over Jack's mouth, silencing him mid-sentence.

"I'm not interested," said Brad. "You can stay here until we return and I work out how to get you back to the boat."

Brad looked around at Jill. "And just in case it *is* in Tsukasa's mouth, I'd better take my dentist with me." He pulled her to her feet. He looked at Matti. "You too."

"You're not just going to leave him here?" asked Jill of Jack to Brad.

Brad looked around at Jack. "Good point. He'll probably try to escape again."

Brad reached into his backpack, produced a set of antique ankle-cuffs, and proceeded to attach one of the cuffs to Jack's ankle and the other to the metal frame of the folding sofa bed Jack was now sitting alone on.

"Where are we going?" asked Matti as Brad ushered her and the still-bound Jill out of the apartment, pulling the curtains and locking the door behind them.

"Mount Gower, to visit Tsukasa," said Brad Lawrence.

It didn't take Jack long to get the gaffer tape off his mouth, although it took a lot longer than he thought it would. He was able to get his bound hands up to the tape, but not behind his head, where Brad Lawrence had thoughtfully stuck down the end of the length of tape that was now, as Jack started to breathe more urgently, threatening to cut off his air supply. This made him think of the band Air Supply, and so horrified was he that he might die with the woeful pop song *Love and Other Bruises* going through his head, that he redoubled his efforts to survive.

Thanks to the fact that the hair on his face created an extremely impermanent seal on the gaffer tape, Jack was able to use this to his advantage by slowly working his lips around either edge of the tape, and began chewing on it like a dog with its favourite squeaky toy. Soon, as a result of this gnawing action, combined with his hands pulling on either side of the tape on his mouth, the tape finally snapped and he took a well-deserved panting break to catch his breath.

Breathing heavily, he looked at his wrists, still bound with gaffer tape. He could either attempt to chew through them or call for help. He decided to call for help. Unfortunately, calling for help wasn't much help, because his cries of "Help me! Help me!" sounded just like the muttonbirds' chorus of "Pick me! Pick me!" only down an octave.

In fact, had someone in one of the nearby apartments actually been listening, it would have sounded to them like a baritone budgie had joined the muttonbird choir.

Unfortunately for Jack, no one nearby *was* listening anyway and so, reluctantly, he started chewing through the gaffer tape around his wrists. When he was about halfway through, he started to wonder why the makers of gaffer tape didn't offer a series of pleasantly flavoured gaffer tapes, just for this very purpose, instead of the unpleasantly adhesive-flavoured one he was currently munching on. Then it occurred to him that gaffer tape wasn't made to be eaten in the first place, so writing a letter to the manufacturer suggesting the idea, would probably be a complete waste of time. He wondered though, considering how oddly his brain seemed to be functioning, if it might have some hitherto-unknown psychotropic properties.

Soon he managed to get a wide section in his mouth and pulled on it until he was able to unwind the remaining gaffer tape and finally free his hands.

That only left the ankle that was chained to the metal frame of the sofa bed. He looked at the situation, completely puzzled. With no tools and no cutting implements at his disposal, he was stumped. He started wondering why it was that Brad hadn't killed him earlier, half wishing that he had, so that at least he wouldn't have had to suffer the indignity of being ankle-cuffed to a sofa bed.

The only reason Jack could come up with for why Brad was keeping him alive was that he liked to either make his murders look like accidents or disappearances, and perhaps that was what he was planning for Jack, Jill and Matti, even though she still thought she was safe.

In desperation, Jack pulled his cuffed ankle back hard in an attempt to budge something, only to have the entire sofa bed slam into his ankle. When he had stopped swearing, he knelt down and looked under the sofa bed. It was on wheels!

Jack wheeled himself and the sofa bed over to the glass sliding door that opened out onto the patio. Brad had cleverly placed a broom handle in the exterior sliding groove of the door so there was no way it could be opened from the inside. Jack thought for a minute, and then decided that if he couldn't open the sliding door, he'd have to go through it. He started to slowly manoeuvre himself and the wheely-sofa, backing and filling, until the sofa bed was now between him and the door.

Dragging his cuffed ankle and the sofa bed with it, Jack made his way as far back from the sliding door as possible, until he was virtually up against the refrigerator in the kitchenette.

He turned around and assumed a crouching position with his hands on the armrest of the wheely-sofa. He now had a clear line of sight to the sliding door.

With a beach towel over his head for protection, Jack took aim along the back of the sofa bed, then employing a kind of odd hopping gait, charged towards the sliding door, pushing the sofa bed in front of him. The sofa bed connected with the glass door with force and ... kept going, showering glass all over the apartment, the patio floor and the towel-headed coroner-on-holidays.

Once out on the patio, Jack manoeuvred and manhandled the sofa bed around the wooden outdoor table, and two outdoor chairs, then down the two steps to the path that led to the driveway.

The driveway itself hadn't seemed that steep to Jack in the past, but that was because he was usually either walking down it, or riding a bicycle. This was the first time he had pushed a sofa bed up it, and even though it was on wheels, it still seemed steeper than it had ever been before.

As he pushed the sofa bed up the driveway, not just one voice in his head, but a whole committee was trying to work out just what he thought he was going to do when he got to the top of the driveway with a sofa bed still chained to his ankle.

By the time he reached the top, he still hadn't quite worked out exactly what he was going to do, but he knew it involved the golf cart he'd parked there an hour or so earlier – the very same cart, it turned out that was nowhere to be seen when he finally arrived at the top of the driveway.

It was *definitely* here, he thought to himself. He looked around, brow furrowed and sweaty. Had Brad Lawrence taken it? It seemed doubtful, especially as Jack had heard Brad's four-wheel drive Volvo start up and drive away, while he was gnawing through gaffer tape.

Brad could have somehow attached the golf cart to the back of his Volvo and towed it away he supposed, but why would he bother to do that when he could have just taken the keys out of it, or pushed it off the road?

On the other hand, perhaps the golf cart's rightful owner had come along and taken it back, which was fair enough, thought Jack, considering he had 'acquisitioned' it in the first place.

How Jack was planning to drive a golf cart with a sofa bed chained to his ankle, he hadn't quite worked out yet. He thought he might be able to somehow pile the sofa onto the back of the golf cart, reach the accelerator with one hand and steer with the other, but he wouldn't be able to work out the final configuration unless he found the damn thing.

He dragged the sofa bed out into the middle of the road so that he could look around. It didn't help matters that it was close to pitch black, there being no street lighting.

Jack stood in the road, right at the very point where the road starts to gently slope away from the driveway, a slope that continues all the way down to Lagoon Beach on the other side of the island, some nearly two kilometres below.

In the dark, Jack didn't realise he was standing on the edge of the sloping road. As he turned around to check if the golf cart might be in the pandanus bushes behind him, he absent-mindedly heaved the sofa bed around and over the lip of the crest of the hill, giving it just enough momentum to drag him off balance. He fell backwards, fortunately landing on the sofa bed, but unfortunately giving it even more momentum as it began to slowly roll down Ned's Beach Road.

Suddenly Jack was seeing stars – largely because now he was lying on his back, facing the sky, with the one leg that was in chains dangling over the back of the sofa bed as he rolled headfirst down the road.

The stars Jack was seeing now seemed to be moving at an increasingly rapid rate as the sofa bed headed down the ever-steepening slope. Suddenly they disappeared behind the canopy of banyan trees that Jack was now beginning to realise posed a serious threat to his wellbeing, should the sofa bed plunge off the road and into one.

He was now hurtling down Ned's Beach Road not unlike an upside-down tobogganist.

He tried putting his chained foot on the ground as a brake, but it was too late, he'd gained too much momentum for that. So, using all his weight, he hurled his body violently to his left and managed to spin the sofa bed around so that now his feet were at the front and his head was at the back, resembling a sofa bed version of the luge event at the Winter Olympics, should they ever be held on Lord Howe Island, at 2:15 in the morning.

By craning his neck forward, he could now at least see where he was going, which would have been a good thing had he not been heading for the first of several nasty corners.

Jack leaned hard against the back of the sofa bed in an attempt to get it to turn to the right, with no success. He pushed harder against the back until suddenly, and with an almighty twang of inner-springs, it folded down into its 'bed' formation, so that Jack's sofa-toboggan was now more of a sofa-catamaran.

This proved to be a positive development, because Jack found that he could now steer to some extent. With arms stretched out like a short chubby Jesus in a Hawaiian shirt, he gripped both sides of what was now a bed on wheels and, by pushing down on one side, was able to lift the wheels on the other side off the ground, allowing the craft to take corners after a fashion – a fashion that probably wouldn't be catching on in the near future, as Jack was terrified.

The corners were coming up with increasingly rapid regularity, as were the kind of humps that made the sofa bed momentarily airborne. All the time Jack was hollering at the top of his lungs – not words so much, as a long guttural "Aaaaghhhh!" occasionally punctuated by the odd "Fuck!" and "Shit!" as the sofa bed either 'got air,' or returned with a thump to the ever-steepening asphalt beneath it.

A huge corner was now approaching and to compensate, Jack leaned hard to the right with all his strength and weight, only to have the entire vehicle spin on its axis, leaving him hurtling headfirst once again. Tilting his head backwards over the end of the bed, Jack was again able to see where he was going, except this time everything was upside down, and the top of his head was frighteningly close to the road, which from his point of view, now appeared to be above him.

Jack had to perform a complete rollover if he was going to be able to maintain what little control he still had over the hurtling road-furniture. He waited for the next bump, then used the air created between his body and the sofa bed to do a mid-air body-flip, landing face down on the sofa, and now riding it like a huge land-based surf-mat on wheels.

The speed at which Jack and the sofa bed came around the last bend on Ned's Beach Road is unknown. If you had been able to ask Jack at that very moment he would have replied, "fucking fast!" However, he would later have said that same speed was actually "fucking slow" in comparison to the speed he was *about* to reach.

The road straightened out, becoming much steeper and from Jack's perspective began to resemble a tree-lined asphalt-covered downhill ski ramp. About 50 metres down the slope, the craft began to get the death-wobbles. Jack dug his now-white fingers deep into the edges of both sides of the sofa bed as its wheels shook sickly beneath him.

The sofa bed's black plastic roller-wheels could no longer take the punishment the road was dishing out. One by one they began to tear, wear or simply grind away underneath the comfy juggernaut.

All semblance of control was now lost. As its worn wheels became imbalanced, the deep-padded vehicle began to rotate, slowly at first but soon fast; round and round like a hurdy-gurdy gone wild.

Jack screamed like a big girl and clung on to the craft with every available part of his body, even some parts that technically were unavailable for clinging-on-with duties.

As the view swung repeatedly past him, he momentarily caught a glimpse of exactly where he was, which was heading right for the very same monster Norfolk Island pine tree across the road from Thompson's store that had tried unsuccessfully to kill him on Day One.

Jack squealed and buried his head into the plush foam padding of the hurtling sofa bed. But just when it seemed like impact was only nanoseconds away, the runaway sofa bed's rear back wheel completely disintegrated and the frame hit the asphalt, raising a shower of sparks, but spinning the vehicle on its axis and miraculously, away from an almost certain fatal tree-hugging.

The sofa bed now scraped past the closed shops that lined the lower end of Ned's Beach Road and, even though they did seem to be slowing down, Jack couldn't help worrying that the sparks from the craft's wheelless back leg, which were aimed directly at his chain-tethered be-sandalled right foot, might somehow set alight the rubber infrastructure of his sports sandal, giving him a hotfoot he wouldn't forget in a hurry.

As the flaming chariot scraped past Humpty Micks Café, it began to turn sideways and proceeded to broadside towards the intersection of Ned's Beach Road and Lagoon Road, the corner bolt that held the frame together getting shorter and shorter as the road wore it to nothing.

Finally, the sofa hit the grass embankment in front of the beach. The jolt momentarily sent it up in the air once more, where the frayed corner bolt popped its rivet, thus freeing Jack's tethered leg. The whole mess plonked down onto the grass, facing the intersection it had just carved up, where it sprang back into its original upright sofa configuration.

Jack himself landed comfortably on the sofa in the reclining position, with one arm supporting his head, as if watching a late-night movie on an imaginary television in the middle of the intersection. At that very moment, a lone ute came along Lagoon Road from Old Settlement Beach direction.

"You look comfy," said Mike, sticking his head out of the driver's window, and looking in Jack's direction.

It was indeed fortunate for Jack that among Mike's many jobs on the island he was also the resident plumber, and happened to be carrying a pair of heavy-duty bolt cutters in the back of his ute that made quick work of the vintage iron cuffs around Jack's ankle.

It was also fortunate that Mike was still pissed enough to agree to take Jack to the top of Mount Gower, even though it was 2:30 in the morning, and pretty close to being pitch black.

Now free from his mobile sofa-bed prison, Jack jumped in the passenger side of Mike's ute, and they headed off into the night. On the way, Jack got Mike up to speed on the various murders and plot twists.

"I don't believe it. 'Old Three Eyes' is a ruthless killer who has kidnapped two of the most attractive visitors to the island in recent memory? And there's a dead Japanese geologist on the island who has the directions to a fortune in gold somewhere in his mouth? I don't believe it," said Mike.

"You said that already," said Jack helpfully.

"Why didn't he just shoot you all?" asked Mike.

"Yeah, I suggested that," said Jack. "He's got some plan to make it all look like an accident."

Mike shook his head again. "I can't believe he chopped poor old Diana Dawson up into little bits, crumbed her with bread and fed her to the kingfish. She was his wife too."

"I know. He's pure evil," agreed Jack.

As they passed Pinetrees, one of the oldest, if not *the* oldest hotel on the island, Mike asked Jack a good question.

"What are you going to do when you catch up to him?"

"That's a good question. I have no idea," said Jack.

"Can you arrest him?"

"No, but I can recommend that he be arrested."

"He's also got a gun and two hostages," added Mike.

"One hostage and one 'I don't know' – possibly hostage."

"What have you got?"

Jack thought for a while and replied. "The element of surprise?"

They drove past the airport. Even though Mike's special edition 'Morpheus Mica' Holden SS 6.0 litre DOHC V8 ute was capable of 240 kilometres per hour, they were only 'tootling' along at 40 kilometres per hour.

"Can't you go any faster?" asked Jack.

"40's the speed limit, mate," said Mike, earnestly. "And it's double-demerit points over Christmas."

"Are there any traffic cops or speed cameras on the island?"

Mike looked around at Jack, and a grin of recognition came over his face. He gripped the steering wheel and put his foot to the floor. The SS V8 took off like a rocket, within moments easily setting a new Lord Howe Island land speed record for non-winged vehicles.

They hit 120kph halfway past the airstrip and kept going faster, the angry growl of the V8 engine echoing across the tarmac. At the end of tarmac where the road turns sharply to the right, Mike stomped the brakes and did the mother of all screechies, turning the SS's wheels around to run parallel with Blinky's Beach on their left, and sheering a good quarter of an inch of rubber off the tyres on the ute's 17-inch low profile chrome powder-coated alloy wheels. Mike grinned like a loon. You didn't get to do this kind of thing much on Lord Howe Island.

"Merry Christmas, Mike," said Jack, grinning back.

"Best present I ever got, mate," smiled Mike, flooring it once more, the ute taking off in a cloud of dust and burning rubber.

Blinky's Beach disappeared in a flash. Cobby's Corner and Lovers Bay loomed on the right and disappeared just as quickly. Mike slammed on the brakes once more and the SS came to a screeching, steaming halt.

"What did you stop for?" asked Jack.

"We're here," said Mike. "That's it. The sealed road's run out."

"How short *is* this island?" asked Jack.

"Pretty short, mate," said Mike.

"What about that unsealed bit?" asked Jack, pointing to the unsealed road that was directly in front of them.

"What? In the ute?" he looked at Jack incredulously, but he could tell Jack was serious. Mike shrugged and shook his head. "Okay, you're the boss." And they took off once more, this time a little slower along the sandy dual-tyre tracks before them.

A kilometre and a half later, the two tyre tracks stopped and were replaced by a single narrow walking track. There was no way Jack was going to make Mike drive any further. It just wasn't possible.

They parked just near the beach on the lagoon side of the island. It was still dark and they had a quite a walk in front of them before they even got to Mount Gower, which was an extremely tough climb even when you *could* see what you were doing.

Fortunately, Mike was well prepared. He jumped out of the cab and began to throw some things in an old backpack he had in the back of the ute.

"Have we got time to pack?" asked Jack.

"I've done this before mate, and believe me, there's a few things we're going to need, mate," said Mike, cunningly managing to say 'mate' twice in the same sentence.

Mike put the backpack on his back. "Here, catch!" he said, as he threw Jack a small nine-LED waterproof aluminium torch, which fortunately Jack managed to catch, despite his innate clumsiness, and the fact that it was pitch black and the torch wasn't on. In fact, Jack didn't even know what it was that he was catching before he caught it, and then still wasn't sure even after he had turned it on and temporarily blinded himself by shining it right in his eyes.

And off they took along the thin sandy track that led away from the beach and into the darkness, even though all Jack could see for some distance were the purple and blue blotches of nine-LED after-images burnt into his retinas.

On their right, they could hear the sound of the ocean waters gently lapping the rocky beach, on their left, the crazy bird orchestra that is the Lord Howe jungle.

They had a four-hour walk in front of them to the eight-hundred-and-seventy-five-metre summit of Mount Gower, although Jack hoped to do it in less, for Jill's sake. Brad Lawrence had already killed at least one person by pushing them off a cliff, so obviously he knew how to do it.

Plunging through the ever-darkening forest, Jack picked up the pace, and strode ahead of Mike, who was younger, fitter and more experienced in climbing Mount Gower, but who also had a full backpack on, and 'being pissed with nothing better to do' isn't quite the same incentive as 'must save the woman who actually likes having sex with me and may be the love of my life'.

They soon emerged from the forest into a grass-covered clearing dominated by the towering dark presence of Mt Lidgbird – a virtual wall of black to their left.

While Jack wheezed and caught his breath, Mike knelt down and took his backpack off and opened it up.

He took out two bike helmets, handed one to Jack, then ripped off a long strip from a roll of gaffer tape and handed that to Jack as well.

"Gaffer your torch to your helmet," said Mike, proceeding to do just that to his own helmet. Jack followed suit. They put their helmets on and turned on their now gaffered-on head lights.

Jack turned his head around to check out his now-illuminated near surroundings. The grassy slope in front of them appeared to peter away into almost nothing. The path seemed to meld with the cliff face.

There was a thick, coarse weatherworn rope handrail tethered to the cliff face above a narrow ledge that seemed to disappear into the night.

"What's that?" asked Jack, pointing and shaking in horror. And also just shaking because of the climb they'd already done.

That's the notorious 'Lidgbird Ledge', mate," said Mike, taking a length of nylon rope out of the backpack.

"We don't have to go around there, do we?" asked Jack.

"That's the only way," said Mike apologetically.

"Did I mention I have a fear of heights?" Jack tried to say nonchalantly.

"Good thing it's dark then. You won't be able to see how high we are," said Mike passing the nylon rope around Jack's waist and tying it fast.

"What's this for?" asked Jack, looking at the nylon rope.

"It's your safety line," said Mike, now tying the other end of the nylon rope around his own waist. "This way if you fall, I'll be on the other end of the line."

"Yes, but what if _you_ fall?" asked Jack, wondering how quickly he could untie the knot at his waist if he had to in a hurry.

"Don't worry. I've done this plenty of times when I was just as pissed," said Mike. Jack thought this news was hardly reassuring.

Now harnessed together like a two-pack of pack mules, they set off across the ledge into the darkness, Mike taking the lead.

In the back of his mind, Jack feared that he might be turning into a hobbit. He'd never looked more like a Bilbo.

As they reached the weatherworn rope handrail, just how high they were became apparent. Salty cold air was rising with some speed from the depths below.

"Ah, refreshing!" joked Jack feebly. He knew he had to do this despite his fear, so he decided he might as well try to jolly himself up. It wasn't really working.

Looking down, all they could see was the cliff disappearing into nothingness, with just the raging growl of the huge ocean swell crashing against razor-sharp jagged rocks coming from below to reassure them that there was in fact something down there that was probably best avoided.

As he took each tentative, shaky step, Jack held as tight as he could to the slightly damp rope and tried not to look down at the churning water below.

Following Mike's lead, he hooked his hands under the rope, turned his back to the abyss and his face to the cliff, and slowly inched along the ledge sideways. Jack fought desperately to keep vertigo at bay and his feet on the slippery sloping ledge.

Halfway across the ledge the updraft began to batter them. It was just at this point that Jack's nose got itchy. He craned his head forward so he could scratch it on his hand, and in doing so, lost his footing, but fortunately not his arming, and landed on his bum on the wet ledge with such force that it dislodged his bike helmet from his head, which he had failed to correctly attach.

Time slowed down, allowing Jack to fight off the natural urge to try to catch his helmet, but also allowing him the opportunity to watch in terror as his helmet, the gaffered-on torch still shining, proceeded to bounce, crash and tumble all the way to the ocean far below, illuminating the downward path Jack himself very nearly also took.

When it hit the water, the foam padding in the helmet made it buoyant, and they both watched as the tiny light was repeatedly dashed against the rocks at the foot of the cliff.

"Wow, the light's still going!" said Mike, clearly impressed.

A huge wave rolled in and smashed the floating helmet against the rocks and the light went out.

Jack pulled himself to his feet, pale and sweating. "Keep going," was all he could say. He desperately wanted to be on the other end of the ledge.

It was another two hundred metres around the curve of the cliff face until the so-called 'Lower Road' reached the relative shelter of the Erskine Valley, where Mount Lidgbird meets Mount Gower. Safely across the ledge, they stopped for another breather. Mike pulled a big bottle of water from his backpack, and they shared some of it.

They managed to traverse the next kilometre along the relatively flat, palm-covered terrain to Erskine Creek quite quickly, where they stopped for another drink, and as this was the last source of water, Mike refilled the bottle from the creek.

Soon they were back on the track that was now climbing ever more steeply to the top of the valley, which brought them to the so-called 'saddle' between Gower and Lidgbird. Jack wouldn't have been surprised to see an Orc or a possibly even an Ent.

"Do you want the good news or the bad news?" Mike asked Jack.

"Good news, please," said Jack in between breaths.

"We've only got about a kilometre to go," said Mike.

"And the bad news?" asked Jack.

"Most of it is vertical," said Mike. He went on to explain how they were now four hundred metres up, but there was still another four hundred and fifty metres to the summit of Mount Gower.

Mike wasn't kidding. They began the next section, climbing virtually straight up over enormous boulders with ropes bolted to them, and so many perilous ledges that Jack was almost beginning to get used to his fear of heights, as he clamoured ungainly over rock after ledge after boulder.

In a way, Jack was glad that he had lost his flashlight, if not the helmet that was attached to it. Without illumination, he didn't have to stare too closely at Mike's arse, which was hovering just above his face most of the way up. This way, at least it wasn't spot-lit.

The sky was becoming lighter now, and they could see the outline of Lidgbird by the spectacular display of stars not obliterated from their field of vision by the mountain's dark black mass. But the further they climbed, the mistier it appeared, not because Lidgbird was becoming shrouded in mist, but because they were.

Gradually, the slope began to ease off and they entered the strange, moist, cloud forest that covers the top of Mount Gower's plateau like a strange, moist cloud-forest toupee.

Through the mist, weird prehistoric palms mingled with moss-covered trees that also housed a variety of rare ferns and exotic miniature orchids. It could easily be the setting for a dinosaur movie or a gothic-swamp-horror movie. If a raptor, the creature from the black lagoon, or a redneck zombie were to jump out from the darkness, Jack would not have been surprised.

By now the two of them had developed such a rhythm that even though there was no danger of anyone falling, they didn't bother to untie the rope that joined them at the waist.

Over a number of small forest-covered ravines, Mike led Jack across the top of the plateau, to its very western edge, expecting at any minute to come upon Brad Lawrence, Jill and Matahina. But they were nowhere to be seen. The only life they encountered were the local woodhens, mildly curious about these odd nocturnal visitors to their realm. But when the woodhens discovered the visitors weren't going to give them a handout, they disappeared.

Suddenly they came to a clearing – a large flat wet rock that backed on to a wall of cloud.

"This is it, mate," said Mike. "This is the spot where Boz jumped."

"Then where *are* they?" asked Jack, perplexed.

Mike shrugged.

"We couldn't have passed them, could we?"

Mike shook his head.

"I thought we'd catch up with them along the way," said Jack.

Mike shrugged.

"There isn't another way up is there?" asked Jack.

"Nope," said Mike. "But there is one other way down." He pointed over the edge.

"I'm sure that Lawrence's plan was to come up here to find the remains of Tsukasa, which for some insane reason he thinks might be on that ledge with the hat and shoes," said Jack, nodding his head in the direction that Mike had just pointed. The wall of cloud. He wondered ...

"They couldn't have accidentally walked off the edge, could they?" asked Jack.

"Anything's possible, mate," said Mike, taking the water bottle out of his backpack. "But Brad Lawrence is an authorised tour guide. He comes up here at least once a week. I reckon he'd know not to walk off the edge."

They sat and waited, unsure of what to do, and not quite ready to commit to the walk back down. Mike pulled out a packet of potato chips which they shared while they watched the sky slowly turn lavender, as somewhere beneath them the sun must have been approaching the curve of the horizon.

It was deathly quiet – just the wind and the occasional mournful wail of a currawong that perched unafraid in a nearby tree.

"I suppose we'd better head back down, then," suggested Jack. They both quietly got to their feet, and Mike put his backpack back on.

Suddenly, a figure emerged from the mist. It was Jill. She was wet, exhausted and bedraggled from the climb, but to Jack, she looked beautiful.

"Oh my god, you're alright!" said Jack, running towards her and then stopping suddenly when the rope around his waist connecting him to Mike went tight.

By then Matahina had emerged from the mist, followed closely behind by Brad Lawrence, brandishing his Iver Johnson.

Jack scratched his head. "How did we beat you up here?"

"We thought we'd wait until it was a little lighter," said Brad Lawrence.

"We watched a couple of episodes of *Curb Your Enthusiasm*," said Matahina.

"Off the satellite?" asked Mike.

"Boxed set," said Matti.

"Cool," said Mike.

"Shit," said Jack. "That means I could have just gone to Brad's house and not had to climb all the way up this fucking mountain."

"That explains why we didn't see your car at the start of the track," said Mike thoughtfully. Jack just looked at him, incredulously.

Mike, a big man, decided it was time to take action so they could all go home. He took a step towards Lawrence, with his hand outstretched.

"Come on, Three Eyes," said Mike. "Hand it over. Time to give yourself up, mate."

Brad shook his head. "I don't think so. And don't call me 'Three Eyes'. How would you like it?"

He aimed the gun directly at Mike's forehead. Mike shook his head and stepped forward just as Brad began to squeeze the trigger of the Iver Johnson. The five-shot cylinder rotated the next chamber into line between the barrel and the hammer, which was now pulled back as far as the spring would allow it. A millimetre more pressure from Lawrence's finger was all it took to bring the hammer down on the .32-

calibre centre-fire shell. The bullet exploded out of the gun and into Mike's skull right in the middle of his forehead.

A family of currawongs scattered in fright as the noise echoed through the trees, and a puff of cordite-flavoured smoke filled Mike's nostrils as he went down, blood gushing from the perfectly circular wound, like thick red water from a broken tap, his head shaking violently and involuntarily with the force of the flow. Matahina and Jill screamed in unison.

"Oh you *arsehole!*" shouted Jack.

"What did you say?" asked Lawrence, now turning and training the Iver Johnson on Jack's forehead.

"I mean, 'Good Shot!'" said Jack apologetically.

Brad began to apply the slightest of pressure to the Iver Johnson's trigger.

"No, don't!" cried Jill, jumping towards Brad, grabbing at his right arm. Angrily, Brad brought the back of his hand and the pistol forcefully down on Jill's cheek, knocking her over, so that she landed hard on her bum.

Before Jack could move, Brad trained the Iver Johnson back on him.

"No, I was right. You *are* an arsehole," said Jack.

"Fine," said Brad, acquiescing to Jill's request. "While I've got you here, I may as well put you to work. Look over the edge."

Jack glanced towards the misty abyss just a few steps away.

"I'd rather not."

Brad squeezed on the trigger. "Look over the edge or fall over the edge," he smiled, evilly.

"Okay," said Jack reluctantly. He took a step towards the edge of the cliff, slowly dropped to his knees, then crawled on all fours in the direction of his greatest fear.

Craning his head reluctantly over the edge, his eyes involuntarily screwed shut, Jack briefly opened one eye and then shut it again.

"I can't see anything," he called back to Brad.

"Look again. Properly," said Brad.

Jack looked again, this time with both eyes, directly down. Through the shifting mists he could see the dark volcanic rock that made up Mount Gower, disappear into the ocean, way, way below. But what he couldn't see was the Japanese geologist's pith helmet and shoes.

"I can't see anything," shouted Jack over his shoulder. "Maybe they blew off the ledge."

"Look again," ordered Brad.

Once more, Jack kept his vertigo at bay and stuck his head out over the edge of the cliff. The rock that he was now lying on, which formed the top of the cliff, seemed to be jutting slightly out, and he could see that its smooth dark surface stretched below him for over a metre or more, obscuring the ledge beneath it from view.

He crawled back from the edge, shaking his head. "It looks like the ledge must be underneath this rock. But I can't see it."

Brad wasn't satisfied. "Well, you're going to have to go down there then."

"What?" questioned Jack in disbelief.

"What are you worried about? You're already on a rope," said Brad, pointing to the thin nylon rope that still connected Jack to Mike's body, three metres away.

"But I haven't got a helmet," said Jack feebly.

Brad pointed to the corpse. "You can use Mike's. I'm sure he won't mind."

Jack approached Mike's still-warm body, and squatted down beside it. He couldn't believe that here he was, leaning over yet another corpse while he was meant to be on holiday.

The torch gaffer-taped to the side of Mike's helmet was still on, so Jack turned it off. There was a lot of blood and it soaked Jack's hands as he undid the helmet's chin strap and proceeded to pull it off Mike's punctured cranium.

Jack poured a pool of warm blood out of the helmet. A couple of small chunks of bone attached to grey matter and matted hair also plopped out onto the moss-covered ground. Jack grimaced. Jill and Matahina gagged.

Only Brad seemed to be enjoying the proceedings. With the gun, he signalled to Jack to put the helmet on. Jack obeyed, feeling the warm sticky residue in his hair. He tightened up the chin strap.

"What about the other end of the rope?" asked Jack. "What are you going to tie it to?"

"What's wrong with him?" asked Brad, pointing to dead Mike. "He's heavier than you."

"Yeah, but he's not exactly going to take an active part in holding on," said Jack. "What about a tree?" he suggested.

Brad shook his head. "Where's the fun in that? I know. Let's tie you to your girlfriend. She won't let you die if she really loves you."

"But I weigh more than she does. I'll just pull her over."

"It's okay," said Matahina. "She can hold on to me."

"See?" said Brad. "Now untie the rope, and tie up your girlfriend."

Jack had always looked forward to the day when he would be ordered to tie up his girlfriend. However he'd always imagined that the order would come *from* his girlfriend. The fact that it was coming from an insane killer while everyone present's life was in real danger, and that the rope first had to be removed from the body of a recently executed corpse, somewhat diminished the order's erotic effect.

After untying the rope from around Mike's waist and wiping some blood off it, Jack began to tie it as securely as he could around Jill's waist. He looked into her eyes, and she was looking right into his eyes.

"I'm sorry for being such a wimp," he said.

"You're an *alive* wimp, that's all that matters," she said. A tear welled in her eyes and rolled down her right cheek. He wiped it off and smiled.

"Look at us," he said. "We only met a few days ago and we're already tying the knot."

Jack handed Jill the end of the rope, which was now protruding from a knot at her waist.

"This is secure, but it's also a quick release knot." He looked her right in the eyes. "If it looks at any point that I'm about to drag you anywhere near the edge, pull the rope. The last thing I want to see is you following me down there."

Jill let go of the end of the rope. "It's not going to happen." She kissed him. The kiss seemed to last a thousand years but was actually only a split second before Lawrence interrupted.

"Enough kissyface. Over the edge." He motioned towards the lip of the mountain. Jack moved reluctantly to the edge.

Jill rotated the knot in the rope around her waist until it was in the middle of her back. Then she faced away from Jack, and braced herself, her legs apart and slightly bent, ready to anchor him. Matahina stood in front of Jill almost as if they were dancing. They put their arms around each other, and both spread their legs slightly to give them the best bracing position to support Jack's 80-plus kilogram body.

Jack looked at the 25-year-old Polynesian princess and the 32-year-old female dentist, their legs and arms entwined, not to mention ropes being involved, and realised he was largely going to miss another of his greatest fantasies.

He faced away from the cliff, got down on all fours, and slowly backed himself towards the edge. He expected to be more frightened than he was. He felt strangely calm, as if he was already dead, which he figured he would be, pretty soon anyway.

He lowered his feet and knees over first, and gripped the edge of the cliff with his thighs and his stomach, like the extreme sport version of an ab-crunch.

Then he slowly lowered himself until he was almost wholly over the edge of the cliff, with just his arms, shoulders and head above the edge in front of him, holding on to some scraggy blades of grass growing in a shallow indentation of soil in the middle of the rock.

"I'm going to brace my legs on the cliff wall and have the rope take all my weight, okay?" he called out to Jill, who was facing away from him. He realised it was potentially the last view of her bum he would ever get.

"Okay," called Jill, as she and Matti braced themselves. Jack grabbed the rope.

Jill was surprised. He didn't seem that heavy. However it was early days yet. Endurance would be the key.

Jack couldn't believe he was hanging over the edge of a cliff by a rope attached to two very attractive women. That's how shallow he was. He could hear them groaning and grunting above him, and was slightly disturbed to find he was getting aroused. This unfortunately made him look down at his groin, and it was then he saw for the first time that he was dangling (or at least the parts of him that *were* dangling) by a thin nylon rope, 875 metres above the ocean.

Suffice to say, almost immediately *everything* was dangling. His arousal swiftly subsided, as did any semblance of confidence he had. His head swum with the wooziness of fear, his mouth for some reason instead of going dry, flooded with saliva, but he couldn't swallow it for fear he would choke. And the last thing he wanted to do was drown on his own saliva while hanging off an 875-metre cliff.

His feet slipped off the slime-covered cliff wall, and he was now just hanging from the rope, his eyeballs spinning in his head, moaning to himself in a pathetic way that was somewhere between crying and wailing, as he swung out over the vast amount of air and height between him and certain death.

Then, still moaning, he swung back in. Head first. Into the cliff face. "Oh *great*, now I've got concussion," he thought to himself. Blood trickled down the side of his face from underneath the helmet, and for a moment he thought it might be a cerebral haemorrhage, until he realised that it was Mike's blood and not his own.

But somehow the blow centred him, and by concentrating on the task ahead and not the fear, he was able to get his feet back on the cliff face and his hands back on the rope.

He heard a voice from above. It was Brad Lawrence.

"Have you found it yet?"

Jack's eyes scanned the cliff face in front of him, as he tried desperately not to look directly down. He couldn't see the ledge because it was still obscured by the massive wall of stone.

"No," he called back up. "You'll have to lower me down a bit further."

With the already-tight rope stretched as far as it would go, this meant that Jill and Matahina would have to move themselves closer to the edge. They both looked down at their feet, grabbed each other a bit tighter and shuffled towards the cliff edge.

Beneath them, Jack inched down, still bracing his body with his feet on the cliff face, in what he imagined was classic abseiling technique, but was actually a far cry from it.

Above him, Jill and Matahina seemed to be slow dancing towards the edge. But because Jill was walking backwards, she couldn't see where she was going. This meant she couldn't see the tuft of moss her left heel was shuffling up to. As a result when she hit it, her foot stopped, but Matahina and the rest of Jill's body kept going. She fell backwards, dragging Matahina down on top of her.

Below them Jack dropped suddenly, about a metre. This resulted in Jill being instantly dragged on her back, out from under Matahina and straight towards the edge. She screamed. Jack screamed. Matahina screamed. And grabbed Jill's ankles as they came scraping past her hands.

Jack stopped falling with a jerk. Above he could hear clapping.

It was Brad. "Bravo!" he said. "Have you guys been rehearsing? That was amazing!"

Matti was now spread-eagled on her stomach, her face flat against the cold rock and holding on to Jill's ankles for dear life.

For her part, Jill was on her back, the rope around her waist pulled tight, and her back lying uncomfortably on top of the slipknot and the rope that was leading over the edge to Jack. She had her arms out wide, and was griping the ground with all her might.

Jack was now swinging two metres below the top of the cliff, making an almost constant "woah"ing noise, as he swung around and around.

When the cliff came into view, he looked up, and right in front of him he saw *it* – an inverted pith helmet decorated with a tarnished gold star. In it was a nesting tern, looking moderately perplexed by the intrusion of this strange creature dangling and woahing in front of it.

Next to the nesting tern was a small pair of men's black patent leather shoes, but this time, unlike the images on Boz's camera, they were not being worn by a second tern.

"Found them!" he called out above. "I've found the hat and the shoes."

"Is *he* there?" Brad shouted "Is the Jap there?"

"Can't see," Jack shouted back. "I have to get closer!" Using the momentum he already had, Jack swung towards the edge.

Getting just within reach, he tried to grab the ledge, but as he did, the mother tern leaned out over the rim of her helmet-nest and pecked him on his chubby little pinkie finger. Jack squealed like a girl, and lost his grip.

He swung out again, and swung back in. This time he approached the ledge outside the mother tern's pecking range. He grabbed the ledge and held fast – then felt a sharp thump on top of his helmet and a shrill squawk in his ear. It was the father tern returning from sea with a mouthful of baitfish.

"Bloody hell!" shouted Jack. "Piss off!"

He had a hold of the ledge now, and realised that it wasn't a ledge at all. It sloped down and opened into a dark cave-like crevice in the side of the cliff, about a metre wide – a crevice that would only really be visible from where Jack was now hanging.

"It's not a ledge," Jack yelled up to Brad. "It's a cave."

"Can you see Tsukasa?" Brad called back.

Jack peered into the crevice, but couldn't see a thing.

"It's too dark," he yelled.

Then he remembered the flashlight that was gaffer-taped to his literally bloody helmet. Holding on to the ledge with his left hand, he reached up with his right hand and pushed the switch, which turned it on. He felt an instant pain in his hand and realised that the father tern had taken another swipe and drawn blood. It had also deposited a small amount of half-digested baitfish on the back of his hand. He shook it off with a look of disgust.

Next he peered deep into the crevice in front of him. With illumination, everything changed. He could now see, less than a metre from his eyes, the mummified head of Captain Tsukasa Kobayashi of the Japanese Imperial Army, staring, albeit without any eyeballs, right back at him.

Jack flinched in shock and lost his grip, sending him swinging back out over the abyss, where the father tern took another swipe at him, and then the rope swung him back to the ledge. This time, Jack grabbed the ledge again and held firm.

Above him, Jill and Matahina were approaching breaking point.

"Please hurry up Jack," called out Jill in desperation. Sweating, she craned her head around to look at the rope. It was beginning to fray at the point where it was rubbing against the lip of the cliff.

"Hang in there. I've found him. He's in the cave," called Jack.

"He's not still alive, is he?" called Matahina.

"Not for a while," called back Jack.

"Just get the head!" shouted Lawrence.

"I'll try," replied Jack. He looked closely at the sunken face before him. It still had skin, though now dried like leather, and most of its hair, although there were a couple of patches that Jack figured had either been salvaged by sooty terns for nesting material, or gnawed off by a rat or rodent of some sort.

Balanced on what was left of the corpse's nose was a pair of round wire-framed spectacles. The glass was cracked in one eye, and the corroded arms were held in place on one side by a mummified ear, but on the other side seemingly by nothing, as that ear had long ago dropped off, and was now resting like an extra thick potato crisp on Tsukasa's narrow bony shoulder. As a result, the glasses sat a little wonkily.

But most importantly, the sunken face had a huge impressive set of choppers. Teeth. Two gleaming white rows of them, with one gold tooth right in the centre that twinkled slightly under the light from Jack's torch.

The body of the long-dead geologist was facing the crevice opening, and sat cross-legged in the lotus position. But all Jack needed was the head. He figured that after several decades of aging, the skull would probably separate from the body without much effort, so he held on to the ledge with his left hand and reached in with his right hand.

The head was just out of reach. He needed to get further up onto the ledge. To do this he would have to swing out and swing back in again. He pushed himself off backwards, away from the ledge.

Above him, Jill saw another strand of nylon pop at the fraying point.

"Jack, I wouldn't do that if I were you," she called out.

Jack swung back onto the ledge, this time a bit higher. He leaned in to the crevice and managed to get his hand on the mummified head. But it wouldn't budge. And it was hard to get a firm grip on it, because the skin had been worn smooth with age.

Jack stretched his arm as far as it would go, took hold of Tsukasa's still jet-black hair and pulled on it, hoping it would bring the skull with it. It didn't. Instead, he had a handful of hair and lost his purchase in the process, sending him swinging once more into the abyss.

With the blood and fish goo on his hand now covered with hair, he looked down to find he now had a hairy palm. "I knew this was going to happen eventually," he thought to himself.

Above him, another strand of nylon unstranded. The rope that was supporting him was now only half its original width.

Jack swung back onto the ledge. This time he was more or less balancing on the ledge on his chest. He reached in and grabbed the skull by the face, and shook it vigorously. The remaining ear and glasses fell off, but the skull itself wouldn't budge.

"Come on!" he shouted. He shook it some more, but still it held firm to the body. In frustration, he stretched his right arm out, and with his open hand whacked the dead Japanese geologist in the side of the head with such force that it knocked the skull clean off the spinal column and into the darkness.

At the same time, this act of wanton violence and corpse-tampering sent Jack swinging off the ledge and over the abyss again.

"Shit!" he exclaimed, as he once more swung back out into space.

Jill, despite the agony in her whole body, had kept her eye on the fraying rope. Matahina, gripping Jill's legs, was at breaking point. Both her arms and Jill's legs were now shaking with exhaustion. She knew she couldn't hold on much longer.

"Hurry up Jack," called Jill. "The rope is going to snap!"

Fortunately Jack didn't hear that bit, as the male tern was squawking angrily at his face.

"I'm going to have to go inside this cave," he called out.

"Just bring back the fucking head, you imbecile!" barked Brad, now clearly getting frustrated. If Jack couldn't fetch the skull, Brad had decided he was going to have to shoot them all and climb down there himself.

Jack swung back onto the ledge but failed to get a hold. He was now feeling surprisingly, and perhaps foolishly, relaxed about swinging in and out over 875 metres of sheer nothing. He pushed himself off the cliff wall with his feet, hoping to give himself enough momentum for the task at hand, but not realising that in the process he had broken yet another strand of nylon rope above him. There was now only one mini-strand of nylon separating him from a horrible and possible slow death, seeing as how things tend to slow down for those last few seconds as you watch the world come racing towards you at terminal velocity.

He swung back towards the cliff face with as much momentum as he could muster, and as he approached the ledge, swung his legs up like a high jumper, using the rope as a fulcrum.

At that point the last strand snapped. Jill screamed. Matahina sighed. She was close to exhaustion.

Underneath them Jack was surprised when his body followed his legs over the lip of the ledge as he tumbled into the crevice. He pulled the remaining rope in and saw the frayed end. His good luck was certainly holding.

He called out of the cave mouth. "Is everyone alright up there?"

"Oh my god, you're alive!" shouted Jill in relief. She now was desperately peering over the edge, but couldn't see him at all. "Where are you?"

"I'm in the cave," shouted Jack.

"Get the fucking head!" shouted Lawrence. To Brad, this was possibly an even better turn of events. They could now lower the backpack into the crevice, get Jack to put the skull in the backpack, pull it back up, and leave Jack in the cave to die. Brilliant, he thought. That's one whole body I won't have to get rid of.

Brad ordered the two women to their feet.

"Get that backpack off the body and tie it to what's left of the rope," he ordered Jill, pointing to the dead Mike, now lying face-down in a pool of blood, the backpack still strapped to his body.

Jack sat up, and dusting himself off, shone the flashlight on his helmet at the headless corpse sitting in front of him. It was amazingly well preserved he thought, considering how long it had been there. Tsukasa's Imperial Japanese Army uniform was still recognisable, although tattered in places. There was little skin remaining on the bones of his fleshless feet, but his hands still looked remarkably like hands, just very skinny freeze-dried hands. Only the bones of a couple of his fingers poked out.

Jack couldn't help himself. He had to examine the corpse closer. It was sitting in the classic meditation pose, legs crossed, back straight, hands cupped in the middle, palms facing up. It appeared that Tsukasa had returned to his monastic training at the very end.

Jack imagined the former monk sitting serenely here in the lotus position, facing the ocean, as the sun set over the horizon, the warm, balmy breeze on his face helping him to concentrate on 'the here and now', and slowly fading off into nirvana, or the happy Amida Buddhaland, or his next life, depending on what school of Buddhism he belonged to.

But a further examination of the corpse suggested it wasn't quite such a pretty picture. Pulling up the legs of Tsukasa's trousers revealed two badly broken ankles and some attempt by Tsukasa to splint them, with strips of material, probably from his shirt, and some thin sticks. However, from the discolouration and dark stains in the cloth ties, it appeared to Jack that septicaemia had set in, and probably gangrene as well.

It was more likely that Tsukasa was meditating to overcome the horrific pain he must have been in. And towards the end, it was probably all that he *could* do, as he would have been completely incapacitated by the two broken, pus-and-blood-oozing ankles.

Jack scanned the cave with the flashlight helmet. It wasn't high enough to stand up in, and narrowed at either side, but mostly it was dry and fortunately free of spider webs.

A short distance to the left of where Tsukasa sat was the blackened earth and charcoal remains of a small fire. To his right, and also within his reach, was a pile of thin bones. Bird bones, Jack deduced.

Jack looked at the pith helmet and shoes on the ledge. They were also within Tsukasa's reach. Were they meant to catch water dripping down from the overhang above? It was possible. Or were they there to attract the seabirds that it appeared Tsukasa had been eating?

Over in the left-hand corner of the cave, Jack could see where Tsukasa's skull had rolled after being slapped off its spinal column moments earlier. He crawled over on all fours, like some kind of Victorian-era miner, to retrieve it.

When he reached it, the skull was face down in the dirt. Jack picked it up to check out the now-legendary teeth that allegedly led to a 'heart of gold', turning the skull like you would a coconut with a series of small tosses.

The face came into view – hollow eye-sockets, shrivelled nose, the skin tight on the bony bridge. Under that, thin lips pulled back and dried in a grimace that reminded Jack of a snap-frozen bonsaied pony for some reason. But something was missing – the teeth Jack had so clearly seen when the skull was still attached to its body.

Jack had distinctly seen two sets of gleaming white teeth. Now all that remained was a gaping black maw, barren of choppers except for a couple of lonely molars at the back.

Jack scrambled about on the floor of the cave, and soon came across a set of dentures. He examined them as closely as he could with the helmet flashlight, but couldn't see any hidden message on either the fake teeth or the inside of the pink resin gums. Maybe they had misinterpreted Tsukasa's haiku completely. Maybe the directions to the gold weren't in Tsukasa's mouth at all.

There was no gold tooth in this set of false teeth, so Jack deduced they were the corpse's bottom set. Nonetheless, he put them in his trouser pocket, then back on all fours, continued his search of the tiny cave floor, and soon had another larger set of choppers in his hand. This time there *was* a large gold tooth in the centre. They also had a large curved plate made of the same mock-gum coloured material as the other set. Jack turned them over and looked at the underside of the plate. Nothing.

He flipped the dentures over again and discovered that there, scratched into the pale pink resin of the top of the plate, were two numbers:

3 07 36.68 S

152 38 11.42 E

That was it. He had the exact coordinates to an alleged vast gold resource somewhere in Papua New Guinea. It seemed completely ludicrous to Jack, because he'd never been driven by dreams of material wealth, vast or otherwise.

He put the set of choppers in his shirt pocket, and just sat there on the dirt cave floor, completely exhausted. The cave was eerily silent.

"What is he doing down there? Spring cleaning?" said Brad with a shake of his head.

Inside the cave, Jack attempted to assess his situation. How was he going to get out of here? He couldn't climb out by himself, and it was unlikely that Brad would let him, unless he had the teeth on him.

What Jack needed, he decided, was some kind of weapon he could use on Lawrence. He frisked Tsukasa's bony torso. There was nothing on him. Not even a penknife. There were no laces on his shoes, nothing on his clothes. For some reason, he didn't have a belt. Maybe it had been taken from him by his Aussie guards.

Jack briefly considered taking one of Tsukasa's rib bones, but felt he'd desecrated the dead man's body enough already by knocking his head off and stealing his false teeth.

But a sharpened bone might be a useful weapon if he could get close enough to Brad to use it. He crawled over to the pile of gnawed and charred bones on Tsukasa's left.

He imagined that Tsukasa, crippled, would have waited patiently until a tern or a seagull perched on his ledge, and then with great speed and the element of surprise, grabbed them, and wrung their necks. Yet looking through the pile of bones, Jack noted that some were bigger and thicker than others. And amongst the mostly white and grey feathers of seabirds, were a number of brown and tan feathers. The Lord Howe Woodhens! Either they were wandering into this cave somehow, or Tsukasa was able to get out and catch them. And if that was the case, there must be another way out of the cave, besides the one with the 875-metre first step.

It made sense, because the likelihood that when Tsukasa had jumped from the Catalina he had landed on a ledge that was more or less under the lip of the cliff face was extremely slim, if not outright impossible. More likely, Tsukasa landed somewhere on the Mount Gower plateau, breaking both his ankles on impact, and then crawled around until he found this cave for shelter, which being a trained geologist probably wasn't as difficult as it might seem.

Jack grabbed the longest and sharpest bone he could find in the pile. By its size, he figured it was probably a muttonbird thigh bone. He slipped it in his belt.

He heard a voice from above. It was Jill.

"Jack, can you hear me?" Jill called.

"Yes, I can hear you," answered Jack.

"Have you got the head yet? Our host is getting impatient."

Jack needed more time to find the cave entrance. "I'm having some difficulty separating the head from the body," he called up. He didn't like lying to Jill, but under the circumstances it was justified.

"Let us know when you've got it," pleaded Jill.

"Will do," replied Jack, before scurrying on all fours to the furthest darkest area of the cave. There, the cave narrowed and met a shaft that appeared to be covered at its top. This must be the entrance, thought Jack.

He now scurried back to the centre of the cave, picked up the head of Tsukasa, and reaching into his trouser pocket, pulled out the lower set of false teeth. He checked them under the torch light to make sure they definitely were not the ones with the map coordinates on them, and carefully placed them back in the corpse's jaw.

With the head in his hand, he crawled over to the crevice opening, and shouted back up. "Hello! I've got the head."

The next thing he knew, Mike's empty backpack was dangling in front of him tied to the remains of the orange nylon rope he'd earlier been dangling from himself. Reaching out he grabbed the backpack.

Another voice called out from above. This time it was Brad himself. "Put the head in the backpack, Jack," he ordered.

"But what about me?" called Jack.

"Just put the head in the backpack. Once we've got that, we'll throw the rope back down for you," replied Brad.

"How can I trust you?" called Jack.

"What difference does it make?" replied Lawrence. "I'm going to kill you anyway. Would you rather a slow death in a cave or a swift death up here?"

"If that's the case," argued Jack, "I may as well just stay here, with the head."

Brad was angry now. "If you don't put that head in the backpack in the next fifteen seconds, the next thing you're going to see is your girlfriend flying past your window on her way down. Would you like that?"

Jack gave in. "Okay. I'm putting the head in the backpack now." He loaded the shrivelled head into the backpack.

"Sorry, mate," said Jack to Tsukasa, zipping the backpack up.

He shouted back up. "Okay, the head is in the bag. Take it away."

Jack pushed the bag off the ledge and watched it being pulled up from above. Next he scurried on all fours to the other cave entrance, and began to climb up the dark narrow shaft, using exposed tree roots as steps. Jack could tell that Tsukasa must have excavated this shaft to a certain extent, but couldn't imagine the pain and determination involved in that task.

The shaft became narrower and narrower. Clearly Tsukasa was a much thinner man than Jack. It was getting awfully cosy by the time he reached the very top, where the entrance to the shaft itself was covered by a large flat rock.

Jack locked his knees against the sides of the shaft and pushed with both hands on the rock above him. But the rock wouldn't budge. He was now glad that the shaft was so narrow. If he were to lose his footing, he too might also break both his ankles, just as Tsukasa did. He wondered how that would appear if he couldn't get out. Eventually they'd find two corpses, both with their ankles broken, and one with their head missing. They might deduce that Jack had eaten Tsukasa's head.

Above him, Jill and Matahina, lying on the ground, their arms over the edge, carefully pulled the backpack up to the top of the cliff, while Brad hovered above them holding his Johnson.

Jack pushed again on the entrance-covering rock – it still wouldn't budge.

Jill and Matahina had now raised the backpack back up to the rock platform they were lying on.

"Hand it over!" demanded Lawrence. Jill dutifully complied. Keeping the gun trained in their direction, he began to open the zipped-up main compartment of the backpack.

Below, Jack was contemplating the possibility that the rock lid covering the cave entrance simply would not open. It probably hadn't been moved since 1948. For all Jack knew, an entire tree might be growing on top of it. Or worse, Brad Lawrence could be standing on it.

Then again, if Brad Lawrence *was* standing it, and Jack *could* open it, it would knock Lawrence to the ground, and Jack could then spring out of the shaft and wrestle him into submission.

The likelihood of events going even remotely that way was extremely slim, but it was all the impetus Jack needed. He climbed his legs up another 'rung' of the tree-root ladder to give himself extra spring, pushed his shoulders and the back of his still-helmeted head hard up against the cold dark rock, and pushed with all the strength he could muster.

The rock gave, and Jack burst out of the shaft spectacularly, about two metres behind where Brad was now squatting with the skull on his lap, the set of lower choppers in one hand, and the Iver Johnson in the other.

Brad, Jill and Matahina all turned to face Jack, who unfortunately was now stuck in the entrance of the shaft at just above his waist. He couldn't have planned a more ridiculous entrance if he had tried. He looked like an overweight gopher, or perhaps more appropriately, a Jack-in-the-Ground. Jill stifled a laugh, but was relieved to see Jack more or less above ground. Matahina gawked, and Brad Lawrence just looked perplexed.

Brad looked again at the false teeth in his hand. He was toying with the idea of shooting Jack then and there, but was more concerned about the teeth.

"There's nothing on these teeth, no markings, no map …"

Jack had to think fast. "Yes there is." He made a flipping gesture with one hand while digging the other hand back down into the shaft to find something, he didn't know what. "There's markings on the other side".

Brad flipped the dentures over. Jack's hand found the dagger-like bone in his belt. He considered it, but he was too far away from Brad to do him any damage.

He fumbled through his trouser pocket and found the toothbrush, toothpaste, sunscreen and a comb, which might all come in handy if he was staying there a week, but not very useful right at that moment.

Then he remembered something else. He felt into his other trouser pocket and his finger slipped into a tight cold cylinder. It was his bottleneck slide – the one he would rather have been using on his Dobro back at Hightide Apartments, instead of wasting his holiday on all this unnecessary 'skullduggery'.

The Jim Dunlop Heavy Pyrex Blues slide was made from high-quality boron silicate, heat treated and 'annealed' – a process of heating and cooling – to make it tough and less brittle. It was cold, hard and heavy and perfect for getting the best blues sound out of a resonator guitar. Jack knew all this because he'd researched it extensively online before he chose the one he considered ideal for his purposes. He was a little obsessive that way.

Brad was still examining the false teeth in his hand. He had just reached the point of realisation that these definitely weren't the map-yielding dentures, when Jack called out, "Hey, Brad!"

Brad looked up. Jack knew he had one chance. He gripped the bottleneck slide between his right thumb and forefinger, and in one lightning-fast movement, pulled his right arm out of the shaft, back behind his head, and threw the piece of tempered Pyrex as hard as he could.

It was a rare shot. Even though Brad was only two metres away, Jack wasn't known as a tosser, or at least that kind of a tosser. He didn't have the greatest hand-eye coordination, and had missed targets much closer. But this time he was lucky. Before Brad could really work out what was happening, the bottleneck slide was hurtling through the air in front of his eyes, and then connected dead centre with his forehead, smack dab on target with the huge mole right in the middle of his forehead.

Although he was only squatting, the slide hit with such force that Brad went down backwards, losing his grip on the gun, which skidded into some nearby bushes. His head hit the rock beneath him, and he passed out. Tsukasa's skull went up in the air, landed on the rocky ground and cracked like an egg, emitting a small grey cloud of desiccated brain matter.

Jack scrambled out of the hole. Jill rushed to embrace him. "Thank god you're alive," she exclaimed.

"Yeah, it's pretty fucking amazing!" said Jack, smiling. He gave her a quick kiss, then rushed over to Brad. The slide had split his mole and blood was oozing out. Jack picked his trusty bottleneck slide up off the ground, wiped Brad's blood off it, and put it back in his pocket. He never realised before how handy a bottleneck slide could be. Everyone should carry one, he thought to himself.

"Quick, we'd better tie this prick up, before he comes to," Jack said, grabbing the rope. As fast as he could, he tied Brad's hands and his feet. Jill grabbed the backpack, and just for good measure put it over Brad Lawrence's head and tightened up the zipper.

"I hope he suffocates," said Jill bitterly.

"Maybe he'll roll off the cliff in his sleep," added Matti.

"We can only hope," said Jack.

Brad was starting to regain consciousness. He let out a low guttural moan. And began to shout. "What the fuck's going on? Untie me! Get this thing off me!"

"Does it smell like mummified head in there Brad?" asked Jack, and the girls laughed.

"Come on. We'd better get out of here," said Jack, then he, Jill and Matti headed back off through the palms and ferns of the moss forest to where the track back down the mountain began.

It was becoming light now, they were exhausted but elated, and still in a hurry to get as far away from Brad as they possibly could.

Jack was justifiably a little trepidatious about leaving him there, because even though Brad was tied up, he could still get free. Jack himself had proved earlier that even the most incompetent of escape artists are sometimes successful. But the alternative was to take Lawrence with them, and they were all too exhausted to cope with a prisoner as well. As far as Jack was concerned, Brad could just lie there and rot. But Jack figured that as soon as they were back in civilisation, he would call the authorities on the mainland, and they could send a police chopper to pick Brad up. And Jack could get back to his holiday, his girlfriend and his guitar.

The mist had lifted by now, and as they hurried down the side of the plateau, they were afforded exceptional views of the island below and the huge expanse of ocean beyond. They even had a rare glimpse of Ball's Pyramid, 23-odd kilometres to the southeast, jutting six hundred metres out of the ocean like the tooth of some gigantic shark. However, at this point in time they weren't really interested in taking in the view. All they were interested in was getting the hell out of there.

They clambered down the rocks and boulders with little concern for minor injury. Skinned knees and nicked hands weren't a problem at this stage of the game. Exhausted, their legs like jelly, they simply *had* to keep going.

In some spots the descent was even more terrifying than the climb, yet not nearly as terrifying as the events they'd already witnessed, or the prospect of being in the presence of Brad Lawrence ever again.

Yet despite all the sliding, slipping, swearing and grunting, the trio soon made it down the steepest part of the descent to the relative flatness of the valley between Lidgbird and Mount Gower.

At a clearing on the bank of Erskine Creek, they were so dehydrated, all three got down on all fours and drank like dogs from the water's edge. As they were splashing water on their faces to wash away the sweat and grime they'd accumulated in their adventures, they were alarmed by a frightening sound. A gunshot echoed through the valley.

"Oh shit!" shouted Jack. "Run!"

All three jumped to their feet and ran as fast as they could away from the sound. While they were running, Jack looked at his right upper arm. Blood was soaking through his shirt.

"Fuck!" he exclaimed. Still running, he rolled up his sleeve to see a thick gouge carved into the flesh of his upper arm, right in the spot he'd been planning to get a tattoo of a hula girl one day. It wasn't a deep wound, the bullet had really only grazed him. But he was bleeding like a stuck pig, and now that the shock had worn off, it was actually beginning to hurt.

The graze pointed down, which suggested that Brad was still some distance above them. He must have escaped and followed them down and then, somewhere on the steep slope above, caught a glimpse of them drinking, and took a pot shot.

"Um, I hate to state the obvious," said Jill, running just in front of Jack. "But did we leave the gun up there?"

"I'm afraid so," said Jack, who was trying not to draw attention to his wound in case it upset Jill and Matti even more.

Matti, who was in the lead as they ran along the path, turned around and said to Jack "You're not very good at this, are you?"

"Hey, I got us this far didn't I?" retorted Jack. "This is the first time I've ever had to deal with a *live* villain. Normally I just deal with dead ones."

They were soon approaching the end of the valley, their bodies burning, their lungs bursting. Both of Jack's knees were beginning to scream in pain every time his feet came down on the hard soil beneath them.

Then within metres of the grassy Lidgbird Ledge, Jack's left kneecap gave out, and he stumbled to the side. Unfortunately, his left foot had stayed put, which meant as he fell he twisted his ankle and screamed in pain as he went down.

"Ah, shit, fuck shit, cunt fuck shit, fuck!" he shouted, clearly upset.

Jill and Matti stopped and turned back.

"Are you alright?' asked Jill, putting out her hand to help Jack up.

"I think so," lied Jack trying to get to his feet. He took a step, and winced in agony. "I think it might be sprained." He actually thought it might be broken, but he compensated for his innate tendency towards hypochondria and toned it down to a sprain.

"Ah guys," said Matti, pointing down the path. "He's coming."

Off in the distance but moving fast, they could see the shape of Brad Lawrence lumbering along the track.

Jill and Matti each put one of Jack's arms around their shoulders, took his weight, and together they hobbled off, like contestants in a mixed-sex five-legged race.

"Sorry about this, ladies" said Jack, wincing in pain.

"That's okay," said Jill "We're used to it. We've been carrying you all day, buddy," she joked.

"Isn't it always the *girl* who sprains her ankle?" she added, adding insult to injury, literally.

"That's right, I'm a big girl," agreed Jack before squealing with pain just like one, as he took his next step.

Soon, but with much discomfort, they reached the beginning of the Lidgbird ledge.

"How are you going to get around *that?*" asked Matti.

"I'll be alright now that I've got a rope to hold onto," lied Jack. "You two go ahead. And get help."

As Jill and Matti moved away from him along the ledge, Jack looked up to see Lawrence getting closer and closer. Jack grabbed the rough, weatherworn guide rope and, hooking both hands under it, slowly and painfully began to edge himself along the ledge.

As the two ladies disappeared around the curve of the cliff, Jack tried hard not to look down to the swirling water a hundred metres below, almost wishing that it was as dark as it had been when he had passed this way several hours before. At least then he couldn't see how far he had to fall.

The pain from his ankle was almost unbearable, and the pain from the bullet graze threatened the grip of his right arm, but he was tenacious, and determined to make it. Step by painful step he slowly made his way along the ledge, finally, exhausted, reaching the other side.

Jack paused to catch his breath; he could hear Jill and Matahina running, clambering and sliding down the path below.

No sooner had Jack caught his breath, than he noticed Brad coming along the ledge, almost bounding, his eyes full of rage, blood still dripping from the mole Jack had cracked with his bottleneck slide.

Jack high-tailed it out of there, sliding on his bum for the first metre, then hopping, loping, and on occasion crawling on all fours through the kentia forest-lined path that led down to Johnson's Beach.

He was actually rolling when he came out of the forest into the clearing in front of Johnson's Beach. There was no time to stop. He knew Lawrence could only be a short distance behind him and gaining fast. Jack hauled his body onto the sand and kept crawling, dragging his sprained ankle behind him.

At the water's edge, he knew he could go no further. He propped himself up on a large black rock just where the sand met the water, and waited for Brad to catch up with him. Hopefully he could stall Brad long enough for Jill and Matti to get help, or at least get away.

It wasn't long before Brad emerged from the kentia palm forest and, gun in hand, lumbered towards Jack.

"I see your girlfriends have deserted you," said Brad, walking up to within metres of Jack. "That's too bad."

"It's all over Brad, give yourself up," said Jack, somewhat brazenly.

"No," said Brad, levelling the Iver Johnson at Jack's chest. "It's all over for you." He began to slowly squeeze the trigger.

Jack painfully raised his right arm. At its end he held Tsukasa's top dentures, the gold filling twinkling in morning sunlight.

"Is this what you want?" asked Jack, and with a flick of his wrist flung the choppers spiralling into the air, out over the crystal clear waters of the lagoon.

Brad and Jack watched the dentures fly over the water seemingly in slow motion. Also watching was a hungry kingfish that surfaced directly under the falling falsies, its enormous purse-like mouth gaping to catch what it assumed was a free feed.

Just as the dentures were almost at the blue lips of the fish, now in fast motion, a sooty tern dived from above and snatched them from the sea creature's snapping jaws.

The tern flew up and over Jack and Brad's heads, and with the dentures in its beak, looked for all the world as if it was smiling at them. Brad raised his arm and trained the Iver Johnson on the tern and, with steady aim, fired. The shot echoed off the cliffs of nearby Mount Lidgbird, cordite filled the air, and with a puff of white feathers, the seabird fell to the beach, about six metres from where Brad stood.

"Wow, good shot!" said Jack. "That's too bad."

"Why do you say that?" asked Brad, now training the gun back onto Jack's still-heaving chest.

"Well," said Jack confidently, "you said your great-grandfather only gave your great-grandmother three bullets. You're out of bullets, buddy."

Brad nodded, impressed. He tossed the gun in the air, caught it by the barrel, and held it like a club. "It doesn't matter. What I'm going to do to you will be more fun *without* bullets."

Brad advanced towards Jack, a strange non-human look in his eyes. Jack got to his feet, and braced himself to take the blow that was only seconds away.

"Your great-grandfather was right to warn your great-grandmother about the Germans," said Jack with a smirk. "We're deadly."

Then something neither of them really expected to happen, did happen. As Brad brought the butt of the gun down towards Jack's head, Jack raised his left arm, and blocked the blow. At the same time, Jack threw his entire body weight forward, and with his injured right arm, thrust the jagged point of the muttonbird bone he'd pulled from his belt, through the synthetic material of Brad's khaki shirt, in between his ribs, and directly into the centre of Brad Lawrence's heart.

Brad's mouth gaped. He dropped the Iver Johnson in the water that was now lapping at his ankles. He looked at Jack and made a guttural gasping noise.

Jack pushed the bone in deeper with the heel of his hand and smiled.

"Merry Christmas, Mr Lawrence."

Brad fell backwards into the water, blood gushed from the wound in his chest and mixed with the sea water that was now flowing into his open mouth, causing him to cough and splutter slightly as his life drained away.

Jack considered briefly dragging him ashore and applying first aid so that Lawrence could stand trial for the crimes he had committed, but thought the better of it. Brad Lawrence really deserved to die. And Jack was saving the state and the department a lot of money this way.

Jack fetched the Iver Johnson from the shallow water Brad had dropped it in and, wet, bloody and exhausted, limped to shore. He dragged and hopped to the spot where the sooty tern Brad had so expertly shot, lay dead in the sand, the set of false teeth still clenched in its beak. It looked decidedly odd and particularly comical. Jack wished he had a camera with him to take a picture.

He knelt down beside the dead bird, and prised the prized plate from its black beak. Jack looked up to see a four-wheel drive approaching along the grassy edge of the shoreline. After it stopped a short distance away, Reg and Mick jumped out, and ran towards Jack.

"Mate, are you alright?" asked Reg.

"I've been better," smiled Jack, "but I can't complain."

"Where's Lawrence?" asked Mick.

"'He sleeps with the fishes,'" replied Jack, who was beginning to wonder if he would speak in clichéd movie quotes for the rest of his life.

As Reg and Mick helped Jack back to the four-wheel drive, Jill and Matti pulled up in Mike's ute. Jill jumped out and raced over to them.

"If I have to say, 'Thank god you're alive,' one more time today, you're going to wish you weren't," said Jill.

"Never," replied Jack. She smiled and they hugged.

Matti turned up and joined in the hug.

"This is the best Christmas yet," said Jack wallowing in their womanly embrace.

Reg and Mick left Jack and the girls in their group-hug and retrieved Lawrence's body from the shallows.

"We don't want to frighten the tourists," said Reg, as they carried it past to the four-wheel drive.

"Ew!" said Matti. "What happened to him?"

"'Revenge of the Muttonbird'," smiled Jack.

"I guess we'd better take him up the Fish Co-op and put him in the deep freeze," said Reg, as he shut the back of the four-wheel drive.

"Good thing most of the seafood's been taken for Chrissy lunch," said Mick. "Otherwise there wouldn't be any room for this bugger."

On the drive back into town, Jack was silent. It was the first time he had killed a human being, or indeed anything, since he'd given up trying to keep indoor plants some 20 years ago.

He didn't feel guilty about killing Brad, but he did feel pissed off that it had to come to that. Especially while he was on holiday. But most of all, he was tired.

They stopped at Humpty Micks Café , and Jack used the public phone to ring his boss. Being Christmas Day, she didn't answer, so he left a message on her machine, explaining what had happened, and when he reached the end he added, "Oh and one more thing – I quit. I'm giving up death and devoting the rest of my life to life. Merry Christmas." And with that, he hung up, feeling better than he had in years.

Back at Hightide Apartments, Jack, Jill and Matti went to their respective apartments to wash and sleep, even though it was only mid-morning.

But neither Jack nor Jill could sleep very long. That much adrenalin in the system takes a while to dissipate. Around about 4:00pm Jack got up to discover his ankle was starting to feel a bit better. Now he could hobble around quite easily, and it only hurt as much as the rest of his body. Oddly, the all-over pain created a kind of buzz. Maybe this is what masochists are into it for, he thought to himself.

He grabbed a beer from the fridge, and his Dobro from where it had rested against the wall for so long that dust was starting to settle on it.

He sat down on a chair on the balcony, slipped his trusty bottleneck slide on his finger, and started to play what sounded more country than blues, or possibly country-blues, but with a definite hint of alt-country, Americana, or possibly even Appalachian folk. Whatever it was, it sounded, not sad, but somewhat defiant although with a hint of lament, or possibly regret. Not bad for a guy who wasn't used to the Dobro's tuning, and hadn't entirely mastered the slide, except the art of throwing it. Whatever it was, it sounded pretty good, so he kept playing.

Pretty soon Jill heard the guitar and came out. She was wearing her hibiscus-print sarong again, and her hair was wet from just having a shower.

"What's going on? I thought someone was strangling a cat!" she said, smiling.

Jack stopped playing, and looked hurt.

"Just kidding," she added. "Keep playing."

"Man, talk about 'tough love'," said Jack, and he started playing again.

Jill grabbed a beer from his fridge and joined him, clapping and tapping her foot in time. For a moment they were happy hillbillies.

After a while they soon realised how hungry they were, which made them happy hungry hillbillies. Jack remembered the prawns he'd bought earlier, and brought them out, with some bread, dipping sauce and another round of beers, and they both tucked in.

Matti joined them not long after that, yawning and scratching herself, wearing just a bikini top and a pair of short cut-off jeans. She snagged a couple of prawns, but when Jack and Jill invited her to join them for dinner, said she'd have to pass because she promised to visit Mick, who was pretty upset about his best mate Mike's murder.

Jack and Jill volunteered to come with her, but Matti shook her head and said they probably deserved some time alone, and left with a wave and a wiggle that made Jack wish he were a younger man. Then again, he thought to himself, the bird in my hand is probably worth twice that.

The sun was starting to go down now, so Jack went to the kitchen and brought out the marlin fillets he'd bought at the Fish Co-op what seemed like ages ago, but was actually only yesterday.

"No you don't," said Jill, jumping up and taking the tray of fillets off him. "It's my turn to cook." The holiday just kept getting better.

They opened a bottle of Pierro Margaret River chardonnay with dinner, and later when they were starting to feel no pain, Jack insisted they go for a swim.

They grabbed their towels and the bottle, and somehow managed to make it down to Ned's Beach. The sun had only just gone down and sky was a glowing dome of amazing pinks, oranges, and blues. Amazingly there was no one on the beach.

They put down their towels and the bottle, and almost slid into the warm, refreshing ocean.

"Ah, the curative powers of salt water," said Jack after surfacing like a hairy dugong, and wiping the water from his face.

Like dugongs, or at least a dugong and a sexy lady dolphin, they frolicked in the shallow water. Jill wrapped her legs around Jack's legs, and they kissed. And kissed again. And then one more time.

Then Jill gave Jack a funny look.

"Something's come between us," admitted Jack.

"Yes, I can feel it," replied Jill.

"How does it feel?" asked Jack.

"You tell me," she said, grabbing Jack through his boardshorts.

"Feels good," said Jack, a huge dugong smile on his face.

Jill led him up the beach by his dick and they made love, on their towels, under the stars.

Postscript

Six months later, Jack was at the wheel of what was now his boat, and indeed his home, the *True Love 2*. Sitting at the flybridge helm with his hands on the wheel, he wore black Ray-Bans, a new old Hawaiian shirt, board shorts and a very distinctive hat – an authentic Japanese Imperial Army pith helmet, complete with a now-polished gold star – Tsukasa's old hat in fact. Yes, he had actually taken the pith. He scanned the seas for the entrance to the reef the *True Love 2* was approaching.

Much had happened in the previous six months. After Christmas, a team of detectives from Sydney flew to Lord Howe Island, and Jack had to go over the whole case with them.

A charge of manslaughter for the death of Brad Lawrence was dropped, because Jack was clearly defending himself against a known killer. Also Brad didn't appear to have any friends or relatives to kick up a stink about his death and, generally, everyone agreed he was a bad man and the world was a better place without him.

There was a coronial inquiry in which Jack gave evidence. It found that Brad Lawrence was responsible for the untimely deaths of Harvey Jacob, Boz Boswell and Mike Hunt, and probably responsible for the deaths of Diana Dawson, and

Norman Gimbell. Bert Slater, it was decided, probably just fell off his stool playing the pokies.

Jack was right about Harvey Jacob's powerboat too. The cost of repairing it after Jack had beached it and Brad Lawrence had gutted it, and shipping it back to the States, was more than his relatives were willing to pay, so Jack managed to pick it up for a relative song. Of course, he had to sell his semi in Erskineville to do it. But it was time to move on.

Next he went about getting his license, so he wouldn't park it quite as badly as he did last time. The repairs to the *True Love 2* were paid for by selling his story to *60 Minutes*. She was repaired and refitted at Berry's Bay in Sydney and, once she was complete and seaworthy, Jack moved himself, his guitar, his best Hawaiian shirts and anything else he thought he might need on board, and headed back to Lord Howe Island.

The reason for his return was Jill. She'd extended her dental tenure – and why wouldn't you, thought Jack. If you have to be a dentist, you may as well be one in paradise.

However paradise wasn't perfect for Jill because Jack wasn't there, so she was waiting at the pier when he arrived, and held her breath as he successfully brought the *True Love 2* up alongside without damaging it at all.

After catching up with Mick, Reg, and Suzie and meeting Heather for the first time and her new baby, Byron, Jack welcomed Jill aboard her new home, and they sailed, or rather motored, off into the sunset.

Their first stop on their maiden voyage was to Aitutaki, to attend Matahina's wedding. She'd gone home after Christmas, got to know the Polynesian prince she was betrothed to a little better and realised that even though he was far from drop-dead gorgeous, he had a beautiful soul, and decided that the arranged marriage wasn't such a bad idea after all.

After the wedding ceremony, and a few days spent exploring the amazingly blue lagoon of Aitutaki, Jack pointed the *True Love 2* in a westerly direction and they departed.

Their first stop was Fiji, then Santo in the Vanuatu group, and the Solomon islands, where Jack made them take a rather lengthy detour to visit an outer lying reef known as Ontong Java Atoll – but curiously sometimes referred to as Lord Howe Atoll, even though it has nothing to do with Lord Howe Island, except that they were both once named after the same bloke.

From there, the *True Love 2* headed west towards their destination, the map coordinates that Tsukasa san had etched into his dentures over 60 years ago.

As they entered the channel in the reef, Jack felt a tingling in his loins. This may have had something to do with the fact that he was sporting a new piece of nether-jewellery. He had replaced his old palang with the centre pin from Brad Lawrence's great-grandmother's Iver Johnson 1900, double-action revolver. "Now," he had told Jill, "I can honestly say "Iver Johnson in my pants.""

Jill joined him on the flybridge, looking tan, taut and terrific in a red polka-dot bikini, a pink straw cowboy hat and big oval sunglasses.

"Is that it?" she asked Jack, pointing with a tilt of her hat to the huge tropical island in front of them, because her hands were full with the two Tusker Ice beers she was carrying.

"According to the teeth, it is," replied Jack, looking at the choppers that were sitting next to the compass on the flybridge consol.

"It's huge!" remarked Jill.

"Yep," replied Jack, steering the *True Love 2* parallel with the shore.

"And there's our gold mine."

As they motored around its southeast edge, they noticed an increasing amount of human activity on the island's flat lip, behind which a tropical green ridge loomed.

Rounding the headland that the ridge created, they could see that it was in fact the enormous C-shaped crater of a still-active volcano. White smoke rose in places, and the lush green was replaced by a huge open-cut mine in the heart of the crater.

The shore was lined with demountable huts operating as accommodation – for workers in some cases, offices in others. A massive refinery loomed up next and, soon, as the water turned from deep blue to muddy brown from the tailings discarded after processing, they found themselves in the company of a number of gigantic ore-carrying liners.

"It looks like a tropical Port Kembla," said Jill, herself a former Wollongong girl.

"Lihir Island," said Jack, "but it was known as Sanambeit Island back in Tsukasa's time."

He took a swig of Tusker and continued. "Part of the Lihir group or archipelago. The island was briefly occupied by the Japanese army during World War II."

"That must have been when Tsukasa came here," said Jill.

"Presumably," said Jack. "However, it held no strategic value to the Japs, so they lopped off the head of the local Portuguese priest and left."

"Maybe that's why Tsukasa didn't tell them about the gold," postulated Jill taking a sip of her beer. "His brother was a priest, so perhaps he felt they'd gone too far."

"We'll never know," said Jack.

Jill picked up the binoculars that were lying on one of the padded vinyl seats, and focused them on the mine. Monster yellow trucks ploughed ore-laden back and forth along the tiered levels of the open-cut mine, while giant bulldozers dug deeper and deeper into the steaming red-raw soil.

"What a massive operation," she exclaimed.

"It's the largest gold deposit in the world, or so they tell me. The mine is actually *in* the caldera of an active volcano. It was first surveyed – this time round – in the early 1980s."

"How do you know all this?" asked Jill.

"I've done my research," said Jack, pushing a book on the island out of Jill's sight.

"So Brad Lawrence was a little late," asked Jill.

"Yep," replied Jack. "About twenty-seven years too late. Too bad, too. Tsukasa was sitting there all that time, waiting for someone to find him, and discover the gold."

"I wish it had been us," said Jill.

"Not me," replied Jack. "I've got all the gold I'll ever need, right here." He smiled and took a swig of Tusker.

"Are you talking about me, or the beer?" asked Jill.

"Both," said Jack, giving Jill a kiss, then taking another swig.

www.ingramcontent.com/pod-product-compliance
Lightning Source LLC
Chambersburg PA
CBHW031108030726
47496CB00002BA/436